CIVIL TWILIGHT

C I V I L
T W I L I G H T

A DARCY LOTT MYSTERY

SUSAN DUNLAP

COUNTERPOINT

BERKELEY

Library of Congress Cataloging-in-Publication Data

Dunlap, Susan.
Civil twilight : a Darcy Lott mystery / Susan Dunlap.
p. cm.
1. Women stunt performers—Fiction. 2. Attorney and client—Fiction. 3. Murder—
Investigation—Fiction. 4. San Francisco (Calif.)—Fiction. I. Title.

PS3554.U46972C58 2009
813'.54—dc22
2008051632

ISBN (10) 1-58243-452-2
ISBN (13) 978-1-58243-452-0

Cover design by Kimberly Glyder Design
Interior design by Megan Cooney
Printed in the United States of America

COUNTERPOINT
2117 Fourth Street
Suite D
Berkeley, CA 94710

www.counterpointpress.com

Distributed by Publishers Group West

10 9 8 7 6 5 4 3 2 1

To Edith Gladstone

CIVIL TWILIGHT

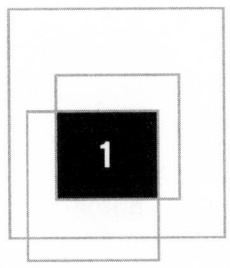

1

"I NEED A FAVOR, Darce. An easy one, this time."

"What, and ruin your reputation?"

An instant passed before my brother let out a hoot. "Where are you?"

"At the zendo. I'm doing that car stunt downtown tonight, the one on California and Market. I want to get down there and scope out the street. It's"—I didn't want to say *dangerous,* not to him—"a one shot gag and—"

But he was talking over me. "I need you to . . . hang with a client . . . just an hour or two. Take her window shopping, to the beach, for a walk, get her mind off things." When it comes to attorneys, my brother Gary's a virtual Goliath's nightmare. Which means when one of his Davids calls at 3 A.M., he's there, pronto. Gary's a hero to his clients—and to me. He's always taking huge chances—financial and legal—and when he says there're things I don't want to know, I believe him. He'll go to prison himself to protect a client's rights, but window shopping? Not hardly.

"So, what are these terrible things she can't be thinking about: Indictment? Jail?"

"Divorce."

"Hey, if she needs a hand to hold about that, she's in the right place." He'd had three of his own.

He started to say something, but must have thought better of it.

"Besides, you don't handle divorces," I pointed out.

"This is different."

"Different *how?* Divorce and what else?"

"Listen, are you going to do this for me or not?"

He was my nearest and closest brother, but the truth was all I really knew about him were the parts of his life that could be easily discovered, not the nooks and nuances of who he was. Until recently, I'd steered clear of San Francisco and my entire family. Now I was cautiously feeling my way back.

"Okay, okay. Sure."

"Great. I appreciate it. I mean it."

"So when do you need me?"

"Now."

"*Now!* The shoot's at six-thirty! It's almost five now!"

"She's waiting at Washington Square. Her name's Karen Johnson."

Jesus. "Okay." What was I thinking? "But only for an hour," I added.

". . . Darce?" His tone had changed.

"Yeah?"

"Rabbits it."

Our old childhood signal was barely out of his mouth when he clicked off. So I couldn't ask him just why I shouldn't mention it, particularly to the one for whom the code had been created in the first place—our oldest brother, John, the cop.

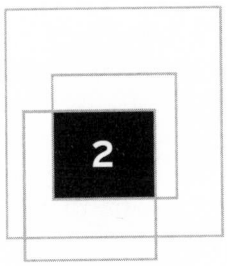

2

WHEN I FIRST spotted her, she was on the steps of Saints Peter and Paul Church, staring at Washington Square as if the park were the most fascinating, delightful spot imaginable. Turning, she smiled at me as if I was just what she'd been waiting for. It was an appealingly disingenuous expression and one that automatically made me suspicious. The eggshell blue linen tunic and slacks she wore looked expensive, as did the cut of her subtly streaked blond hair. Her face work was as good as I'd seen on any movie set. A first lift, as opposed to the nibble your own ear look of a third or fourth. It gave her the aura of a coddled twenty-something, one at odds with the lines already re-establishing themselves between her brows. But her hands nailed her age as over forty. Sinews in them revealed a past that involved heavy work; one pinky was twisted halfway around so the nail faced away from the other fingers. She had a salon manicure, but two nails were chipped and had been clipped short and chipped again.

"You've got to be Gary's sister," she said.

"Right."

"I figured. You have the same walk."

"You're kidding." I run miles every other day, I take aerobics, dance, kill myself on machines in the gym. Gary works his butt off, but he's sitting on it the whole time. Only metabolism and missed meals keep him thin; his muscles have to be hanging three-toed from his bones. "That's not exactly a compliment. His office is a block from here. Bet he didn't walk with you, did he?"

She did a flash assessment and laughed. "Prove me wrong. He said you were a big-time jock—you'd take me running."

"He told *me* to take you shopping."

"Really?" she said, as if that added to the challenge. Then she caught my eye and laughed harder, the way my sister, Gracie, and I would over Gary's foibles.

Who was this woman? And why did she need a babysitter? Why hadn't Gary just told me what was going on? Now I was dying to know. Considering how he'd set it up, he was all but begging me to pry. But I was tilting toward liking Karen, didn't want to cause her more distress than whatever she already had. Damn Gary! "Where do you want to go? Embarcadero? Marina Green? I've only got an hour, but I'll see that you get back to Gary."

"Somewhere high up with grass and big trees and shade. Where would you take a tourist who wants the best view of the city?"

Ours is a knockout city and we San Franciscans are ridiculously proud of it. Few things please us more than an appreciative tourist. "High up, trees, great view: you're talking Coit Tower. From there, you can see the entire city, the Golden Gate, Alcatraz, Berkeley, the works. I have to warn you, though, the run up's an extreme sport."

"You're on." With that, she pushed off like a sprinter, her worn running shoes at odds with the elegant linen pants that billowed out as she cut across Washington Square Park.

Behind us evening rush hour traffic crowded Columbus Avenue, heading toward the onramp for I-80, 101, 280 and Route 1 along the Pacific. The sky was clear—unusual for July in San Francisco—the air just a bit too warm for decent running, as she'd find out when that burst of energy evaporated. I could have paced myself to follow along until that happened, but, well no, I couldn't make myself come in second. I came abreast of her crossing Stockton and started up the gentle incline without breaking stride. "I misjudged you."

"You're not the first."

"Who're the others?"

She eyed me, and a moment later laughed. Then she picked up the pace.

"What's Gary handling for you?"

"Divorce."

"Gary doesn't—"

"Doesn't what?" she snapped.

I jolted back, then to cover my shock, skirted wide around a guy in chinos and tweed jacket arguing with himself, or sporting a Blue Tooth I couldn't see. Gary does an odd of combo civil and criminal suits, but he steers clear of divorce cases. Unless he suddenly, for some bizarre reason, had changed.

"Sorry, Darcy," she said when I circled back to her. "I didn't mean to sound so abrupt. It's just . . . well, you know, the usual. Big stuff to me, old hat to the rest of the world. I was so undone over the weekend I imagined I saw my ex, Matt, here. I just wish there was a divorce debit card I could swipe through and have the marriage deducted from our account."

"I understand, believe me. It's never easy. I was married for a couple years—no kids, no goods, no bad feelings, and even so it was hard." Nothing between us, because, as my husband had explained to his attorney, my favorite brother Mike had been missing for years and there was a hole in my life no one else could fill. In fact, the guilt, the grief, the ever-present not-knowing and imagining gnawed at all my brothers and sisters—and I didn't want to think how much it ate at Mom. "We're not great successes at marriage in my family."

7

My explanation wasn't quite the truth, and neither was Karen's, I was sure. Oddly, that felt like a connection.

She must have felt it, too. "Don't blame yourself," she said. "Things happen."

The street was as steep as they get without being stairs, the sidewalk narrow. I hung behind, giving her time alone. Who was she? Had the divorce unhinged her? Damn Gary, why couldn't he have told me more? My gag was at 6:30. I needed to be on the set, doing a walk through, checking under the hood, double-checking the brakes. When I flipped on the ignition it would be too late.

We crossed an alley and took the two steps up to the sidewalk. Ahead, Greenwich grew even steeper. A little red Smart Car coughed as the driver downshifted and swung into the tight turning circle that ended the block at the park. "The park," I called out as I came up beside her and started up the red stone steps into the sudden greenness. Only pride kept me from panting. Her breath, too, was coming fast, but she wasn't complaining, nor slowing down. Telegraph Hill Boulevard, the two-lane loop to Coit Tower, bisected the stairs. As we ran in place, cars whipped by on the straightway, but when they rounded the next curve their drivers would find themselves idling in a line, waiting for the few parking spots by the tower.

"You are in damned good shape, Karen."

"And you."

"I have to work out every day to keep ready for work. What's your excuse?"

"Muscle memory."

"From?"

"Another life." She caught her breath, and again, and for a moment I thought she'd pass over my question. "I had a job years ago, hauling stuff up a cliff. For months. I'd see that old concrete building in my dreams. At the end of the season I looked like an anatomy text picture. Every muscle outlined. But not anymore. Then I'd've left you in the dust, girl."

"Where was that impressive job?"

She tightened and then gave her head a shake, laughing the way you do when you've suddenly realized something that's perfectly obvious. "Alaska. I've done my share of uphill employment. I was hauling fish in Sue—in Alaska. Luckily, I've had easier jobs since."

"You'd have to have. But listen, don't worry. Whatever's going on, Gary'll take care of you. He's the best."

"I know. That's why I hired him." She hesitated. "Darcy . . . it's not as if we're friends . . . "

"Yet," I said.

"Right. I . . . wanted to . . . "

I glanced over, but suddenly she wasn't there. She was in the middle of the roadway.

Brakes screeched.

"Karen!"

The car was between us.

I raced around it. "Karen!"

She was standing over a teenager in jeans and T-shirt, lying on her back on the sidewalk, clutching a phone.

The driver's head poked out the window. "Idiot!" he yelled. "Look before you walk into traffic! Fucking cell phone!"

The girl pushed herself up, face dead white, and defiantly snapped open her phone. The driver reached for the door, hesitated, shook his head, and shot off down the hill.

"I knew what I was doing!" The girl's voice was shaky. Karen started to reach out to her and caught herself. "I wasn't going to get hit! You didn't need to shove me!"

"Sorry. You okay?"

"Fine. I'm fine. I didn't need any . . . Well, maybe you . . . Maybe I . . ."

Karen shrugged. "Never mind."

The girl gave her a nod and hurried across the roadway and down the steps, her flip-flops slapping the pavement.

Karen watched her go, and I had the sense she was more undone than the girl.

"Are *you* okay, Karen?"

"Maybe I did overreact. Car wasn't *that* close."

"They come at a good clip down this road. But listen, if you've got to err—. Like you said yourself, things happen."

"I—" She swallowed and for an instant I thought she was going to cry, or laugh. Instead, she stared up at the tree tops until her face shifted into the same expression she'd had looking at Washington Square. "What a great park! Smell the trees! In Alaska we waited so long for spring we hated to miss a moment of sun or scent. Is that a cedar? The tower? How tall is it?" She eyed the obelisk that commemorated the firemen who saved the city after the 1906 great earthquake and fire.

"Hundred feet."

"More. Surely more."

"You're right, of course. I was thinking of a koan."

"How do you step off the hundred-foot pole?"

"Yeah," I said, surprised. "How'd you know? Are you a Buddhist?"

"No. I just read it somewhere. Love the idea. Maybe someday, when I have more time . . ."

The path ended at the boulevard. Cars in the up lane idled in line. In the down lane, one paused at the stop sign, then drove smugly on.

"How do you progress off a hundred-foot pole?" I'd chewed on that particular koan in my time. It was intended to be about life after enlightenment, but for me it was just about life. I knew how to push my way up in a business where the standards were for men, how to make myself climb higher than anyone thought I could, do stunts others had failed at, how to balance on the top in the wind. I could climb the pole, but to step off, into nothingness, that was a whole 'nother thing. "So, Karen, how *do* you step off the hundred-foot pole?"

"You let go."

"A hundred feet up?"

"You step off the pole and the rules don't matter anymore, because you're already dead."

"Wow. Spoken like a roshi."

"No, listen, I just mean—it's logical isn't it? Better to take your shot downfield than hang on waiting to get sacked."

The football reference surprised me, coming from her. "But still—"

"Falling, you only break your neck." The path ended and she started across the road. A car jerked left to avoid her. She stepped back, shrugged, and said, "You're a stunt double. Maybe you *don't* break your neck if you do it right. What d'you think?"

"You couldn't pay me enough. But that's not the Zen answer. Actually, it's never the Zen answer."

She let out a laugh as if the oddly unnerving interchange had never occurred. The cars backed up and she scooted around the line, skirting the stopped cars, jumping back as passengers got out to walk while their local hosts sat in the exhaust-snorting line. She was taking it all in like it glistened. She reminded me of how I'd felt at the end of long Zen sesshins, walking down the street after days of sitting zazen and seeing everything crisp and bright and wonderful.

I wondered the same thing I had half an hour ago: Who was this woman who needed a babysitter? Who was this non-Buddhist who'd

11

danced around this koan like it was a Maypole? I hesitated, then decided: "Karen," I said when we got to the circle at the top, "you want to get dinner?"

She started, then a smile spread across her face. "I'd really like that. But my treat. Let's go somewhere really nice. Somewhere"—she caught my eye and laughed—"above our element."

"How far above do you have in mind?"

"One of those places you need to seriously bribe the maitre d'. Somewhere with a view."

I glanced at my watch: 5:02. "I'm going to have to go get ready for my stunt. But listen, it's at California and Market. Why don't you come down and watch when you're done with Gary? It's a car gag, bouncing off a run-away cable car. A pretty big deal. Water gushing. Ambulances and fire trucks all over. They're going to close Market Street and the Embarcadero. I'll leave word to let you onto the set. The schedule calls for a twilight shot, but I can't swear how long it'll run. Come around eight. If it's still going, you can watch the action. If it's over, we'll go eat." I added, "Above our element."

"Sure," she said, so offhandedly it was hard not to feel dismissed.

A horn honked. I turned to glare. "Hang on, Karen, that's my brother."

"The missing one!"

"No, no. My oldest brother. Give me a minute, okay?"

She looked at me curiously. "Darcy . . ."

"Yes?"

"Nothing."

"No, tell me!"

"Okay. None of my business, but . . . your missing brother. You don't want to beat yourself up. 'If only I'd noticed . . .' 'If only I hadn't said . . .' you know? I don't mean to intrude, but you assume something happened and he fell off the pole. Maybe he made a bad decision afterwards. It's easy to jump; hard to climb back on."

I didn't know what to say. I wondered what Gary had told her, and why.

"None of my business. It's just I've had friends . . . and . . . don't be so hard on yourself."

The horn beeped again. I headed toward it and when I turned back, Karen was walking toward the parapet.

John was pulling into a legal parking spot, something he rarely troubled to do. That meant he hadn't swung around the waiting traffic, Code 3'd it up the down lane, and parked in the crosswalk, which would have saved him twenty minutes. He was dressed in a suit that fit better than any I'd seen on him. He looked good; he looked *not* like a cop. "You here on a case?" I asked, leaning into his car window.

He ignored my question—his family trademark—and opened the door, forcing me to jump back. I took that to mean Yes. He put an arm around my shoulder and walked us toward the west side of the circle. I have affectionate siblings, but John is not one of them. His arm around my shoulder historically meant I was about to hear something unlikely to improve my day.

"Amazing view, huh?"

"Yeah, John. Same as it's been for a century." I shifted my shoulders, but he held on tight. "You passing yourself off as a tourist? Keeping an eye on someone who can't spot an unmarked?"

"Just here to think."

"About annexing my shoulder?"

"About Mike."

"You drove an unmarked car, sat in a line of exhaust-spewing cars for twenty minutes, so you could park your official vehicle in a civilian spot in a crowded tourist attraction and not look at the view, all so you could have some thought about Mike that you haven't considered in the twenty years since he disappeared?"

"This new lead you think you've got. You're not going to find anything there."

He squeezed my shoulder in a way he never had the entire time he was barking orders and complaining that we younger kids were out of control. Something was going on with my oldest, stiffest, most wary-making brother. I waited.

"I've been all over. I've checked every possible lead from San Diego to Seattle and beyond. I've had PIs on retainer."

"And you kept them all to yourself? Did you think—"

"You want to hear about each dead end?"

I turned toward John, trying to read him. "This conversation could be about Mike, but it's not, is it? What's the matter, John? Are you okay?"

"Sure." He bent near and hugged me. I was so stunned I didn't move. Then I hugged him back, feeling like I was in the middle of a stunt and hadn't read the script.

"Who's your friend?"

I followed his gaze and saw Karen through John's eyes: a slim, attractive blonde checking her phone messages as she waited for one of the telescopes to free up. She caught his eye and smiled, a sweet, longing expression. He wasn't a bad looking guy. None of the star quality of Gary, but he was in decent shape, graying at the temples, and today sporting a lime green shirt that set off the green in his eyes, evincing a sartorial concern I'd never seen him show before. He'd sure dressed for someone. But not Karen. As for her, I felt sure she ached not for John, but for the sweet closeness she assumed we shared. John, though, was seeing something entirely different. He was smiling back with a hesitant, vulnerable expression. His whole being screamed: vulnerable.

Be careful, big brother! You're out of your league with her. What you need—What he needed was to snap him back to himself. "You've had a PI on retainer? And he's never found a lead to Mike? Maybe what he's found is a patsy."

"Patsy! You don't know what you're talking about."

Ah, that was the John I knew.

He put his arm back around my shoulder, but this time to herd me to the walkway where he could hold forth more privately. "I don't walk onto your movie sets and decide I can do stunts, do I? But you assume you can do missing persons better than the police. I'm the professional, I—"

"John!"

"What!"

"Your car. That's your car! Someone's stealing your car!"

A woman screamed and grabbed a toddler, as the car shot past. Karen Johnson was at the wheel.

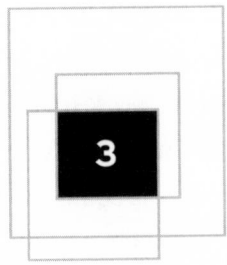

3

"SHE STOLE MY CAR!" John yelled at me as the unmarked shot across the parking circle onto the exit road.

I ran after. Skidded to a stop. No way I'd catch her. The exit road had no traffic, and only one stop sign. You don't boost a police car, then brake for stop signs.

I raced for the sidewalk, jumped the parapet into the trees and underbrush. It wasn't a dead drop but close. I skidded tree to tree. Below was the Lombard curve where the road ended. I had to catch her there. If she beat me, she'd be out into the warren of North Beach streets, in an unmarked black car made to draw no attention.

I slammed into exposed roots, grabbed for a tree trunk, swung around it. The hill was steeper, rockier, the drop to the curve almost straight down. I shot a glance at the road. Car barreling down. A family started across, jaywalking. Car kept coming.

"Karen!" I yelled. "Karen! Stop!"

She wasn't braking. Wasn't slowing. She was going to hit them.

"Get back! Get your kids on the sidewalk!"

A siren shrieked. I stumbled, leapt, landed hard ten feet down on the cement.

The car shot by, siren suddenly keening. The family huddled at the edge of the macadam; the woman flat out on the cement.

I ran into the road, after the car. Karen turned left onto a side street—out of the park, into North Beach—and when I reached the street she was gone. There was only one way she could have turned, but at the next corner there were more options and more at the next after that. She was out of sight, but in the distance, the siren screamed. The siren was still on!

No problem. I stopped, gasping for breath. John would have called in the theft. By now every patrol car in North Beach would be closing in. The woman had been an idiot to steal the car, and a lucky idiot not to have killed anyone, but now, pinpointing herself with the siren, she was just a run-of-the-mill dolt.

I stood, catching my breath, listening for new sirens, for sirens converging. Instead, silence. I tried to gauge where the sound last came from. No luck. I dug out my phone and called Gary. Gary's machine. "Gar, get ready for a call from Karen. Whatever trouble she had an hour ago, it's nothing to what she's in now. She stole John's car, his unmarked police car! Hey, what the hell's going on? Call me!"

I hurried up the path. I needed to get to my brother before backup arrived. Before a uniform scooped him up and spit him out at the scene of Karen's arrest, wherever that would be. How was I going to explain this to John? I slowed my pace. I couldn't explain it to myself! I liked Karen. Liked that despite whatever was going on with her, she was interested in Mike. And me. *Don't beat yourself up!* She'd paused to say that on her way to steal the car!

I was impressed by her immediate, certain response to the hundred-foot pole koan. *You are atop a hundred-foot pole. How do you proceed?* Letting go, I knew from reading rather than experience, meant not releasing your grasp and falling in terror, but rather stepping out of the past, out of who you are, into the next moment, whatever that moment brings. It was about walking though a door to the unknown. But was it stepping out of your life as a soon-to-be-divorced woman to drive away in a stolen police car?

What could possibly have spurred her to do such a crazy thing? Chance? The keys, obviously, had been in the ignition. *That* was going to make John look great. "Just-so John," as he was called behind his back in the department, was now going to be just a laughingstock. Cops don't leave the keys in the car. Civilians in San Francisco don't leave their keys, not unless they're hot to be pedestrians. The one small saving grace for him would be the muzzling of his biggest fun-poker—Gary would be silent, indeed.

Gary with his hush-hush client, John suddenly gone irresponsible, and . . . Karen . . . What the hell was going on here? I needed time to think. But time was the one thing I didn't have.

A couple speaking German ambled down the steps. I veered around them and headed up. I wanted to beat the reinforcements John would have called, but not by too much.

What could have made Karen pull a crazy stunt like stealing a police car? I asked again, as if it was the koan. I was walking slowly now.

How do you proceed off a hundred-foot pole?

You step forward.

But something triggers that decision. According to John, chance is a bigger cause of crime than the law-abiding would like to believe. But he sure wasn't going to make that argument in this case. Not and have the fault be all his own.

I rounded the top of the stairs onto the observation circle. No patrol cars. Good.

"John!"

His eyes were jammed to a telescope pointing far right and down into the bushes. "See anything?"

"What do you think? No! She . . . took . . . my . . . car!" He was almost yelling. Behind him people moved away fast. "What the hell got into her?"

"I don't know, John!"

"You brought her here!"

"It was a fluke."

"Fluke? Yeah, right!" He turned and strode back from the parapet, got a car-length away, charged back, planted himself inches from my face. "You brought her. How come?"

"I didn't *bring* her. I'd just met her. She wanted to go for a run; I only had an hour. We were in Washington Square. This was just the logical place—"

"Washington Square, a minute from Gary's office. Gary! He's behind this," he shouted at me, light dawning, "isn't he?"

"Stealing a police car? Are you nuts? I've kept away from our family all of my adult life. I hardly know either one of you. But that's just crazy."

He was pulling in breath through clenched teeth, eyeing me like I was a suspect. "It's Gary, isn't it? What did he tell you?"

He told me to rabbits. Why had Gary insisted I not tell him? Gary was my buddy, but he was what I loved in guys—a brat. Could John possibly be right?

His face was growing purple. I'd never seen him this out of control. He dug his fingers into my arm. "Don't you clam up to protect him."

"Let go of me!"

His grip loosened. I jumped back.

"Not Gary, huh? You saying *she* set us all up? What do you know about her? You tell me! Why did Gary say to bring her here?"

Ah. "Gary didn't. He only told her I'd take her running. He didn't say where."

"So *you* chose Coit Tower?"

"No, she wanted a high spot with a view and trees . . . oh."

"Exactly. What did she say to you?"

"She's getting a divorce. But she didn't go into that. She just about got killed shoving a girl out of the way of a car. Driver was furious."

"Really?" For an instant he seemed taken aback.

"Yeah, just as suddenly as she decided to take your car. People *do* lose it in divorces, you know."

"What else?"

"A Zen koan; she talked about that, and about Mike."

John barked out a laugh. "Your two favorite subjects!"

"Hey, I don't—"

"What else did she say?"

"Nothing! No, wait. There was one last thing, but it's not going to help you. She was trying to be kind. She said, don't beat yourself up—meaning me—about Mike."

He nodded, his lips tensed into a slight sneer I knew all too well. "So you liked her, right?"

"What's wrong with that!"

He took a step back and shook his head. His expression said I was an idiot. "If someone's your friend, they're okey-dokey and the rest of the world just doesn't understand. You're sure you see something the rest of us're too thick to get. Your friends, you'll move heaven and earth to justify them. You've always been that way. Used to be Mike, now it's Gary. So Gary couldn't have set this up . . ." His voice trailed off and I had the feeling he found it hard to believe Gary had purposely sabotaged him either. "If it's Mike, he must've walked out of the house one Thursday in a bubble

21

of innocence and been spirited off to another life. Because you adored him, there has to be some very fine, all-redeeming reason a forty-three-year-old man can't walk back in the door now and just say, "I screwed up."

I just stared. Then I said the only possible thing. "Fuck you!"

A patrol car, lights flashing, raced up the down lane of the exit road. When John spotted it, he jumped back and the expression on his face was not that of a police detective relieved to have a ride back to the station. Nor did he take the all too familiar gritted teeth inhalation of one prepared to take a ribbing. His expression was momentary; the next instant he was walking toward the car, leaning down toward the driver. But during that moment, I could have sworn his face showed a flash of fear.

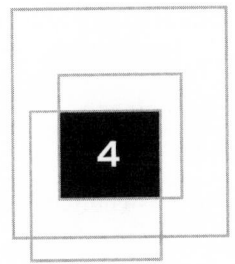

4

I RAN TOWARD the patrol car.

John glanced back at me, got in and slammed the door. The car sped away down Telegraph Hill Boulevard.

"Damn you!" I was so furious—so hurt—and stunned by his attack, my temptation was just to let him deal or sink. What I needed to do was get to the location and get ready for my gag. It was already 5:30. In an hour I'd be turning the ignition key. But there was no way I could just let John go, not as out of control as he'd been.

I leapt the observation ledge, skidded between pines and cypress, pushed off and leapt for the plaza.

They were almost at the Lombard curve. I slid down the double railings, swung forward and hit the sidewalk.

John glared out the window. He still had that panicky look. The vehicle picked up speed, nearly hitting a cab. Both paused momentarily. John made some kind of signal, and the patrol car shot away.

I yanked the cab door open and flung myself in. "Hang a U."

"I can't do a U here!"

"Of course you can. John will cover for you. He's not paying you to lose him."

"He's not paying me at all."

"He will when we get there. *If* you don't lose him, Webb."

Webb Framington Morratt hung a U, shooting me across the leather seat, then hit the gas. He was on what he called an unofficial retainer from John. Very unofficial. I wasn't sure the range of things he did for my brother *or* their legality. But he definitely wouldn't want to offend him. "Keep him in sight."

"He didn't tell me to trail him."

"Of course he didn't. When he called you, he figured he'd be sitting back here with me. He didn't figure you'd screw around so long a patrol car would get to him first."

"I didn't—"

"No matter. Just keep up because I don't have the address."

When we got there, John would be livid, Webb Morratt would be outraged, and the next time I needed to make use of Morratt I'd pay for it. But that would be then; this was now. "John uses you because you can tail a car in traffic. Because you *say* you can. Don't give him reason to doubt it. Your record for honesty isn't the best."

He grunted, but did step on the gas.

I braced my feet as we shot through the narrow North Beach streets, the cab swaying as Webb whipped around corners.

What was with John? If he'd stayed up nights planning the cut, he couldn't have pierced deeper. Mike was four years older than me; I'd adored him. In a family where siblings paired off, he was my other half. I told him everything; he told me . . . less than I'd realized. When he disappeared, I was fifteen. As a family we held together; individually and in private we fell apart. John, for his part, just plowed on. Why this outburst now of all times?

Morratt was watching me in the rearview mirror. I took a breath. "Tourist season, and you've still got time to hang around for John."

Morratt scowled, his round pink head scrunched like a ball a retriever had just had a go at. The ball unwrinkled a bit. He hesitated, fighting his urge to sound off. It was a losing battle. "What'd you think, John's my patron? I do some work for him. He's front of the queue, but he's not keeping me in gas. There've been times I've missed airport runs for him. Fast fares. It's a big loss I incur for John."

If I'd been biting my lip I'd have bled to death. "But you could pick up fares at Coit Tower the times you dropped him off, right?" I was trying to make sense of it all.

"I never dropped him off there."

Was he lying? Damn! What was my brother doing up there that he was so hot to hide? Wait a minute. "So you've just *picked him up* there."

He nodded, with a grunt.

Of course. "Cheapskate. You mean he'd have called another cab to get him up there? So he didn't have to pay you to wait?" Pay him to sit around enjoying the view while the meter ticked? To note whatever it was he was doing up there. So Morratt could tell me.

He studied my face in the mirror. Now he had his eyes on the rearview the whole time. The road was incidental. "Yeah."

"There were times he called you, right, and you dropped everything, right, and then he wasn't ready and you had to sit around and wait, on your own sweet time, right?"

His eyes narrowed. Even Webb Morratt had a limit. Just as I was deciding on a different approach, he said grudgingly, "Nah. If he made me wait, he made it up."

"And when you had to go out of your way to take his friend down with him, was that on the meter, too?"

"Nah, that wasn't the problem. It was him driving around dead silent after, going crazy if I said two words. You know what a bummer that is

25

when you're alone hauling hack all day and finally you get someone you can shoot the breeze with and he clams up, plus makes you clam, and even—get this—turn off the radio. Like a tomb. And when he—"

A horn honked.

Morratt shot a glance out the window. Traffic was almost stopped. Ahead on the left was the Ferry Building and for a moment I wondered whether there was a reception or rally there. Then I spotted the cause of the hold-up. It was the set. *My* set, where I'd be doing my stunt in—yikes!—fifty-five minutes. As I'd told Karen Johnson, Market Street was closed for two blocks, from here up past California Street, which was where the action would be. I could see two fire engines and an ambulance, and a huge crowd—workers stopping on their way to the Embarcadero BART station, streetcars out to the Castro, Glen Park, the avenues, or buses to the East Bay.

The black-and-white stayed on the Embarcadero under the Bay Bridge and cut right on Brannan. From there it was an easy shot to the bridge entry at Second Street. If John got on the bridge, I was sunk. No pedestrian walk. But he didn't. He shot across Second Street on Brannan. He was headed toward the Mission. Damn! Toward the Hall of Justice. He'd flagged the patrol car to take him back to the police station! Ahead, the light was turning red. John shot through it. I thought the police were being more careful about jumping lights now that the city was making a big deal about it. Morratt followed.

Was this really a prank? Karen Johnson an actress set up by Gary to ensnare me? I'd even asked her to dinner. But I couldn't believe—

Like John said, I couldn't believe it of Karen, nor could I of Gary. Definitely not.

He passed Sixth Street without slowing, without veering from the left-hand lane. The Hall was at Seventh and Bryant, one block north.

I watched for his taillight, but cops don't always announce their intentions. Still, when he neared the corner without signaling I wondered if I'd been made and he was just running out the game. In the distance a siren pierced the air.

He crossed Seventh, kept going. Between Eighth and Ninth John turned around and the driver hit the gas. I had been made. But he was almost into the mix of streets under the freeway, not a place to lose someone. What was he doing here in the Mission? He *was* a detective; maybe in the middle of all this, he'd been called to a dead body. Maybe by now Karen Johnson and her appropriation of his unmarked car had been shoved out of his mind.

The siren was louder. John's car picked up speed on the Fifteenth Street hill. A truck pulled out and across at Caledonia, blocking the entire street.

Metal crunched. The siren went dead.

I got out and ran through the stopped traffic, across the blocked street, pushing hard, up to the corner at Valencia, then started down the hill.

The patrol car John had been in was double-parked, the driver standing behind his open door. The focus of his attention—everyone's focus of attention—was ten yards further on.

There, in front of a trio of well-kept Victorians was a black-and-white, engine steaming, grill crunched into a fire hydrant. Two officers stood next to it shaking themselves, first arms and then legs, as if to prove they were in better shape than their car. A woman in a royal purple velvet sweat suit—the type you'd never dream of sweating in—and sling-back heels was striding angrily into the house. On the sidewalk, San Francisco Police Department Detective John Lott—my brother, John—looked devastated.

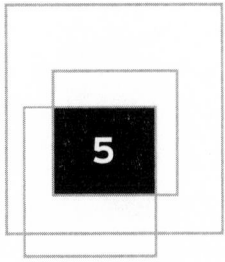

5

THE SWEAT-SUITED woman turned back toward the house and motioned John over with an imperious flick of the wrist. She looked furious.

He was pretty near boiling over himself. As he strode toward her, no one but a sibling would have known how close to the edge he was, but I could tell that from the brick-stiff fingers on the hand he was fighting not to make into a fist. I didn't envy the velvet woman this encounter. John had never touched any of us younger kids, but he could degrade, humiliate and disgrace all with one phrase. It had made us wary and his friendships brief.

The woman stood on the stoop in her spike heels, he on the walk. Still, he had a couple inches on her and it looked like he could tuck her under his arm. Her expression said: Try it! She was probably in her fifties, but well cared for, with dark hair slant cut to her chin line. She raised a hand. A bracelet sparkled, diamonds all around. Definitely not a woman planning to sweat. Without raising her voice enough for me to hear five yards away, she lit into John.

I had to stop myself charging over to protect him.

She spat out a few more words, turned her back and tapped up the steps. It appeared she'd out-Johned John.

He looked close to snapping. It wasn't just anger, there was something else—something I couldn't quite put a name to.

"What was *that*?" I demanded.

"Darcy! Get out of here *now*."

"What *was* that?" I repeated, ignoring him.

"Later."

"Tell me *now*."

He leaned forward. "Later!" I could have sworn the expression on his face as he looked at me was fear. Then it vanished and he motioned one of the patrolmen. "Cordon off the block from the corner—"

I checked the time. I had to get to the set. A stunt double who keeps the whole production company waiting, won't be working again—ever!

But I couldn't leave John like this.

I scanned the crowd behind us—a large, holiday-spirit kind of group—for the person who'd know what'd happened, and tell me quickly. An elderly man, in beaked cap and Giants jacket looked eager to talk—too eager. A flicker of sunlight glistened off the aluminum handle on a stroller, but I discounted the mother holding on. Too distractible. Then I spotted a woman in jeans holding a coin pouch and an empty container of soap. I sidled up next to her. "What's going on? Did you see the whole thing from the Laundromat across the street?"

She glanced at her watch—*right choice!* "Six minutes on the dryer. Okay"—she looked over at me—"yeah, I heard the siren, but, I mean, who pays any attention to sirens? It was the brakes that got me. Cop must've been standing on the brake pedal. The black car—looked like an unmarked—it cut into the oncoming lane, siren going, but even if you're a cop with the siren, you can't just do that, you know? No one expects a car coming at you head on, even a cop car. She sideswiped it"—she pointed to the patrol car across the street—"and it went smack into that hydrant. Unbelievable."

"Where's the driver? The woman?"

She shrugged. "My washer was down to two minutes and there are only six dryers and I wasn't alone in the place, so I grabbed a cart and ran it across the room to save a dryer. She must've backed up. Next thing I saw she was shooting around the corner down there. From the sound of it, she must've cut off a couple of cars doing it. It's just a guess, but I'd say she didn't have the light with her."

"After that?"

"Gone. She stopped after that turn. Probably the horns and brakes and everything stunned her. She stopped, like she was about to be a good citizen and not leave the scene. Then, like, you know, she must've realized she'd hit a cop car, not just the other one, and decided to get out while the getting was good."

"So?"

"Squealed off. Jesus, talk about hit-and-run!"

"They didn't go after her?"

"Couldn't. They'd have had to be hooked to a tow truck!"

When I'd told Karen Johnson I'd misjudged her, I hadn't known the half of it.

Two patrol cars pulled up, double-parking a few feet to our left. My companion took a step away from me and I got the feeling I had pressed too hard. But, now or never. "Any guy in a suit come here a lot?" I glanced in the direction of John. Without meaning to.

"Yeah," she said, picking up the implication I hadn't intended. "Look, I've got to go get my clothes." I let her go.

It couldn't be. Not John. Officers from the arriving cars now hurried toward him. A curtain shifted in the Victorian's window. There was someone looking out. Was she watching John, in his expensive new suit, and the shirt that brought out his eyes? John, furious and fearful.

I tried to see him from my just-departed informant's perspective. She had to be wrong. The crowd was dissipating now, thinned by the monotony of the action. I made my way toward him.

There had been suspicions about John. When I heard any such innuendoes I put them down to the usual departmental resentments. John could be overbearing. He *was* overbearing. Gary and Gracie, Mike and I had bitched about him throughout our childhoods. John, The Enforcer.

I had lived away from San Francisco all my adult life. When I looked at John now I still peered with the wary gaze of the teenager I'd once been. For the second time today, I asked myself who was this man.

As if to remind me of the answer, John turned toward me. "Get out of here! Now!"

Instinctively I planted my feet. I have a long history of staying in John's face. "You want me out of here? Get someone to drive me to the set!"

Normally, he'd have chewed me out loud and long. Now, he grabbed my arm, walked me to a patrol car, and shoved me in the cage. "Take her to the movie set, Jenkins. And don't answer any questions."

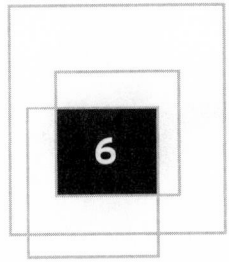

6

THE GUARD AT the set checked me in.

"Duffy's right here," he said, grinning.

He wagged his black stump of a tail. It was a big statement for a dour Scotty. But Duffy adores being on the set. I keep running into people who remember him from this western or that romance. He's done Fala three times that I know of in FDR biopics. There's a mystique about him. In a business that puts a high premium on superstition, he's viewed as such a good luck omen the directors send cars for him.

I'd inherited him when his previous owner scarpered minutes before the sheriff's arrival on a location set in the high desert. He'd paused only to leave me Duffy and a bag of what I assumed would be dog supplies but turned out to be lock picks and a few other useful items that explained the fellow's hasty departure. He'd never come back for Duff. On the lam or in the can; I chose to believe the former.

We walked on to the base of California and I stood a moment staring at the eerie sight. The California Street cable car shoots down the slope from Nob Hill nearly to the Bay. It stops abruptly just beyond the corner of Drumm, where the intersection smacks up against Market. Traffic pours down California, shoots across Drumm, then merges in one great lump ready to shove across Market on a light that's never green long enough. There, old green streetcars with tiny high windows, resurrected from the streetcar graveyard in Brooklyn, and sunny orange cars with big happy windows, retired from Milan, ferry excited visitors up and down the broad thoroughfare. But not tonight. Tonight Market was blocked off, traffic detoured to Mission. Drumm was silent, and nothing moved on California. The last time I'd seen it this still was right after the Loma Prieta quake.

Just above the intersection, a cable car sat empty. At the west end of the block, another was poised to head down. Cardboard mock-up autos, created in studio, lined the downhill lane as if waiting for the light to change so they could shoot across Market to points south and east.

"Running behind," Jed Elliot, the second unit director greeted me. "Only half an hour."

I shrugged, trying to hide how relieved I was. Location costs—equipment, salaries, site fees—were big budget issues for producers and no one wanted to be responsible for delays that threw production into the next day.

Elliot and Duffy eyed each other. Then Duffy jumped into his chair.

The fingers of fog were reaching over Nob Hill, less than a mile west of here. Thirty minutes was about as long as the *thin* fog shot would hold. Once it got its elbow over the hill, it would punch down thick and heavy. After that Jed Elliot would be dealing with a night shot and the lighting would need to be reworked, not to mention all the script adjustments. There was going to be heavy pressure to wrap on the first run-through. If we did manage to start at 7:00, we'd be fine, though.

Karen Johnson had been going to meet me here at 8:00 P.M. Instead, where would she be by then? Where was she now? In jail? In San Jose? San Francisco's a peninsula, so there's only one way to go if you don't dare take a hot car across a bridge. And John . . . What had she gotten John into? I'd liked her; but now. . . I just hoped Gary'd picked up my message.

I walked up the block and around the corner to the stunt car, a shiny burnt-orange convertible that would look great in the shots—assuming we still had some light. The modifications had been minor—extra air bags, padded lap harness that wouldn't show, a good sized weight in the passenger side of the trunk. This part of the gag would be straightforward: around the corner, clip the uphill cable car, shimmy my own ride as if losing control, side swipe a couple junkers, appear to straighten out and crash into the downhill cable car. It was a precision run, meaning it had to be done in one take. The light wouldn't hold, and the junkers could only be hit once without looking like, well, junkers.

"Straight fiction shot."

The cameraman laughed.

In the final cut the scene would show the actress I was doubling speeding across Front Street to the corner of California, glancing across at the wedge of the 101 California building that juts toward the corner like a sharp cake knife. Assuming the street made a gentle 45 degree curve, she'd continue alongside the building, not realizing she was in the middle of the intersection. Because the building side road was an illusion, it required, after clipping a cable car, cutting left, sharply and instantly. It'd be a great visual.

A bit of poetic license was the slope. In the final cut I'd be shooting down the steep incline of California Street. That incline, however, was actually four blocks west. Between Front and the Bay, the street was flat. Put a marble on the sidewalk here and it'd stay dead still. Tomorrow I'd drive the incline. Later that shot would be edited in.

I checked the tires, slid under the chassis to make sure everything was connected. This little orange sports car wasn't new, but it wasn't a junker of the caliber I'd driven in other gags. The problem with those old cars is there's a reason they were junked and that probably didn't happen at the point when they had one hard ride left in them. I'd slid under one and found brake cables dragging.

With this car, though, everything looked good. It was the second unit director's job to make sure it was. Still, Jed Elliot wasn't the one who'd be slapping it into two eight-ton cable cars. A stunt double who wants to live triple-checks everything. It scared me how close I'd come to not having enough time. I walked to the corner to eye the slide patch. The slippery base had been laid the width of the cable car plus five feet beyond, to allow me to spin while on it and be off the edge the moment I needed traction to pull out.

I slid in, clasped the belt, visualized the gag: from turning the key, letting up the brake, feeling the pressure of the gas pedal under my foot, to picking up speed as I turned onto California, then hard-righting the wheel to skid right, and sending the tail left to clip the cable car. I ran through it, started again, this time visualizing the front of the cable car, the "60" in the middle of its front end, feeling my arms and shoulders thrust right as I pulled into the skid. I felt the impact, saw the skid, the steering wheel spinning back through my hands, the clutch as I pulled left into the turn, brushing a dummy dressed to represent a terrified tourist. A yard beyond that would be the low ramp. I needed to yank the wheel full left so I hit the ramp already into the turn and got enough centrifugal force for the 360.

Fifteen minutes to go. Ahead, the crew was adjusting one of the in-place cameras set against the corner of the building. There'd be other fixed cameras rolling and, once I started, the camera cart with a driver every bit as skilled as I was would be ahead on my left. It was going to be a tight run for him. He'd have to be as aware as I was of the ramp. If he was too close when I did the 360, I'd slam him into the wall.

I began to picture it one more time, now focusing on the end of the run. But when I closed my eyes, the picture in my mind was not the street in front but the road leading up to Coit Tower. And Karen Johnson. How could she have done something as stupid as stealing a cop car? Was it a publicity stunt? She sure handled the car like a getaway driver. Could John possibly be right about Gary setting the whole thing up? Giving her directions to Madame Velvet's house where John was so unaccountably thrown off his stride, and anxious for me to be gone.

But if Gary didn't set it up, if she had stolen the car on her own, could she have known John would be waiting at Coit Tower? Not impossible. Webb Moratt knew. And just what was John expecting, all dolled up in his suit like that?

John! I kept coming back to his expression—more like anguish than simple anger.

"You okay?" Jed Elliot leaned toward the window. He looked barely warm enough in a heavy fleece jacket and watch cap.

"Fine." I willed myself not to shiver in the fifty degree night, sitting there in a spaghetti string halter. *Be tough, shoulders!* "I've done plenty of car work."

"Sure." He meant that he didn't know me, yet.

"I was fine driving this baby yesterday, right?"

"Three minutes. Fog's good, but the light's going faster than we figured, so we need to do it in one."

Keeping my hand relaxed on the wheel, I smiled up at him. "Right."

As he walked away I eyed the road ahead. The cameraman stubbed out a cigarette and slid into his cart. In the thickening fog his little open vehicle looked like a refugee from a soapbox derby.

Even if I'd just been driving here to dinner—meeting Karen Johnson for a shared meal "above our element"—I'd be slowing down and paying attention to headlights as the first bit of fog blurred the air. Had this been real life, here on California Street, cars would have been bumper

37

to bumper, taillights glowing like Christmas balls. Jed had done a good job simulating it. He'd set up dummies, cardboard mock-ups of a BMW, Mercedes, two Hondas and a Ford, with the two breakaway cars I'd hit. Beyond the cardboard set-up was the spew cart, the obligatory display of fruit or vegetables, or in this case fish, that would be hit, depositing its contents all over the road. However, the fog was Jed's friend: even the oldest dummy would look fine tonight.

John! Where was he—

Focus! Focus or die! I exhaled oh-so-slowly and tried to clear my mind.

"Thirty seconds!"

"Engine!"

I turned the ignition. It seemed an eternity before it caught. Outside I heard the grunt of the camera cart starting up.

"Clear the set! Get off!" someone yelled. I shot a glance across the street. Was there someone in eggshell blue over on the sidewalk? Could Karen really be here? "Action!"

I punched the gas. Continuity would pick up ten feet before the corner, where I left off yesterday. I needed to hit 30 there. Fog smeared the windshield. The car burst through it, like stepping off the hundred-foot pole. *Focus!* 25, 30. I eased the wheel left, as if falling for the illusory road next to the wedge of 101 California.

The first cable car loomed, and I jimmied the wheel in "panic." The camera cart cut in close. I hit the slip pad, yanked the wheel hard right. Then the skid, and I was slamming the rear fender into the front corner of the cable car. Fog blurred the street. I cut left, down California, shimmied onto the cable car tracks, overcorrected full out, smacked the first junker, bounced left, hard-righted into the second. The dummy pedestrian popped out. I skimmed it, slammed the brake.

The car lurched—hard-right, hard-left—as I hit the ramp and clung to the wheel. It bounced, spun, going wide toward a lamppost on the far sidewalk. The front bumper missed but the rear smacked it. Metal crunched. Drifting out of the circle, I yanked the wheel back into the spin. The second cable car was two yards to my left. I went up over the sidewalk, slammed into the fish wagon from the back. Big, sloppy, silvery fish flew against the windshield. Slime turned the glass gray. I couldn't see anything.

The cable car was dead ahead, the passengers' bare legs dangling from the outside benches. I stood on the brakes. The shrill squeal cut the air.

A fish flew over the windshield into my face.

"Sheesh!" I said as I pulled to a stop and someone opened the door. "Did you have to get day-old fish?"

He didn't react.

I snapped the belt free and was out of the car. "The cameraman okay?"

Another fish hit me. "Jes' fine, thank you."

Shoes hitting pavement, disembodied cheers came through the fog. "Good work!" Jed was calling. "You get it all?" he was asking. In reply, the cameraman was flinging another fish. Duffy was barking, then he leapt into my arms, making everyone laugh.

I'd lucked out. This time. What a day it had been since that call from Gary. It scared me how closed I'd come to losing focus. I had a fire gag coming up in a couple days. Fire's fire. If I couldn't focus then, I'd die.

It was night now. The streetlights blurred the road surface under the fog and I was glad I wasn't the one making sure every dead fish was swept away. Duffy jumped down. I headed west toward the corner where I'd started. It was just the second unit—the stunt crew—here tonight. They'd be a few minutes packing up before we met at Harrington's, the site of the per diem. It was the few minutes I needed. Common sense told me this was the last place Karen Johnson would come. Common sense said I'd imagined that flutter of blue cloth.

But, still, I wasn't ready to rule it out.

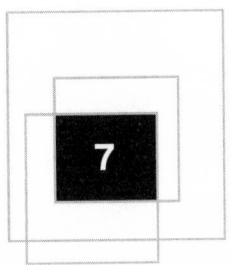

7

THERE WERE A LOT of places Karen Johnson could have been in the vicinity of California and Davis. None panned out. I called John's cell. No answer. Ditto Gary. By the time I walked back down the hill toward Harrington's the euphoria from the gag had evaporated and I was tired, worried, and frustrated. Duffy, on the other hand, was annoyed and hungry.

"Come on!" Jed was just leading the crew inside. "We've got a section at the far end of the bar."

"Reserved?"

"Commandeered."

"Yeah, we weren't very restrained last night," a tech chuckled. "Hey Darcy, your drive was great. You got a lot of distance with those fish. Brad's still out with the broom and searchlight. Poor guy."

"Thanks. But, listen, I'd better eat out here with Duffy."

"Bring 'im!"

"Yeah, he's one of us!" The crowd, about a dozen strong, surrounded us and we moved inside as one. If the bartender noticed the small black shape, he didn't let on. We pushed tables together and ate in a single very loud group, with shrimp on the table, beef strips under it. Duffy, who was not the sort to lower himself to beg, or bark in a no-bark area, never had his mouth empty long enough to reconsider. I had grilled calamari and a beer, and enjoyed being part of a crew again, not to mention hearing their praise.

"Hey, guys," I called out when there was a trough in the noise level, "did you notice a blonde woman in a pale blue linen pantsuit standing by the curb? I thought I spotted her there just as I was starting the gag."

"And you didn't pull over and check her out?"

"You'd done another three-sixty maybe you coulda caught 'er."

Everyone was into it.

"Listen, if you remember you did see her, call me."

"She a friend?"

I hesitated. "Truth? I don't know. But I do want to see her again."

"I'll be going over the dailies," Jed said, waving the waitress over to get the tab. "I'll call you if I spot anything."

"Thanks." I gave him my card, not that I expected him to have her on film. But it doesn't hurt for the second unit director to have your card in his pocket.

An early morning call loomed for everyone but me, and by half past nine people were cutting out.

I left Duffy outside while I used the ladies' room and when I came out the street was empty, or nearly so. Only Brad, the guy in charge of fish removal, was still at work, him and the last of the police detail double-checking to make sure no civilian tried to follow my route down the road. The cops were laughing at the idea of a fish wagon down here in the financial district. Movie location duty was a plum and I wasn't surprised to see a guy John's age sitting in his warm car. I tapped on this window.

"Yes?" he said questioningly. "Oh, hey, you're Lott's sister. I heard you were working this set. It you that did that drive?"

I nodded, pulling my totally inadequate fleece vest tighter around me.

"You made it look real. *Real* real! When you hit the pole—great driving."

"Don't let on to anyone on the set, but that wasn't exactly planned."

He laughed. "What about the fish wagon, you supposed to hit that?"

"Yeah, but not so I ended up wearing it." I shivered and turned up my collar.

"You need a ride? If you don't mind riding in the cage."

"What I need's a favor. A big one. I need to get my dog home to Mom."

"John's mom's still there? When him and me were tight—years ago—I had some great times out there. She still make that stew?"

"Always has some ready. She'll be very pleased to see you again. A guy who makes a special trip to bring her her favorite furry child, you're going to just about be enshrined."

Duffy hopped in the heated car. I gave my mother a quick call and loped the few blocks to the zendo. The building was dark, as were the steps upstairs to the living quarters, which was fine, since I had no intention of staying. I changed into a heavy sweatshirt and jeans, clipped on my pouch and headed out into the fog.

From the zendo Gary's office was a ten-minute walk north on Columbus. It's the second-floor front unit in a small Victorian, on a wedge of corner where two streets meet at Columbus. He could have rented a more impressive office, in a more expensive location, but the charm of this little building suited him. His office was a cupola of windows at the fruit end of the pie slice, like a cherry that's slipped off the crust. If you stand on his desk you can see the Golden Gate.

I rang the downstairs bell. I'd given him a lot of leeway today. I'd dropped everything to distract his troubled client, even without him explaining why I'd been called upon. And despite his hanging up on me when I asked! I'd left a message telling him Karen had swiped a police car, and another after she crashed it. Now, Gary could damn well tell me what was going on.

He didn't buzz me in.

I rang again.

No response.

I jumped back and looked up to catch a flicker of guilty movement. But there was no sign of life.

I pulled out my phone and called. He had to be there. I was sure of it. No answer.

"Damn you! Call me!"

There was only one exit. I could have waited. He'd slept in his office before. He'd be likely to spend a more comfortable night in there than I would freezing on his doorstep. But, thanks to Duffy's previous owner, I was the proud possessor of what looked to be the illegitimate offspring of a door key and a lock pick. I let myself in. If Gary wasn't going to explain things himself, then I'd let Karen Johnson's case file do the talking. It was merely a question of finding it.

The last time I'd been here Gary was about to meet with a new client whom for some reason he wanted to impress. So he'd paid his paralegals double time to file away mail, hole-punch documents and put cases back into the file cabinets. Now it was business as usual: the place looked like it'd been burgled. The conference table in the crust end of the wedge held a frightening mountain of cases. Folders were propped against the walls, piled on the floor and in front of the file cabinet, blocking any possibility of putting them away. It was like Gary had forgotten he lived in earthquake country. His apparent belief—not unfounded—was: out of sight out of mind. He had a system, but it was beyond words. What I did know of it was that the most recent case would be on his desk or nearby. Balancing against a padded chair that itself held a stack of files, I stepped over two piles of folders, edged around the desk and almost fell over the body behind it.

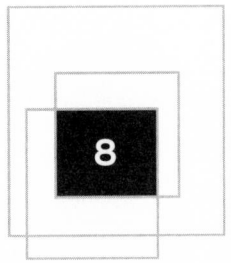

8

I LEAPT BACK, swept the pile of cases off the desk onto the rising figure behind it. That bought me just enough time to reach for Gary's phone and punch in the 9—

"Wait!"

"Huh?" I glared down at the form of my brother John. "What the hell are you doing here?"

"Waiting to get a hold of Gary."

"Back there? You aiming to grab him by the ankles?"

"I wanted to see what kind of amateur it was pulling a b-and-e," he corrected me, as he stood up. "I could have taken a train to the East Bay in the time you spent attacking the lock."

"I'll be quicker next time." I switched on the light and caught the remnant of something on his face. Once I might have called it a "can't control her" look. But I'd seen this same expression when the patrol car had picked him up at Coit Tower. After he'd blindsided me about Mike. Before he yelled at me in front of the crash scene.

"John, what the hell is going on?"

"That's what I want to know."

He was all cop—*we ask, you tell*—now. I could have smacked him. But I wanted answers more. With huge effort, I swallowed my rage and steeled myself to play his game. "Your plan went awry when Karen took your car."

"Your friend stole my car."

"Not *my* friend. The woman you'd been meeting at Coit Tower for how long? I barely knew her, but you, John, you knew her very well. Not as well as you wanted to, you, in your hot guy-on-the-make suit. So, just what were those get-togethers about?"

Was this how cops did it, sucker-punched and watched? If I hadn't been so furious, I would have felt bad, very bad. "You have these clandestine meetings," I went on, "and she steals—oh, no, wait, she doesn't *need* to steal your car. You're her—what?—boy toy? She can just borrow your car. The city won't mind you lending it to a girlfriend. That kind of thing happens all the time. It only creates problems when there's a crash in front of a spiffy Victorian and the buck gets traced to you."

"Are you here to find out something about Gary? Or do you just want to make a scene?" His control was masterful. He wasn't red-faced. His hands weren't in fists. He didn't look like he was about to slug me. Not quite.

"Let me condense my question so you can grasp it: can you explain you and Karen Johnson?"

"It's none of your—"

"Not my business? It's my business, the SFPD's business, the whole city's business."

"It wouldn't have been if you hadn't—"

I shook my head. Just stared at him.

His stared back, his face taut, walling off the machinations going on behind it. "Okay. You're right."

"Right about what?"

"I'm meeting her for a torrid affair. You're just wrong about the Victorian. We're using the Laundromat across the street. It's more practical. We can get a clean load—"

"This is serious."

"You don't think I can have a serious affair?" He settled back on the desk. He knew he'd won.

In his mind I was still his baby sister, in front of whom he'd dangled toys out of reach and spelled out secret words to the other big kids. I could have screamed.

I had to regroup, but not now. Definitely not here. "So what'd you find among Gary's mire?"

"Nothing."

"All your own speedy lock-picking for nothing?" The office looked more daunting a muddle in the light. Even if John or I knew exactly what to grab there'd be less than a ten percent chance of finding it in here. "I'm assuming by your presence here in the dark, without a warrant?"—

He nodded.

—"that your issue is personal rather than police business."

He offered the most grudging of grunts. "But you brought her to Coit Tower. How come?"

"Gary called. Told me zip. I'm as much in the dark as you. I don't know whether he planned the carjacking or she did or she did it on the spur. What do you think?"

I expected him to attack or evade, but he surprised me. He cleared Gary's chair and settled into it. "Dunno, Darcy. There've always been gags and gotchas in the family, me trying to keep control—okay, I know, with a way heavier hand than you kids wanted. Particularly Gary. Three years younger with too much time spent trying to show me up."

I resisted the urge to come to the defense of Gary—and, in fact, all the rest of us.

"But lately . . ."

"Lately?" I prompted.

"Lately . . . The last couple weeks, maybe month, he's been weird. I mean, for Gary. Whatever you may think, he and I are close. There's probably not a single thing outside of Mom and the 49ers we agree on—and even with Mom we've got opinions that don't match—but still we're brothers and I know what Gary's like. I've seen him through three divorces, a couple of huge settlements on cases he was almost sure to lose in trial, one loss that threw him for a loop for months. What I'm saying is I know him. And lately he's been strange."

"Strange how?"

"Called me to meet him for a drink and stood me up. Skipped the Seattle game."

"Maybe he wanted to save himself the frustration."

"Yeah, well, team coulda stayed in the locker room and done that for all of us. But last week he missed Sunday dinner without a word to Mom. Of course, later he fell all over himself apologizing and she forgave him like she always does. But you can guess what dinner was like with everyone trying to make conversation to distract her so she wouldn't have a chance to think what we knew she was thinking anyway."

I nodded. "That afternoon Mike walked out the door . . ."

It was a moment before he said softly, "Yeah. Gary can be a jerk, but he'd never do that to Mom. Never."

I pushed a stack of papers aside and sat on the desk. "And yet, he did. So, why?"

"I don't know."

"But you figure it's got to do with Karen Johnson, right?"

He shrugged.

"You know he's representing her. And you know about her. You could have said, 'Mom, Gary's got a big case that involves a woman I've been seeing for a month. He can't show up for dinner because he's taking her . . . Oh, shit, is that it? Are you both after her? Does Gary have some snazzy new suit, too?"

Now he did go red.

"You let Mom worry? You're worse than he is!"

"No!"

He scowled this time, but I could see that, however momentarily, I had him on the defensive. I needed to take advantage of it.

"Okay, what've you found in here? Anything in the cases?"

"I can't be going through them! It'd break the chain of custody and produce ongoing chaos. Every bit of evidence'd be compromised. Every opposing counsel would be in court. It'd be a nightmare for him."

"Then what *are* you doing here? First you say Gary set you up, that he hired Karen to work you. So why are you waiting around here? He's not coming back. They're halfway to some lodge in Carmel by now. They're in Santa Cruz for dinner. They're drinking margaritas and toasting their success, clicking their glasses and laughing at you. And if they knew you'd been sitting here, in the dark, waiting, they'd be rolling on the floor."

No reaction.

"But that's a crock. How do I know? Because, John, you're sitting here. Because you're not that sloppy with your car. Because it's a whole lot more likely you gave her your car—"

"So she could set up a crash in front of Broder's mistress's place?"

"Not your—"

"You thought *I* was—"

51

"No, no." I was so relieved I could barely corral my thoughts to cover my mental betrayal. "Chief of Detectives Broder? Your boss? His mistress lives in the Victorian? He's going to be after your tail when this comes out."

"He's already eyeing it."

I nodded. John had a lot of enemies on the force. But Broder seemed to have had it in for him for reasons that had made no sense till right now. "So who's footing the bill for this love nest? Is it her house? It's a little pricey for a police salary."

John shrugged.

"Two police cars crash in front of it, the papers are going to love that! Big front-page expose. Broder may be too busy protecting his own tail to worry about yours."

"With luck." But sitting there in Gary's chair, his stiff body hitting the cushion in the wrong places, John still looked like he wasn't leveling with me.

"Know what?" I decided to see if I had any advantage left. "Whatever this thing is, it's yours and Gary's. It could have cost me a job this evening, but forget it. Forget you ever saw me today. I'm out of here." I strode toward the door, nearly tripping over a portable TV. Plunking it on the table, I flicked it on. "You're so great at making up stories, here, enjoy some fiction by the pros!"

The TV burst on. "It's stopped dead, the whole freeway!" a voice shouted over the clatter of a helicopter. BREAKING . . . BREAKING . . . BREAKING rolled across the bottom of the screen. The screen picture was of a roadway empty but for a few vehicles and something small in the center.

"What is that?"

John leaned closer. "It's I-80, coming off the Bay Bridge."

"But no traffic? There's never *no* traffic."

"Stopped. Means something major." He pulled out his cell.

"We're flying as low as we can, Cindy," a male voice said on the TV. "Can't make out exactly what the hold-up is. Traffic's stopped in both directions. There's something on the roadway. I'm zooming . . . it's . . . it's a body!"

The beating of the copter's rotors spiked.

"Say that again!"

"A body, Cindy. I can make out blue, light blue, probably slacks. Maybe blonde hair. We're too high to be clear."

"We've got a report—unsubstantiated—of a shoe falling into the parking area, a woman's running shoe. We don't know if it's connected, but it came down from the same location.

"Blonde hair, light blue pants and top. That's what Karen had on . . . and the running shoes . . . Omigod, John!"

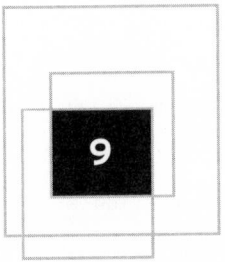

9

IN LESS THAN a minute we were racing for his car. We shot through Broadway, down Columbus and were crossing Market before John had the flasher on his roof. He had his cell on speakerphone. The squawk was coming so fast from so many locations it was almost impossible to make sense of it.

"Freeway's blocked off at First Street. They're detouring drivers off there. Anything east of us'll be a parking lot," he said, cutting west. "Damn, I wish I had a patrol car. But even . . ." His voice trailed off. I didn't need to look at him to know he'd been on the verge of griping about his missing unmarked car, but he caught himself. He, too, was trying to square the idea of the living, breathing Karen Johnson with a corpse lying on the roadway. I eyed him, attempting to gauge whether he was mourning the loss of a lover or puzzled by the violent death of a practical joker. Or if he was worrying about his car and career. My cop brother's a grand master at masking emotion.

Suddenly I was shivering, not from the chill but from shock and loss. "I liked her, when we were running up to Coit Tower. We were planning to go to dinner—'somewhere above our element,' she said. It was going to be fun. She was fun. We'd pick a restaurant where you have to bribe the maître d', you know, the kind of place where you're paying for the view."

"Where?"

"She was going to meet me at the set and decide."

"Last meal, huh? Special place because she knew it'd be her last?"

I stared out the windshield; darkened storefronts flew by. "It didn't sound like that. But I was with her half an hour, and we were running, then panting, then talking about the hundred-foot pole—"

"What pole?"

"It's a koan, one that's always gotten to me. How do you proceed off a hundred-foot pole? Karen said she wasn't a Buddhist, but she knew the answer, or *an* answer."

"A koan that had gotten to you? More than others?"

"Yeah, why?"

He turned left. Ahead we could see the flashing reds on the light bars, the silver-white glare from lines of motionless headlights. "Had you mentioned anything about Buddhism before?"

"No. But when I said a hundred feet made me think of the koan she knew what it was. You're trying to work out whether Gary primed her, right?"

He didn't answer, which meant he was.

"I can't say what Gary's involvement is in all this, but it's not with the koan. She recognized it, and more than that, she knew the general answer."

"Which is?"

"What do you think?"

"I don't have time—"

"Then don't think, just answer. You're on a hundred-foot pole. How do you proceed?"

"Easy. We get that every couple months. Top of a pole? Call the fire department."

"No phone. Just answer."

He hit the horn, pulling around the car in front. "Okay. How'd you get up? Were there handholds? Like a telephone pole? Step-bars? Then you could climb back down again. If not, you'd have to hug and slide. Damn lot of splinters. But the whole thing makes no sense. What's the point anyway?"

"You just made it. You had a perfectly sane response. But it's not the answer. How do you step off a hundred-foot pole? You just do it."

"And you'll fall."

"Yeah."

"And be killed."

"Maybe."

"Dammit, Darcy, look ahead. What do you see? The crime scene for a woman who fell a hundred feet out of a half-constructed high-rise and was killed! What do you Buddhists say to that?"

"I don't know." I could barely get the words out. *Don't know* is a respected answer on many levels. But neither of us was thinking of the cosmic not-knowing now. I was looking ahead at the mass of red taillights flashing up from the roadbed of the freeway above us. I was imagining and trying desperately not to picture Karen Johnson's crushed body in the middle of it all. "The truth is I don't know anything about her, except she said she was here to get a divorce and maybe even that's not true."

Traffic shifted. He shot left, up a ramp and into the construction parking area at the base of a skeletal building. He flashed his ID at the patrol officer on guard. "Where's the scene?"

"Fifth floor. Elevator's over there, sir."

All around us were police, fire, ambulance, and coroner's vehicles. John squeezed his car so tight in between two unmarkeds we had to sidle out and jump back as a patrol car and then a van raced in before we made it to the base of the high-rise.

In another year it would change the skyline, stab the sky higher than many thought safe in a city that lives under the threat of the next big one. Now only the bottom floors had been walled in. Above, it was a skeleton of structural support beams and crossing supports.

"Fifth floor—first open floor?"

"Looks like it."

"Like construction in hell," I said mostly to myself. Flashing red lights dueled, coating the cement in almost constant crimson. Sirens from vehicles trying to slice through the traffic jam and radio squelches fought with shouts from all directions. I kept expecting John to bark at me to get back in the car or away from the scene, but it was almost as if he'd forgotten who I was—or wasn't. Moving between clumps of uniforms and cops in street clothes, he strode purposefully, as if this was his case. I followed as if I was a part of it, too, into the cage of a freight elevator.

"Look," a uniformed guy pointed to the front ceiling corner as the door rolled shut. "Bird's nest? Here?"

"Elevator probably wasn't moving yet when the mama bird made it," a tech said.

"Spiffy address."

"Nah, it's just the freight elevator. They'll be blue collar birds."

"Hey, was that a head? I thought I saw a head in the nest."

"Birds have 'em. Makes flying easier."

A couple of guys chuckled. "But how'd they last here?" the uniform insisted. "You'd think the construction outfit would've—"

"Endangered species?"

"You better check with—"

The cage eased to a stop. "Fifth floor!" a guy in the rear called out. "Ladies dresses, coats, and intimate apparel!"

A ripple of forced-sounding laughter pushed us out the door.

"How many parking levels are there?" I asked. John shot me a look but said nothing.

Someone answered, "Eight, at least. You can afford to live here, then you got more than one ride. Look at the space markers. They're not for compacts."

Level five was an open slab; maybe the walls would be added tomorrow, but tonight there was nothing to keep a determined driver from flying off the edge.

The elevator was in the middle of the square. The southwest quadrant was cordoned. I'd heard John say the biggest cause of trampling a crime scene was off-duty cops rubbernecking. But no one was muddying the scene now. The normal night lighting hadn't arrived and inadequate lanterns formed two lines as if beckoning all to walk between them into the abyss. Too-bright flashes revealed the slab, empty but for the group inside the lantern lines. Crime lab techs were still putting down markers, snapping shots, moving lights, shooting the same thing from a different angle. Everyone else stood in the dark outside of the yellow tape.

"What've you got, Larry?" John asked a guy in a suit.

"Fall. No witnesses, least not yet."

"Just wait. Everyone's got camera phones now. They're all on the horn to TV stations trying for big bucks. You've alerted the stations to that, right?"

"Yeah," he snapped. "But no-one's going to have a shot of the take-off. Fall took what—a couple of seconds? No time to get the phone flipped open. And before she fell, there was no reason for a picture."

"Unless there was," I said. "Unless she was leaning over the edge, fighting someone off."

"We're alert to that, too." He took me in, top to bottom. "I didn't catch your name and department."

"Fell onto the freeway?" John demanded.

"Yeah." Larry's attention snapped back. A slight catch in his voice said he knew better than to offend him. "See that pile-up down there." He walked toward the edge of the slab, stopping with a good thirty inches to spare. John and I looked down—almost *straight* down—onto the freeway. I'd watched this building going up, so close to the roadway that if I'd been a kid I'd've been scheming how to get up here to spit on cars. When it was finished, would they allow windows to open, I'd wondered.

"Only three cars in the pile," Larry was saying. "Miracle it wasn't lots worse. I-80's what—the most jammed road in the nation? We're lucky it's not a fifty engine smash-up. Body flying out of the sky! Some poor slob's lucky she didn't come through his windshield."

Larry was watching John, who shrugged.

He was my age, maybe younger, and although he could have been in charge here, he just didn't have that top dog look. "Well, anyway, I haven't been down there—I've been too busy up here keeping the scene clean—but word is she hit the roadway—I mean, what're the chances of finding a patch of bare road? But she did, smacked down in lane two. Truck ran over her, then a car, then there's brakes squealing, cars slamming all the hell over. Not much left to identify. A couple of drivers are already in SF General."

"They say anything, the drivers?"

"What do you think? Body falls out of the sky in front of you? Truck driver just kept crossing himself. They're lucky to be alive, all of them. We were lucky they didn't think of that before we got in a few questions. She could've killed them. Sheesh, if you're going to jump, give a little thought to the people below, you know?"

How about a little thought for a woman lying dead on the freeway! "If you were in that good shape, you wouldn't need to jump, would you?" I controlled myself before that came out, but still Larry was glaring, and John moved himself in between us.

I stepped away, closer to the edge. The wind was stronger, flapping my sweatshirt and jeans the way Karen's blue linen pants had when she set out across Washington Square Park. I looked down at the freeway, the six empty lanes of this elevated road. I'd driven it a thousand times, easy; every San Franciscan had. I'd sped across the Bay Bridge from Berkeley in the left lane, waiting till the last moment before the Fifth Street off-ramp tunneled down from that lane to cut right. I'd slipped into the middle lane in this area, whipping past slowing drivers eyeing the Civic Center exit, and headed for the Fell Street arm that would shoot me through Golden Gate Park to Mom's. Everybody's got their strategy on I-80. They . . .

Stop avoiding! Focus! The flashers swirled red like traffic lights in the fog-blurred night. They glowed against the black of squad cars. Nothing moved down there. For a moment I imagined I saw Karen's body between them, her bare arms and blue-clad legs stretched out like she was making snow angels, her blonde hair awry. I didn't—couldn't—let myself think about what had happened when she hit, of what was left of her. Couldn't think about her, not yet, not here.

I was looking away. Again I forced myself to stare down at the freeway. It was almost directly below—almost, but not quite. A single lane in the parking area cut between the building and the freeway. I stepped forward. If she—

"Hey, get away from the edge! What're you, crazy?"

I was the least likely person here to fall, but I wasn't going to fight about that. I moved back. "Looks like there's about eight or nine feet between the building and the freeway."

"Yeah, so?" Larry said.

"Do suicides usually take a running leap?"

"There's wind."

"Not enough for that short a drop. If she stepped off the edge, she'd've landed next to the building."

"You forensics?" He eyed me, then John.

"I'm talking the mechanics of falling. To leap that far, you need a running start."

"Look—"

"No, you look. Look at where the road is. If you wanted to jump would you believe you could jump that far?"

"We're not talking about me. We're—"

"A jump like that, it's *Crouching Dragon*. If you had to leap that far between buildings you'd be dead. You'd need to run, to get up speed." *You'd need a ramp, a catcher, a dummy, and a damned good editor back in the studio.*

"Or you'd need to be pushed," John said. "Anyone working on that?"

"I don't know. You'd have to ask the detective."

"Who is . . . ?"

"Broder."

Bad, very bad. Bad enough John's car caused the mess outside of his woman's house. Broder'd been after John already, but now he'd have live ammunition, too, for his hunt. When he found out John's brother was the victim's attorney, that his sister had spent the afternoon with her, and that she'd been able to steal John's car because he'd left the keys in it, John would be not merely toast, he'd be charred crumbs. As for me, I'd be sitting in an interview booth till sunrise. And Gary, who'd set this whole thing in motion, I didn't want to think about him. Whatever his reason, I was sure it was no prank. When he learned how Karen died he'd be devastated. He'd need time, before the police caught up with him, to stop feeling guilty and start thinking like a lawyer again.

When Broder asked, John would have to have answers; he'd have to be straight with him. Which meant, we needed to get out of here. Now.

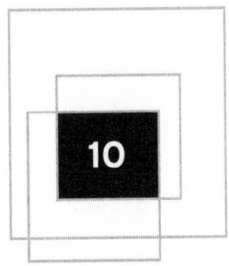

10

JOHN AND I double-timed it toward the elevator. We were twenty feet away when the doors spread open, revealing a detective talking to a woman next to him. It wasn't Broder, but Korematsu. Korematsu liked me, sort of, but he loathed John—big surprise. Still, he was galaxies better than Broder. Best was we avoid them both. Instinctively and without as much as a glance, John and I veered right, picking up speed and heading for the stairs. We weren't fast enough.

"Darcy," the detective said, "what're you doing here?"

"Making myself unpopular."

"Really?"

"'Sarcasm has no place in a police investigation,'" I quoted from a police training handout I'd seen once.

Korematsu snorted. We'd tangled with each other on a previous investigation. "How're you managing it this time?"

"I was explaining the rules of high falls."

"Like Isaac Newton did before you?"

"Exactly. The freeway's about eight feet away. No amount of wind will blow a falling body that far."

"We might have figured that out without you."

John had moved behind the only object that could provide him cover—a black sedan parked behind and to the left of the elevator. He was peering in the far window as if doing a preliminary check. The last thing we needed was Korematsu spotting him.

"I can show you what I mean. Come over here." I strode to the edge. "Look straight down and—"

"Hey, you! Get back!" male voices yelled. Someone yanked my arm. Korematsu just shook his head.

"Okay! Okay! Find out in your own good time. Or else subpoena Newton. I'm out of here!" I heard muttering in my wake but didn't stop. The elevator was rising up into sight. I made for the side opposite John and waited as the doors opened. Six men hurried out. When the last one cleared, we'd be hightailing it out of there. I didn't look back.

"So it's Bring Your Little Sister to Work Day?" Korematsu called behind me. He was like the Tibetan monks who could chant two notes at once; his higher tone suggested amusement, the lower one suspicion.

"Yeah," John said, "and I kinda doubt you have a problem with that, the way you've been eyeing her."

I leapt into the elevator. "What the *hell* was that about?"

But John wasn't listening to me. His shoulders were hunched, and he was looking back toward Korematsu. It was like a freeze-frame, all action stopped, cops and techs watching or pretending not to, eyeing John warily, checking out the detective. The scene broke. Korematsu muttered something and started to turn away.

"What're you doing here? I thought this was Broder's case?" John taunted.

"Broder got held up. He'll be here in a few. He'll be surprised to see you . . . both."

Don't comment!

"Nah, he's only got eyes for you." With that John finally stepped into the elevator and I slammed my fist against the down button.

"You . . . !" He was such an idiot words failed me. "Is there some reason you go out of your way to offend people?"

"Skill."

"I'm impressed."

He was grinning. "Listen, it's illusion—something you of all people should know the value of. Now when the question comes up about us being there, no one's going to ask why, they're just going to talk about me baiting him. They'll be thinking about Broder."

"Very clever. But it may not be clever enough. Korematsu's a decent guy, but now . . . You better hope illusion's more important than fingerprint results. You know damned well Broder'd sell you for stew."

The elevator car bounced. The gate opened.

John shoved me out, then grabbed my arm, and pulled me behind a Dumpster.

"Wha—"

"Quiet!"

"Hey I . . ."

"Hold it!" It was Broder.

An aide ran for the elevator, planted himself in the doorway. Broder strode toward it. He was so close I could hear his breathing. I didn't dare look at John.

The group stepped into the elevator and the car rose.

The instant it cleared the ceiling, John and I made a dash for the car. Neither of us spoke.

The car was blocked in. "You drive." He flipped me the keys. "I'll go find out who's behind us and get him down here."

"Don't bother. It's Korematsu's." I recognized the red Mini Cooper.

"Asshole! No wonder he was so fucking smug up there." He started back to the elevator.

I grabbed his arm. "What? You think he did this on purpose? This is a big fucking case and he was racing here! You flatter yourself."

"Screw you. Cops *notice*. That's what we do! Of course, he—"

"Listen!" I hissed. "We're in a tight enough spot. Not just your car—*us*. Show a little sense, for a change."

He shook off my hand.

I grabbed back and turned him so we were glare to glare. "I can get the car out. But you need to stop making things worse."

He hesitated.

"Think how pissed Korematsu'll be when he comes down and it's gone."

He turned toward his car. It was parked at the edge of the lot. That was good. Cars were jammed in on both sides—bad. Ahead was a steep grade and a three foot drop—very bad. If I could anchor a wedge in front, pull the wheel full out to the left and hit the gas hard, I just might be able to . . . to land in the Dumpster jutting out from behind the building.

I bent and checked the other direction. The drop was worse. "If I had a wedge—"

"If you had a helicopter!" John was shaking his head.

"I've driven—"

"—cars they tow and crush once you've had your way with them. Forget it! Not in my car!"

"Okay, then let's just get out of here—"

"I can't leave it. No cop walks away from his car and takes the bus. I might as well get a spray can and write: QUESTION ME! on the trunk." He glared back at the Mini. "Bastard knows this is mine. Bet he was grinning ear to ear when he hemmed me in."

For half a second he was distracted by six burly firemen walking out of the elevator.

I shoved him in the opposite direction. "Meet me on the street!"

"What do you—"

But I was running toward the men. "Hey, can you guys help me? I don't know if it's even possible, but see that little car over there, the Mini? It's got me blocked in. If you could just get it a few feet back."

"You want us to pick it up?" A crew-cut blond raised an eyebrow.

"Yeah, well, I guess it may be too much to expect—"

"No, wait, you've got a winch, don'tcha, Dave?"

"Yeah, sure. If we pulled up the bumper—"

□□□

"You got the fire department to move it?" John asked as he slid into the passenger seat. "How the hell—"

"I flashed my red curls. We got lucky. So now, where're we going?" I stopped for a light and glanced at him. I'd spent plenty of time figuring out where to hide in this city when I was avoiding him, but before, this brother had always been the one pursuing. "How long do you guess we have?" He understood that I meant before Broder, Korematsu, and the gang wanted his head on a platter.

"Ten minutes? Two minutes? As soon as they realize that black car up there on floor five is mine."

"Your car? She drove your car up there?"

"Circumstantial, but yeah."

"Why would she go there? A construction site? Don't they have guards?"

"Unmarked cars aren't that unmarked. Some guards give them a pass. They worry more about thugs carrying stuff out than about broads.

Whatever. By tomorrow they'll be lawyering up and we're not going to know shit."

"But how'd she even think of it? She was a tourist. Wait, maybe that's it! The entrance to that parking lot's really confusing. Plus it's off the most confusing bit of road in town. One minute you're going along Harrison, you make a left onto a city street and suddenly it's turned into the entrance to the Bay Bridge. That parking lot entrance—in the dark, it looks like just another lane, a last chance to keep from getting stuck on the bridge."

"Hmm. Want to know what I was doing while you were diverting Korematsu? Taking note of the scratches on the hood, the blue fiber caught on the bumper."

"Omigod! She was hit? No wonder her trajectory—Omigod, poor Karen!" I coasted through a yellow light. "Hit! She didn't jump. Didn't do a running leap. Hit! Jeez, John, someone killed her! Someone stepped on the gas and—"

"Someone in *my* car. That's what Broder's going to find out plenty soon."

"This is seriously bad," I said, my knuckles white on the wheel.

"You don't want to think *how* bad. If I only get canned I'll be thanking St. Jude. I'm a *sworn* officer. I'm withholding evidence in a capital case."

He didn't say the word prison but it hung between us. ROGUE COP SENT TO SLAMMER. My whole body went cold, imagining the headlines. I reached over and rested my hand on his arm, and he didn't shrug me off.

When I could trust my voice, I asked, "Were you involved with her?"

I thought he'd shake me off now, but he was listening to his own thoughts. "I'm the guy who's always got things planned and double-checked, the guy who'd run a make on his own mother. Things are falling apart faster than I can chase after them. I don't know who I am."

I wanted to pull over and just take him in my arms. But the only reason he could speak at all was the solitude of the dark car in the dark and empty street and me driving on. So I said nothing. Not at first, anyway. Then I thought of something, a question I needed to pose.

"There's a koan that says: a master makes a magnificent cart. If he removes the wheels and the axel and the cart box and all the parts, then what is it? John, what is Karen Johnson now?"

"What was she before?"

I started. That wasn't a bad question: what was the cart before it was built? But John wasn't asking about carts, or about Karen Johnson's essential being.

"Before she stole your car? Don't you know?"

"There are things I know, or things I thought I knew. But nothing I knew or imagined or guessed wrong about explains why she'd do what she did. It's crazy. Like a sci-fi novel where you step into another dimension and everything looks normal until you realize the laws of nature don't hold."

"What do you know? John? John! How'd you ever get involved with Karen in the first place?"

"Gary."

"What did Gary say?"

"Gary, dammit! Where the hell is he?" John flipped open his phone, then closed it again. There was no one he dared call. If you spend your life being a police detective and suddenly your connections, your status, and your power to demand answers are taken away, then what are you?

"Gary got you involved? How? Why?"

"Later. Things're going to close in on us, real soon. Where *is* he, dammit?"

"We're going to have to split up, John. You check his house, Mom's, wherever."

"Those are the first places they'll look."

"Then we need to move fast."

"And you? What are you going to do?"

"Drop me at the zendo."

"You're going to *meditate?*"

"No. I merely want you to be able to be honest about one thing."

He made a gurgling noise I took for a half-swallowed laugh, a grudging admission that I had more street smarts than he'd imagined. Then when I pulled up at the corner of Pacific he squeezed my shoulder. "Be careful—more careful than you ever think you should be. Put your phone on vibrate. Time's 12:02. I'll call you in an hour."

"Yeah," I said, for want of a more appropriate word. How could I not be tongue-tied? Twenty-four hours ago, I'd never have believed I'd be conspiring with him to withhold evidence and stay out of the clutches of the SFPD, his once sacrosanct employer. It was as if the entire fabric of the known universe had turned inside out.

I started toward the zendo. Everything on the block was dark. Even Renzo's Café on the corner was closed. Only the zendo might be unlocked. Once in the zendo I might be able—just for a moment—to step back from everything, to see it all as merely thoughts and sensations, to take away the axle and the wheels of it and sit there in the dark with what it would be.

But I knew Leo, Garson-roshi, would be upstairs. There was no way I could involve him. So I turned back toward Columbus, heading for Gary's office. At the corner I picked up my pace, relieved when I crossed into North Beach by the normalcy of people still eating in trattorias and drinking coffee at outside tables. I was glad to be in a place where tragedy was a burnt pizza crust.

The last time I'd been here—what, two hours ago?—I'd been greeted by a "body" behind the desk. I let myself in.

The room was darker than before. Now the single streetlamp shone mutedly through the fog. I stood beside the door, letting my eyes adjust, straining to catch any sound of breathing through the snore of the foghorn. I couldn't resist checking under the desk first thing, but of course no one was there now. I stood against the wall, as I'd done earlier, looking across the tundra of case folders. Karen Johnson's file could be anywhere, bunched with others by any rationale, alphabetical being the least of the possibilities.

Think like Gary.

I plopped in his chair. It was a high-backed leather swivel. The dim light flowed from the cupola windows behind. Odd that Gary would choose a place like this for its charm and view, then sit with his back to it. But then, I realized, it made perfect sense. His clients sitting nervously on the other side of his desk eyed the view; Gary eyed them.

If I were Gary . . . I pictured Karen Johnson facing him. She'd cross one leg over the other as he shifted the stack of folders he'd scooped up to clear a place for her. She'd be amused by the office, just as I'd been the first time I met Gary here. He'd have put the stack where? I concentrated, channeling my brother's habits of mind, trying to re-create his routines.

If this were her first appointment, he'd make notes on a yellow pad and put them in a folder with her name written on a sticky. By her next visit her file would have a typed label and be waiting on his desk. Even after he'd sent her off to meet me, it would have sat there until he heard my call, or something else sent him racing out of here.

Holding my hand over the flashlight I checked the desk. "Oh, shit!"

Someone had been in here! Someone had been rooting around on his desk. With the insane mess of clutter no one, not even Gary, would realize the place had been searched—no one but me. But I'd been perched on the corner of the desk when I'd been talking to John there, and now that space was piled high. What was going on here? I made for the door.

Halfway there, I stopped. Whoever was here had looked through the cases; he was hardly coming back.

Unless he was still here.

Common sense said: clear the building pronto. It said: call John. But I didn't have time to deal with him telling me to get out quick. *Be careful, more careful than you think you should.*

I walked back to the desk. The concession I made to carefulness was that I knelt on the floor, head just about desk level so I could scan the room as I examined documents. If anyone moved I'd . . . do something.

No luck. I found nothing, and no Karen Johnson–related notes or file usefully presented themselves. But I couldn't leave empty. I surveyed the floor. Folded open was the *Las Vegas Sun.* Dammit, had Gary gone to Las Vegas? Was that where he was hiding out? Or . . . or had he advised Karen to go there to get her divorce? Or for some other reason? Or was Vegas just a neon herring?

I stood. My knees screamed. Gary needed thicker carpeting.

A clock chimed. I panicked, then forced myself to smile. He needed a quieter clock.

It chimed again. Two o'clock. How had it gotten so late? It'd been between eleven and midnight when we left the site, midnight when John dropped me off—when he said he'd call in an hour! He would never, ever be unreliable, especially now. I tried his cell. This number is not accepting calls, the automated voice buffed me.

John, I wanted to yell, where are you? What happened? Why isn't your phone working?

11

I RACED OUT of Gary's office. And found myself standing on the sidewalk, in the fog-thick middle of the night without a clue what to do next. I had three brothers and at this moment they were all missing. My anguish over Mike remained at the center of my life. In the two decades before I gave up my exile and braved the city again, it had been possible to have days when I didn't flash on his taking me on my first trip to the notorious Haight-Ashbury or cutting under the fence to climb around the ruins of the Sutro Baths, and whole weeks when disasters on the news didn't spark new fears about what might've happened to him. Back at home now, as I was, every block held memories of us kids dangling our feet on the cable car's outside benches, pushing through crowds to the edge of the Bay to watch the fireworks explode overhead. But last night, worry about Gary'd eclipsed all that.

And now the crisis was John.

I'd liked Karen. Obviously, John had liked her, too. But she'd grabbed his car and left him to twist in . . . in his own stupidity and whatever else he wasn't telling me. Then she turned up dead! I didn't know what to think— or feel—anymore.

Without conscious decision I found myself walking back toward the zendo. North Beach prides itself on its night life, but there's a limit and

2:00 A.M. on a cold soggy night blew through it. The only things moving on Columbus were sheets of yesterday's papers skittering toward the financial district. I picked up my pace. By the time I crossed Broadway into the Barbary Coast I was admitting to myself that being cold, exhausted, without plan or car was no way to begin a search. Silently as possible, I went in and padded upstairs to my room.

I am the abbot's assistant. He—Leo Garson—is understanding about my work taking me away. But when I am here I make a point of fulfilling my duties. My alarm blasted at 6:30 and at ten to 7:00 I was in the courtyard striking the clappers—polished wooden blocks—three times to announce the morning sitting. Inside the zendo oil lamps glowed but cast no shadows. The large, brick-walled room was cold and the black cushions—*zafus*—on black mats—*zabutons*—lined either side in an unmoving procession toward the altar. I bowed to the altar, lit the candle and broke a stick of incense in two to set in the ash near the sides of the bowl. Waiting sticks, the two stubs were called.

At 7:00 when Garson-roshi entered, I handed him a full stick to place in the middle of the bowl. The pungent aroma ribboned into the room as I took my seat, turned toward the wall and placed my hands in a *mudra,* left hand resting in the bed of the right palm. They say one reason monks traditionally sat in full lotus was so they could fall asleep and not fall over. I've attained this in half lotus. My head drooped; I snapped awake. I'd been dreaming of Gary's enigmatic phone call, me curious but not worried. Again I woke, remembering Karen Johnson. Something about her hadn't been in sync. What? Again I woke, this time with no picture, only the echo of feeling she'd understood the urgency of my search for Mike.

I badly wanted to talk to Leo, to have him brush away my clutter of extraneous thoughts, but to tell him too much would open him to police focus; that would be terrible for him and worse for me. The problem with Leo was his proclivity for answering questions truthfully. Tell him and I might as well cut out the middle man and just call Korematsu for a chat.

I wasn't sitting zazen at all! I was thinking! I might as well be in an armchair with a latte! I inhaled, focused on my breath, noted my pale shadow on the wall, the sounds of breathing behind me, the wind, the rush of traffic, a stomach gurgling. I'd complained to Leo once about my thinking: *I think I'm sitting zazen, but then without noticing I realize I've just been sitting here thinking.* Leo had smiled and said, *Just keep bringing your attention back. That's the practice. Thoughts are illusion. Goals are illusion. Everything changes.* Once again I brought my attention back to my breathing. When the bell rang to end the period. I turned and was surprised to see six people in the room.

Ten minutes later, after I'd put out the candle and sifted the ash so the altar was ready for evening zazen, I caught Leo upstairs. "Roshi, you have a moment?"

"Always." He grinned. Life in this very moment is a basic concept of Zen. Life *is* this moment—this moment—this moment, nothing more. Of course he had a moment. "Sit."

I stepped into his room, a narrow cell like my own, with low Japanese dresser and chair, also low. He settled on his futon and crossed his legs. Instead of the robes in which he'd led the service he now wore black drawstring pants and a T-shirt. The sweater he'd added would be too warm in an hour.

I wasn't about to reveal too much, but there was one question that would cause no problems. "Roshi, how do you proceed off a hundred-foot pole?"

"Forget you asked."

"But—"

Again he smiled. His features were too big for his face; when he smiled it looked like they were about to leap off of it. "Let's take a few steps down that pole. Why, all of a sudden, are you asking?"

"I mentioned the koan to a woman who doesn't sit zazen and she knew the answer . . . well, an answer. She said: You step off."

"Why did you mention it?"

Why had I? We'd been heading to Coit Tower, which I'd mistakenly said was a hundred feet high. But why had I made such a silly error? "I was trying to figure out who she was."

"Because?"

"I thought Gary was . . . I don't know what I thought. It all happened so quickly. I thought . . . I thought he was involved in something secret . . . but maybe for a good reason. Though John instantly assumed he was setting up some prank."

"We see through our own eyes." He glanced up at me. "Things are as they are."

Things are as they are was a deceptively obvious-seeming teaching of his.

"You saw through your eyes, Darcy. You didn't just see your brother, but this woman, and what you took to be their relationship."

"I saw her as a friend. Then as crazy. Then as a woman who'd played my brother. Maybe more than one brother. Then suddenly, she was dead. I don't know what to think."

"Don't."

He was right, I knew. Thoughts would just stumble over each other in my head. But I couldn't help it. "She said she was going through a divorce, but, you know, that wasn't the vibe I got. She was in too good a shape. She was"—I suddenly realized—"someone I could picture Gary dating." *Gary dating! Was that what John pictured?* "She'd plugged into that sudden fascination Gary emits when he's utterly focused on something outside himself. It's a seductive quality, particularly when the object is yourself." I paused, hoping for an observation from Leo but he offered none, waiting for me to go on. "I felt like there was a big exciting secret they shared, not like she was a client Gary was representing but more like they were doing something together. Something that was going to happen fast, because, when we talked about going to dinner she said she wanted it to be somewhere special."

"A celebration?"

I swallowed hard but still could feel my eyes fill. "Or last meal."

"Are you seeing through your eyes now or then?"

I had to think. "Then I'd have said there was an air of last fling, but nothing as dire as last meal."

"Nothing that suggested she was going to jump off a building onto the freeway."

"Omigod! How did you know?"

Leo shrugged. "Korematsu called. He wants to talk to you."

"Damn. Is he coming here?"

"He asked you to call him."

"Did you tell him I would?"

"I said I hadn't seen you, couldn't say when I would."

"Thanks."

"It was the truth. You're not always here for zazen, and I don't expect you to be."

"Thanks." It was a relief that Leo already knew about Karen, but it also introduced other subjects I preferred not to raise. I glanced at him, sitting as calmly as he did in the zendo, as if he had nothing at all but this moment with me to consider. As if by the time he got out of here his sweater wouldn't already be too heavy. Something occurred to me. "When you agreed to come back to the city, after all those years at Redwood Canyon, I'll bet you envisioned all sorts of problems, but never that so many would be caused by your assistant's family."

He let out a hoot. "But, Darcy, I really like them, your family."

"Thanks."

"So, are you going to call Korematsu?"

"Not now. Not on three hours sleep. That'd be a big mistake. I can't have him throwing my words in my face when I not only can't remember my last syllable but barely can find my face."

"You're going back to bed?"

"Can't. I need to find John," I said as if his mention of Korematsu had beckoned my worry about John. "He promised to call me last night and he didn't. His phone isn't working."

"Maybe that's why he didn't call."

"I never thought of that. But it's not the answer, even if for anyone other than John it'd make sense. I was going to hunt him down last night, check at Gary's house, at Mom's, at Lost Sock—"

"Lost Sock?"

"His apartment. He acts like he lives there, but he's almost always at Mom's because he wants to keep an eye on her—not that she appreciates that. The family joke is that John's apartment exists only in his imagination, like the place where lost socks and keys end up."

Leo grinned. "But you don't think John's there."

"He would have called."

"But he didn't."

"Because something happened. Because he had to ditch his phone, because he'd called someone he didn't want the police or someone to know about."

"But they can subpoena his phone records."

"Not right away. He'll buy a week or more at least."

"Then why wouldn't he call you from some other phone?"

"He wouldn't want that number on my record."

"But a pay phone?"

"When was the last time you came across a pay phone that worked? But wait, he might have left a message here, on the land line! Did he?"

Leo shrugged. I leapt for the phone. Two voicemail messages. The first from last night at 9:33 P.M. "Darcy"—it was a woman's voice. The traffic noise in the background was so loud I had to press the receiver against my ear—"I'm so sorry. I would have liked dinner . . . really . . . if things'd been . . . different." She—*Karen!*—laughed. A car door—hers?—slammed. "Later, huh?"

I played it again, desperate to turn back time. Her voice was breathless, just like it had been at the top of Greenwich Street as we stood panting. I saw her again, in the blue linen shell and slacks that made her running shoes look out of place. Her blonde hair blowing in the easy breeze. Back then. But now as she spoke, I felt her drawing away from the phone as if watching for something—no, someone. The person who shut the car door. The person who'd soon kill her? She'd thrust out last words—"Later, huh?" in a single breath.

I stared at the white wall in front of me.

Leo still sat on his futon. Someone else would have been overcome with curiosity, but he was waiting.

Very carefully I saved Karen's message. "I was with her less than an hour, but, the thing is, I was so focused on her, trying to figure out—" I stopped. That was one part of this Leo didn't already know. "It was like a script summary."

He seemed to hesitate, as if balancing the need to speak with the lack of invitation. "Like one version of a script?"

79

That wasn't quite it. "Like the first act was missing."

He nodded. "So you were penciling in possibilities as you went?"

"Yeah."

"Be aware."

"Yeah." I played the tape again in my mind. "Things change. Karen's changed entirely, gone. But her voice, her words are still there. They're not going to change."

"But you will."

"Maybe."

He didn't insist though we both knew he was right. I could understand or could choose not to.

The second message was from Korematsu, telling me to call.

I saved that, too.

Leo pushed himself up to standing. "I'm off to a meeting. And you? What are you going to do?"

"Call Korematsu."

12

I LEFT A MESSAGE for Korematsu, saying I was returning his call, *not* asking how come he was still doing the scut work on Broder's case, much less what was what with that case. Had they found the evidence on John's car? Had they—God forbid—found John? Was Korematsu planning to sit on me till they did? I barely had time to hurry Leo away from the zendo so he didn't muddy the waters I was about to jump into, when an unmarked car squealed to a stop. I walked out into the courtyard to draw Korematsu's attention as Leo turned the corner onto Columbus.

"I'm glad you called, Darcy." Translation: surprised you called.

I nodded. I'd been right: it was a mistake to see him when I was so tired. I needed a shower. I felt like something that had been wadded up and tossed on the floor. Korematsu, on the other hand, looked freshly laundered from his light blue shirt, his dark brown sports jacket to the dark hair that flopped over the corner of his forehead. His skin had the shine of scrubbedness and his eyes looked sharper than coffee could create.

"What were you doing at the scene last night?"

"Come this way." I led him into the zendo to the upstairs hall where the phone sat in a nook, punched the number and handed him the receiver. "Listen to this. It's from Karen Johnson."

He stood, eyes half closed as he concentrated on it. He replayed it, then went on to the next message, the one from himself.

"Hey, I only authorized you to listen to that one."

"I'll need the records of all calls to and from this number for the last week."

"No way. This is the zendo phone."

"Nevertheless."

"Fine, you can deal with my attorney."

"Your brother?"

I didn't like the way he'd said that. "Snideness is unbecoming in an officer."

"Fine. In the meantime I need to hear everything you know about the deceased."

"Can we do it over coffee? I've been up— chances are you had a late night, too?"

He hesitated as if loath to admit he was less than a hundred percent, then shrugged. "Sure. Is Renzo's open this early?"

"Of course. He'd be insulted you even considered otherwise."

"What're you drinking? I'll bring them back."

"Double espresso." I was in a better mood than I had been minutes ago, before Korematsu's sarcastic reference to Gary. If he'd had any idea Gary was representing Karen Johnson, he'd have been all over me.

I hoisted myself onto the courtyard wall while I waited for him. It was about four feet high with a curved top, a dicey perch for most people and one that would require some attention from Korematsu. He was going to be firing questions; I needed answers of my own. Any physical advantage I could manage would help even things out.

He held two paper cups as he walked back up the still empty street. When I put out my hands for them I could see that, politely, he hadn't even sipped his yet. I felt a stab of guilt about the wall.

But he swung up easily and looked at me and laughed. "What'd you think? That I was John?"

Was I that transparent? I handed him his coffee. "Nah. It'd take you years of hard couch time to get in that bad shape." I took a sip. Double espresso barely described it. It was syrup. "Did you put sugar in this?"

"Nope. Blame Renzo. He had the lid on before he gave it to me."

"Guess he figured if a cop was volunteering to get me a double at this hour of the morning I must need all the help I can get." I sipped again, feeling the rush of hot coffee flow down my tubes warming my whole torso, that boom of caffeine snap open every pore in my face. *Renzo, I owe you.* "This is Broder's case, right?"

He nodded.

"So how come you're fetching and carrying for him?"

"We don't just assign one detective to a case. You know that, Darcy."

"A high-profile case, you mean?"

He nodded again. Tones of voice can be revealing. A nod is just a movement of the head.

I prodded. "So Broder's just figure-heading?"

"Chief of Detectives Broder is in charge. I am assigned. My assignment is to liaise with you."

"Then 'liaise' for me the status of the investigation."

"We ask; you answer."

"You asked why I was at the crime scene. I asked the status. We bargain; you agree."

"We'll see."

"Puh-lease." Korematsu had worked undercover for five years, an eternity in a small city. He was a master at not revealing. He made John look minor league. What he wasn't revealing was his motive. Was he asking: why

83

were you at the crime scene of a woman you just met? Or was it: why were you and your brother at the scene where your brother's car killed her? Was I a witness or a possible accessory after the fact? "I came to the scene because I saw the story on the news. John got us in. Now you: what's the status?"

"We've got the murder weapon. Your brother's car."

"How do you know it's the weapon?"

"Scratch marks on the hood—"

"It's a police car! They've probably all got scratches."

He shrugged.

There wouldn't have been time to get lab results back. I sipped the coffee. What could I admit without making things worse? What could I conceal without ending up in jail? "She stole the car, you know that, right? After that it had nothing to do with John. Fifty people at Coit Tower were there. You could spend a week interviewing them."

He nodded.

"So what's her background? Her fingerprints have to be all over it. Have you matched them?"

"No."

"Not yet?"

"Not ever."

I stared.

"The steering wheel's been wiped clean. Also the dash, door handles on both sides, and every other surface in the front seat area. When the vehicle in question is one of ours, our techs go over every inch. She must have floated on air and driven it by magic, and wiped her wand clean."

"You've got her body, why don't you print . . ." I read the answer in the look on his face. He didn't try to hide it.

"You don't want to know how badly a body can be mashed. She could have run under a power mower and come out better. Jumping onto a freeway was the worst way to die, for her, for the drivers on the road. How are those people going to live with it? A body flies out of the sky; they can't avoid it, maybe if they could she'd be alive. Maybe they don't kill her, just run over a hand, a leg, a shoe. One woman was hysterical. A guy was next to catatonic."

I lifted my cup to drink, realized it was empty and sat holding it. "I . . ."

"I want you to be prepared."

"For?"

"I need you to identify the body."

The cup was still in my hand, still in front of my mouth, empty. "No." The word was barely audible. "I just can't. I was with her; I talked to her. I liked her. I can't look at her body so mashed up that she doesn't have fingers! I just—"

"Darcy, your brother's a prick—"

"A by-the-book prick."

"True, but guys like that, they're wound tight and a single perfect-storm thing can send them spinning. So I'm not saying he could never be involved in this murder."

"Hey—"

"But I am giving him the benefit of the doubt, which is more than many will. I'm sticking my neck out, not for him; I'm sticking it out for you. You understand that?" He stopped, waited till I nodded, watching me the whole time.

I couldn't think about that now, couldn't let myself wonder. *Any suspect who trusts a cop deserves to be in jail. Another John Lott maxim.* I didn't dare trust Korematsu, despite those yearning chocolate brown eyes, the sweet thatch of dark hair falling over them. He'd never deceived me before.

But I couldn't trust him, not now when what we were playing for was John.

"Right now," he insisted, as if inviting my reservations about him, "we have nothing on this case—no ID, no witnesses after the victim left the crash site. The only thing we know about the car is that your brother signed it out. He never reported it stolen, not when it happened, not when he was standing right beside it at the murder scene, not after he made his memorable exit. And now he's gone to ground."

"But . . ." There was no but.

"Unless some other lead turns up the whole focus is going to be on John. When the public learns that a detective's car is being called the cause of death, the pressure on the department is going to be enormous, unrelenting. All stops will be pulled out and pressure put on every member of your family. Your phones will be tapped, you neighbors questioned, your mother's neighbors, and a make will be run on everyone who walks into this Zen center, including Leo Garson. The story'll be headlines all over the country. After the first day, when there's no update, the press will glom onto Mike's disappearance and speculate about any connection to the missing brother. If it goes on another day, they'll find out about that Victorian on Guerrero and the woman who lives there and her well-placed friend. And then heads will roll. Need I say that there are people in the department who'd go to great lengths to avoid that happening? Throwing John to the wolves is the easiest way. No one's going to object."

I couldn't say anything. It was all true.

"There are only two reliable persons who saw the victim yesterday. You and John. The body is the only thing we have."

I swallowed. "Okay."

13

ONLY AN IDIOT with a secret gets into a police car. *Yet another John Lottism.* Korematsu would undoubtedly turn on the questions as soon as he turned the ignition key.

But he didn't. He just drove. And I sat there leaning against the door, watching his dark brown eye peek out under his hair and glance everywhere but at me. It was so tempting to speculate about him, as opposed to worrying about John, thinking about Karen or imagining what was awaiting me at the Hall of Justice.

Outside pedestrians shivered as sun pierced the fog and retracted. Once we pulled up outside the morgue, any hint of warmth vanished. Inside the building it was just another busy Wednesday morning with officers clacking past, clerks calling out, cell phones ringing, metal trolleys rattling, and everything echoing off the walls.

I steeled myself against the moment when I'd have to step into the icy room and a tech would pull open the drawer and—I couldn't bear to think what I'd see. But Korematsu took me first to an evidence room and a minute later returned with a box the size of a fixed-price postal mailer. "I'm hoping her clothes will suffice."

Her clothes. Such a tiny box. I had to swallow hard before saying, "Me, too." I reached for it, but he waved me off. Carefully, he unfolded the linen tatters that had once been that stylish blue outfit. I swallowed harder. There was barely a square inch of color left, amidst the tire marks, the dirt, the oil stains, the blood, and other soil marks. There wasn't enough material left even to guess whether it came from slacks or a blouse.

"Is it hers?"

"What I can see of the color looks right. It's not like anything for sale right now in the stores. Did you find running shoes?"

"Four—one pair and two singles. Stuff gets dropped on the freeway," he explained, then looked away as he realized what he'd said. "It'll take a while for the guys to put the pieces together. I was hoping you wouldn't have to look at her remains—"

"Was there a button? Same color as the material? The slacks had buttons at the cuffs, for decoration. Inch across. Luminescent, mother of pearl kind of thing."

He opened a smaller box.

"There, in the corner! That sliver! That could be a piece of the button."

He scooped it out with a ladle, laid it against the fabric, and eyed me questioningly.

"I can hardly swear it's the button, but if there was a piece of her button that size, that's what it would look like. What's the rest of the stuff? That thing there looks like a link from a bracelet or necklace or watch, but she wasn't wearing jewelry and her watch had a leather or cloth band, not metal. And the tooth's definitely not hers. Hers were white, probably capped, definitely whitened."

"That's a lot to have taken in if, as you say, you were only with her for an hour, just met her."

Because I was trying to figure what she and Gary were up to. "One of my roommates in New York was a hygienist. What pictures have turned up?"

"Of the tooth?"

"Of her death. A woman drops to her death on Route 80, in front of dozens of drivers and passengers, all talking on their cell phones. There've got to be pictures. Every news station, local and national must've gotten offers, right? And you got those photos from the stations, right? Maybe they'll help me identify her."

Had he been John he would have puffed out and muttered: *cops take, civilians give.* But Korematsu only hesitated a moment before nodding, taking the box with the button and heading out the door. This trusting business wasn't coming any easier to him than to me.

I sat on the edge of the table and turned toward the wall a couple feet away. The pictures were going to be awful and I needed to clear my mind so I could see them without the overlay of the case. I wanted to look for some angle of her body in the air, arms up or down, something to give me an idea of her reaction.

The door creaked. I turned to see Korematsu holding out a sheaf of papers. "I don't know why there aren't a dozen crashes an hour! A body drops in less than a second and ten people have pictures. It's insane. Not good pictures, not useful ones. But just to move the phone in that time . . . !" He shook his head. A wave of hair dropped over his forehead and he pushed it back. "These are the pick of the lot, which'll tell you how bad the others were."

"It was night. Dark up there. I'm amazed—"

"Exactly. This one is the best, but, well, steel yourself."

"I am. Thanks, though." I meant for the thought.

The two pictures were long shots of a blue bundle on the roadway with a truck skidding to its left at the edge of the frame. I couldn't make out any detail and didn't want to, but I forced myself to study the blurry images. In the last shot she was falling, inches above the roadway; she looked as if she was reaching down for it. One arm was out over her head, the other flung to the side. Her legs were spread and one was bent and forward. The shot was from the rear and blurry as if it had been focused on the license plate ahead, with her falling into the frame. "If you blow this up, you should be able to see the button here on her pant leg."

"Anything else?"

"No."

"You've done falls, right? You were talking about it at the scene, or at least so the scene sup kept saying. About how she wouldn't have fallen onto the freeway if she'd just stepped off the edge of the slab. What I'm going to ask now is a long shot."

"Shoot."

"Can you tell whether she had any warning?"

"You mean, did she have a split second to see the danger and react instinctively?"

I eyed the photo again. "A high fall in a gag—stunt—is a whole different thing. You run the tape in your mind, second by second. You know where the catcher bag is and how much time you have to flip or turn and then stretch out so you land on the maximum body surface to spread the force of impact. The whole time you're in the air you're aiming toward your landing. You're controlling every part of your body."

"But this . . . Look, there's no coordination between her arms, or her legs, no attempt to cover her head, or land on her feet, not that that would have made any difference. Her legs aren't together, which she might have done automatically if she'd been a diver. There's nothing about this that suggests any plan or preparation."

He held out a hand for the picture.

"Not that that means anything. Even if she *had* planned it, she'd probably never've done anything like that. Not many people have. And even those of us . . . Hell, I wouldn't look any better about to die. Still . . ."

90

"What?"

"If you're asking my professional opinion as someone who's studied falls, I'd say she never saw it coming."

"A couple tons of metal speeding at her?"

"If I was standing there and you drove toward me, I'd assume you'd turn or stop. It'd never cross my mind—"

"Because I'm a police officer."

Damn! "Because"—I hesitated to say it out loud, as if I'd be betraying John—"I trust you."

He started to raise his gaze to meet mine and ended up giving me too curt a nod. "That'd take a lot of trust."

"More trust than sense."

"What'd John think?"

So that was it! Trust be damned. This was what he'd been assigned to do: use me to peek into John's mind, into observations and opinions John would never share with him. With every bit of acting skill, I forced my face not to tense up, kept my voice calm. "'Relying on trust is the sign of a lazy interviewer.'"

Korematsu's mouth quivered but I couldn't tell if he was restraining a laugh or simply failing to hide his discomfort. "One of your brother's Academy classics. So what did he say about Karen Johnson?"

"He didn't have any basis to judge. I don't know if he even saw her, really. When I got to Coit Tower with her I said I was going to talk to my brother a minute, and she went off to look at the view. Maybe he noticed her, maybe not." I could have mentioned her checking messages, but I was too disgusted with him.

"Cops notice."

"But when she swiped the car I knew it was her, from her hair and the blue. But he was looking at the car, not the driver."

91

"He left the keys in the car?"

Damn! This was exactly what I did not want to get into, which would only dig John in deeper. It was all I could do to control my voice. "You see a woman you know, who's not in running clothes, panting. You—especially if you're John—suspect the worst. Mugging? Heart attack? You jump out to check. I'm his baby sister. Of course he's not going to stop and go through standard procedure while I collapse on the macadam."

"All that time to turn the ignition key."

"I happened to be fine, but it could have been otherwise." Weak. Getting weaker. I gave up. "I don't know. It was a mistake."

"A pretty basic mistake."

"Do you need me to identify her body or not? Otherwise, I'm out of here."

He hesitated again. "Wait in the hall."

I was glad to be ushered out into the world of fast forward. I sat on a wooden bench, felt the slats under my butt. There was a newspaper next to me. I opened it, but couldn't focus to read. So I sat behind it, thinking not of Karen Johnson but of the cart koan: when all the parts are removed, what will it be? Maybe I was thinking of her.

A cell phone was ringing. "I gotta take this. Catch you up in a min," a male voice called.

The quick tap of high heels resounded on the flooring.

"Broder," a man was saying.

Another cell phone rang.

". . . his fine little piece on the side on Guerrero." Same guy. Muffled laugh. I didn't dare look.

". . . oh yeah! Livid, you can just imagine. No, no, not even about his wife. More power to him; my wife'd . . ."

Another newspaper crackling open.

92

I leaned back, ear to the edge of my own paper.

". . . and the smuggling thing."

A hand landed on my shoulder. I dropped the paper.

Korematsu stared down, his expression tense. I couldn't tell how much of the phone call he'd overheard, but if Broder's affairs were gossip in the hallway, Korematsu already knew. Broder's mistress smuggling! The acting chief of detective's mistress, whose house was guarded by patrol cars! No wonder Broder was taking charge of this case, desperate to get it closed before the bombshell burst.

Suddenly I understood the danger to John. Broder'd be taking no prisoners in his rush to nab him. He'd use every bit of his power, influence, connections to pin Karen's murder on him and get him no-bailed. And if John didn't live to face trial, all the better.

I was desperate to run for the door. Instead, I took a breath and followed Korematsu to the viewing room.

14

"YOU SURE YOU want to do this?"

I nodded. Yet, despite my intentions I was not sure at all—and less sure with each step down the short hall into a small, cold room. Two gray metal chairs had been pushed against the gray wall. The door at the far end was wide and I understood the reason.

Korematsu motioned me to sit.

I didn't move. Breathed. Remembered the reactions to the koan when Leo gave a talk on it. *A cart maker built a magnificent cart with wheels of one hundred spokes. If you remove the wheels, the axle, the front and back pieces and even the cart bed, what will it be?* "One big mess," a woman said. "A pile of rubble," a guy added.

A pile of rubble?

The door opened and the acrid smell of formaldehyde gushed in. Instinctively, I breathed through my mouth. A metal dolly rolled through the doorway. A cart. If its wheels were stolen and its bed tossed away, what would it be, I wondered. It was an instant before I realized I was just avoiding looking at the oil-skin-like sheet lying on top of something small and flat.

"You're sure?" Korematsu asked again.

"Yes." But I held my breath and reminded myself that whatever shape the bones and flesh under the cloth were, they were still as much Karen Johnson as they had been.

He pulled the sheet clear of her face. Despite all my intentions I gasped. She looked like a Salvador Dalí Karen Johnson, like the cart when its wheels and axle and bed had been trampled, run over . . . as she had been. I kept my eyes on her, holding our connection. Her face, that face I had noted looked so good for a woman the age I took her to be, resembled one of those rubber Halloween masks flattened in its cellophane bag. But it wasn't all flat, really, just the lower half, like someone had ripped off her jawbone the way you'd tear into the wings of fried chicken. Lucky there was enough lip to cover the exposed bone of her upper jaw because her teeth were gone. That must have been one of them in the box I looked through, swept up off the freeway like debris. *A big mess.* Her eyes were closed, the lids sunk into her skull and I couldn't bring myself to consider whether her eyeballs had been knocked loose, were still in the sockets or not.

My hands went clammy, my head throbbed. The stench of formal-dehyde filled the air. I wanted to race out of the room. I wanted to keep staring at her eyelids that looked almost normal, at her hair that some-one had smoothed down over her forehead. I wanted to pretend the cart was still a cart.

I forced my gaze down. The sheet covered her torso as if she'd sat up in bed and pulled it up under her arms. But I could see her clothes had been cut off or maybe there wasn't anything left of them except for a piece of blue linen jammed so deeply into the flesh of her arm that it mustn't have been worth cutting out. Her blouse had been a shell—sleeveless—so that meant it had ripped open as vehicles hit her, flapped against her arm and been ground in. I pointed to it and Korematsu nodded. "Maybe there's a thread caught inside John's car," I said.

He nodded again, but I had the sense he'd swallowed a comment, probably about the police lab figuring that out without my guidance.

"You haven't done an autopsy. There's no incision."

"Not yet. The M.E.'s backed up."

"Did they do toxicology? Drugs'd explain a lot."

He nodded. He was humoring me, answering questions he'd normally remind me were police business, not mine.

I looked back at her face—half almost normal, half destroyed—and tried to find an answer to this. Common sense said there must have been a desperation in her that I missed. But, even now, even staring at her corpse, I couldn't reconstruct that. Excitement, yes. Recklessness, even. She had been about to step off the hundred-foot pole and was ready to go, not preparing to be herded into a fall.

But none of that was reflected in her body. Right now, I wasn't going to find anything of any use to Karen Johnson or Korematsu. What I needed to do here was for myself. I reached down to touch her hand.

"Omigod! Her hands! They're shredded!"

"That kind of accident . . . hard on appendages."

"You don't mean she tried to break her fall?"

He eyed me questioningly.

"That'd mean," I said, choosing my words with care, "she had some awareness of what was happening. A fall from that height takes less than two seconds—add another second for the horizontal momentum. There wouldn't have been time to assess the situation mid-flight."

His lips pursed.

"You're thinking no one who's gone off a building and about to hit the freeway is going to *assess*," I explained. "What I mean is take in the situation enough to react. Putting out a hand to break your fall is the natural reaction. Stunt doubles have to train ourselves *not* to do that. You coach yourself, you practice, you do a run-through of the fall in your mind, you know the safest landing is on your back, arms and legs out. And still you can barely keep yourself from trying to land face down with your hands and knees breaking the fall.

"But if you were drugged, or if a car you didn't see hit you from behind, you wouldn't have time to even take in what was happening or where you were. You wouldn't be aware enough of the situation to have a reaction."

Korematsu was staring at the floor.

"But that's not how her hands got so mangled, is it?"

"That may have been part of it." He hesitated, as if asking again if I really wanted to know the next thing. "When the body lands, the force flings the arms and legs out. Drivers see the body, swerve, and if they miss the body, likely they run over the hands or feet. Probably that's what happened with the drivers in the first vehicles. In the ones after that, people are essentially driving blind. They know there's a problem, but they can't see what. Maybe they saw the body fall, but they haven't had mental time to process that it's a *body* in front of them. Bad enough it's any object falling out of the sky. It's dark; ahead of them taillights are suddenly glowing. Brakes are squealing, metal crashing all around them. They can't see anything. They're just standing on the brakes and hoping. So whether they run over her—it's a crap shoot. Chances of them braking and being rear-ended into her—" He shrugged. "We're lucky to have fingers. That's the truth. If we get prints, we'll be real lucky. It's not like we're going to be able to send them through the system in the condition they'll be. We're going to need leads to match them." He took a step toward the door.

"Give me a moment." I turned back to Karen, this woman I may not have known at all. I touched a square of flesh on her mangled hand.

I lifted my hand, but the chill of her skin stayed on my fingers as I walked out of the room and started down the hall. Korematsu must have signaled a lab assistant to wheel her body back to the freezer. He was only a minute in catching up with me, as if he wanted to warn me one last time.

Before he could speak, I said, "The killer had to be in the car with her, right? You're not assuming she met him up there on the parking slab . . ."

"Another conclusion we would have reached. I'd be happy to question him if we knew who he was—if we knew who she was. So if you have other information—"

"Look, I've been with her less time than I've been with you today. I couldn't know any more."

"But your brother can."

"Fine. Go get him!" I snapped. This was like dealing with Dr. Korematsu and Mr. Hyde.

"Where is he?"

"I have no idea."

"I think you do."

"You think in error. If I knew where he was, I wouldn't be here; I'd be there." I pushed open the outside door and was relieved to feel the fresh air.

Korematsu caught my arm. "I'll say this to you again," he said louder. "We are on the same side. John ought to be on that side. It's not doing him any good to think he can deal with this off the books. Sure, he's pissed about his car and the brass being furious and the rest of the guys laughing their heads off. I can understand why he doesn't want to run the gauntlet here, why he's set on figuring out what's behind it—beyond his own stupidity. Why he wants to come back dragging a perp or waving a psychiatric record or digging up something more than just her name. But he's only making things worse—a *lot* worse—not showing up here, not calling in, being the kind of irresponsible he'd ride a rookie out of the department for. What I'm saying is if he knows something about this case that he's not reporting, he'll get himself suspended and it'll be what he deserves."

I stopped, turned, was inches from his face. "You've already convicted him, haven't you? He's hiding out. He's doing secret sleuthing. He's too cowardly to come to work. Has it even occurred to you that something might have happened to him? Thought never crossed your mind, has it? I have no idea where he is. And I'm worried. It's not like John, not at all." My voice was quivering, dammit. Now this train of thought seriously frightened me. I pulled my arm free, turned, and nearly smacked into Chief of Detectives Broder.

I looked back at Korematsu, trying to deduce what was show for Broder and what was real.

He eased back a bit. His breathing was shallower, as if to allow more internal room for weighing options. But when he spoke his voice was unwavering and his eyes hard. "I'm going to give you time to get this message to him: if he gets himself in here by the end of the day, I'll cover for him. I'll work with him on this case. Do what you have to. No one's going to be following you. He's made enemies in the department, and a lot of guys will be happy to see him gone. No one's got his back. I'm sticking my neck out, but I'm going to trust you."

"Thank you," I said so docilely a lesser man might have laughed. "I have no idea where to find him but I'll do everything I can. He's being an ass. He'll be here by sundown."

I walked to the street. If I could trust Korematsu then he was on very thin ice here. As for John, there was no way I could find him, even if I had intended to.

I wanted to get back to the zendo. But city running has its drawbacks and there was no good route, with some much worse than others. Hoping to clear my sinuses and my head, I opted for flat and headed back along Howard, on once seedy blocks now in the process of spiffification. I cut left onto the Embarcadero. There was one lead Korematsu might not think of.

I intended a quick stop at the zendo, but when I got there a note was on the door:

> *Come see me—now.*
> *Renzo*

"You read my mind, huh?" I said as I walked into his little café on the corner. Just one of the three tiny tables was empty. The bracing aroma of strong coffee and sweet pastry filled the space. I pulled out a chair, ready to wrap my finger around the handle of the little white cup.

Renzo caught my arm. "Outside."

"Without coffee? What's going on?"

He motioned me to the door. With his greyhound face and gray ponytail, he looked like he'd walked out of City Lights Books after hearing a young Ferlinghetti in 1960. His jacket—cleaned, pressed—was probably circa 1960. He held the door for me and I walked out and followed him down Pacific till we were clear of the café windows.

"That Korematsu," he said, "he may be okay, but I don't really know him. He comes in here getting coffee for you and it makes me uneasy. He looks like he's on business."

"He was."

"Like I say, I don't know him. I've been running this place for forty years. I know the city. I know the police. Korematsu may be okay but his boss—"

"Broder."

"Yeah, Broder. He's shifty."

"He dislikes John."

Renzo shrugged as if to say my point meant little in the greater scheme of things. "Broder's father was a cop and his father before him. They were on the force back in the days when joining was a business investment. Grandpa made his money in protection. Dad was a favorite of drug consortiums."

"Are you telling me—"

"Broder was *going* to be different. He was a stand-up guy. Could have been a twin to your John. Figured he'd wind up chief. But he didn't have the pull. Chief's a political appointment in this town and Broder didn't have the savvy to spot the right connections. Took him a while, but he realized he's dead-ended."

"Interesting."

"I'm not standing on the sidewalk losing business to give you a history lesson."

"Sorry. I didn't—"

"I'm telling you, here's a guy who blew off easy money and lots of it, in order to be chief. All he'd have to've done was looked the other way. But he played by the rules and got zip. His father and grandfather'd say he'd been a fool. He's fifty years old with nothing to show for it. But now . . . *now* he's going to get his. Now, he's seriously looking the other way."

"You mean with the smuggling?"

"I'm not talking any one thing. You poke into any one thing and it's a gateway to the whole business. Trust me, Darcy, you don't want to be the one who sticks her head through that gate."

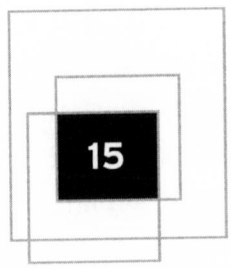

15

"OPEN UP!"

No response.

I pounded.

A shade moved next door.

"Gary, get this door open or I'm calling the cops!"

Fog covered the city all the way into North Beach—thick, damp, cottony. "Gary, I'm going to freeze out here and die on this doorstep and you will never, ever hear the end of it!"

He opened the door. "How'd you find me?"

I pushed into the hallway. The place was a typical San Francisco apartment building—three stories, two flats to a floor separated by the staircase. In each one a hall led past the first bedroom in the front, past the second, through a living room with a window on the airshaft and onto the kitchen and another staircase out back. They were often first rentals for wide-eyed newcomers so delighted to be actually living in the shadow of Coit Tower or near the clubs on Union Street that they didn't care about spending hours each night hunting parking spots.

"Karen Johnson's," I said as I followed him down the hallway to the yellow living room.

He nodded. "But how—"

I shrugged, wishing I was here with a less serious need so I could savor this moment. "You said Karen was here for a divorce. You don't handle divorces. But you've been party to three of your own. You had complaints about the first two attorneys but the third, you called the queen of tangled finance, remember? Erica Ukner."

"Erica wouldn't discuss a client with you."

"Not with me, your sister. But with me, your assistant, it's a different story. I phoned from your office, leaving a message to call back. 'Law Offices,'" I said mockingly, "'Mr. Lott asked me to double-check the local address of Karen Johnson.'" He stared at me, not sure how to react.

"Didn't Karen tell you she was a tourist?"

"Like you told her to? Yeah, Gary. But she has to have a residence in the City and County of San Francisco for three months before a divorce can be filed. Meaning, before you could do whatever you were doing for her. Which was?"

"I can't say."

"I didn't track you down for nothing!"

"Attorney-client confidentiality."

"Your client's dead!"

"Confidentiality survives death."

"Work around it. This is serious. Karen was barely dead when someone was poking around your office."

His mouth twitched, as if he was about to grin.

"Oh, that was you, huh? What'd you take?"

"Everything I didn't want the cops to. I know what can happen. Why do you think John's hiding out. Do yourself a favor, get clear of this whole thing."

"Too late! Okay, tell me this: Why did Karen Johnson steal John's car?"

"Dunno. Really. Since, say, two minutes after I called you, I have not learned a thing that was not on the news."

"Karen didn't call you?"

"Hey. I've told you what I can."

"Okay," I said, trying to peer in through the cracks of his fence of confidentiality. "John said you are the one who set things up."

"Vague."

"Different question: You're covered by privilege. The police can't force you to reveal anything about Karen. So why are you hiding?"

He hesitated.

"Oh, because you know something *not* covered by privilege."

He didn't disagree.

I leaned against the counter, aimed my gaze above his head. "Karen's dead, so it's not something to protect her. It's . . . of course! It's something John told you, something to do with Karen but not your case with her. Now what could that be? The smuggling? She caused a crash in front of Broder's mistress's place. Ah . . . you're not surprised! That wasn't on the news, or not that specifically. So you've been in touch with John. He's okay?"

He hesitated.

"Dammit, is our brother okay?"

"If I said he was last night, it wouldn't mean he was today," he finally brought out.

"What's that . . . ?"

His face hardened. He was one of my dark-haired, chisel-featured siblings with piercing blue eyes. "I'm not saying more, not about anything. You need to get out of here."

Go away, little girl! I was so sick of my older brothers' condescension. I strode back to the bedroom. If Gary wasn't going to tell me anything, maybe the apartment Karen Johnson had been occupying for three months would.

Then again, I decided after going through the cheery, white-walled, flowery bedroom, the plain bathroom, the dark living room without television or DVD player, much less a book, maybe her connection to this place was no more than what was required to meet the residence requirement. "It's like a bed-and-breakfast here, except those places at least have something to read. Did she even spend a night here?"

Gary didn't answer. He'd found a bottle of Merlot—not his taste, so it must have been Karen's—and was trying to edge out the cork with a paring knife. At the rate he was going, by the time he got a drink he'd need it.

I pulled open the refrigerator. The shelves were empty except for a half pound of coffee and a half pint of half-and-half. "Half-fridge?" Companionable humor wasn't likely to lead him into unintentional revelation, but it was about the only ploy I had left.

The cabinet next to the refrigerator held a couple of plastic dishes. On the stove was a single saucepan, probably used to heat water. "Look! A cookbook! Planning to be here long enough to have company?" It was the sole book in the apartment.

"Not mine."

"Karen's?" I picked up *Soups for Summer*. "It's new. Was she the dinner party type?"

He let out a somewhat forced sarcastic laugh and then quickly seemed to catch himself.

"Makes no sense to start cooking now, eh? Who'd she know to ask over? Anyway, the case you've got was about to go big time, right? That's why you were up all night researching; why you needed to do something so immediately that you called me to drop everything and amuse her. If you—"

"Doesn't Mom have this?" He propped the cookbook upright.

I knew he was trying to distract me. "One like it. I'm surprised you remember something like that. The author had a funny name . . . What was it? Plesko? Kresge?" I looked at it: Cesko. That was weird—same name, but definitely a different book. Wait. Same last name, but different first. "And wasn't there some scandal attached?"

Suddenly, Gary had a peculiar expression on his face. He put the cookbook face down.

"What's with this? Is there some connection between Karen and this book?"

He ignored me.

And what was it about, that long-ago cookbook? "One time when I came home from college the cookbook—what was it called? *Apples in Autumn?*—wasn't there. Maybe it'd been gone for years and I just hadn't noticed . . ."

I grabbed it and checked the back flap. The author of *Soups for Summer* was the niece of the original one. "Hey, maybe I can find this Claire Cesko and see what her connection is to Karen Johnson. It says she lives near Redding . . ." I was just joking so I was caught off guard by Gary's reply.

"Maybe not a good idea."

"Why's that?"

"Trust me."

"Tell me. You were the one who got me remembering it. It's just a cookbook."

He said nothing.

I stood up. "Fine. Well, I guess it's not. We'll talk about it when I get back."

"Darce—"

"But before that, you can give me your car."

"You want to take my Lexus to the back of beyond! Think again. Besides, up there it's going to stick out, look a little too, uh—"

"City shyster?"

Only a sister would have spotted the cringe before he shifted, relaunched. "You're going to drive through all those redwoods?"

"I'm over my tree fear," I lied. "Just give me the keys, dammit!"

He hesitated, weighing his responsibilities to his client and the law, to his sister and family. "Okay, okay, but it's crazy to do this cold. There's a PI John knows up there, Les Wallinsky, who's helped out looking for Mike. You need a contact."

"Right."

I had an idea, a necessary one. "Listen, we never had this conversation." I pulled a dollar out of my pocket. "I'm hiring you."

"Good point, everything considered."

I watched him pull out his wallet, insert the bill, slide the wallet back in his pocket, me weighing whether I really had to ask the question that would bring me a barrage of flak. "What's your take on Korematsu?"

"You interested in him?"

"No, no! I don't even know his first name. No, my question is can I trust him." I told him our conversation at the morgue.

"He said he wouldn't have you followed and you believed him?"

"Not enough to come right here. I took a few diversionary measures. But Korematsu? Got an opinion?" He was bound to, I knew.

Gary leaned back till the chair almost toppled backwards. He was a master of the trick. He'd used it to attract women, distract opponents, and by now he'd done it so long the balancing actually helped him focus. "The guy seems too decent to be a detective."

"John'll—"

"John'd be the first to agree. A detective's got to be ready to work a suspect. Nobody's the good cop all the time. What I think about Korematsu is he's hiding something. I'd trust him with the family silver but not with . . . not with . . . I don't know what. Besides, he's reporting to Broder, so you don't need to waste time wondering if you can trust him."

I laughed.

Gary started to speak, caught himself, eased his chair back to the ground with more care than necessary. "Darce . . ."

"What!"

"Korematsu, it's not that he *wouldn't* protect you in this, it's that he *can't* protect you. John can't protect you; he can't even protect himself. If he could he wouldn't be lying low. No one can protect you. Remember how he says: 'Contraband doesn't pass through this city without some cop on the take.' Look, I'm serious about being bound by attorney-client privilege. There are things I can't talk about, even with you." He pulled out his keys and laid them in my palm, resting his hand there for a moment. "Karen Johnson did something that got her murdered. I don't know what. But her killer's out there somewhere. Be careful. Seriously careful."

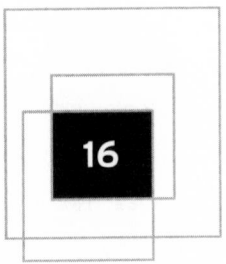

THURSDAY

GARY CALLS HIS Lexus his conference room. Black Rebel Motorcycle Club played from the Blauplunkts in the back. Later I could flip to news updates from London, Karachi, or suburban Mars.

I'd slept at the zendo, sat morning zazen, and driven Duffy to the beach for a run. Ocean Beach is only a few blocks from Mom's house, but Duffy loves to stand on the fine leather seat and peer appraisingly out the window like a right-seat driver. Another owner would blow a gasket at the thought of twenty sharp paw nails scratching across the pale tan leather; another owner would toss Duffy and me onto the street. But likeability is Gary's forte: it's not just that he can sway a jury to his side, but that his client and opposing counsel, expecting him to own the courtroom, make their decisions accordingly. In Duffy's case, a seat cover was all it took for my brother to control the outcome.

It was mid-afternoon before I got out of the city. The Ceskos' town, Star Pine, was three or so hours up I-5. Gary's warning about trees had not only been a jab about the embarrassing phobia that had dogged me since childhood—though I'd pretty nearly licked it—but his comment could hardly have been more unnecessary: I-5 runs from San Diego to Redding without a leaf to block the sun. It's California's tribute to the Jersey Turnpike.

I caught the freeway north of Sacramento. Of course, the car had cruise control, climate control, and lines of buttons that moved the seat up, down, back, forth, heated it, vibrated the back and much, much more. The car moved north but inside nothing changed. So it was a shock when I opened the door at a rest stop near Redding and stepped out into what had to be a hundred degrees.

"You must be Darcy Lott."

"*You're* Les Wallinsky?"

"You look surprised."

"I just assumed—shit, *assumed*—that my brother's contact would be a former sheriff."

"How do you know I'm not?"

"Pigs may fly." I laughed. Without creating a picture in my mind, I'd been expecting a friend of John's to be in his fifties, wearing a shirt that fit ten pounds ago, and a suit that screamed "prosecution witness." But the real Les Wallinsky looked to be in his mid-forties, buff, wearing a work shirt, khaki chinos, hiking boots. Barely taller than I am, he had an adorable knob of a nose, black button eyes, short wiry blond hair, and a killer grin. If he'd been hired by my sister Gracie instead of John, I'd have wondered if he was a gift for my weekend.

"You need to eat?" he asked, glancing at the restaurant next to the parking lot.

"Is there a place closer to Star Pine?"

He grinned. "Okay, but you'll have to hold your appetite for an hour. Oh, and leave that car here."

"Will it be all right?"

"Sure. Don't worry." He motioned to a tan pickup. I followed him and he opened the passenger-side door for me.

"How do you know John?" I asked, once we were on the highway again.

"He hired me." He shot a glance in my direction.

"Why?" I wanted to get this part over with.

"You mean why did he think I could find Mike?"

Suddenly my skin was alive and I was holding my breath. "What makes you think Mike was here?" I hadn't quite believed Gary. But, of course, I'd wanted to.

"He wasn't. Trust me, I've looked. I like Mike. I mean, it's like I know him. I can see why he was everyone's favorite." He glanced over at me again. "And why you were his. No, wait, I'm not coming on, just saying you both have that right-here kind of thing and a lot of go—you more than him. But he had something else. He was like the dog who can always get out of the yard no matter if you got the CIA in to guard it, you know?"

A new person talking about him was like a whiff of having him back. "I'll tell him you said that. He'll like it."

"I'd really love to find him. That list John gave me, of places he figured he could be, I gotta tell you, that's garbage. It's a parent list, know what I mean?"

I laughed. "That's John. It shouldn't surprise you."

"Well, there's no record of Mike. None of the old-timers around here recognized his picture or him in the video Katy shot that last Thanksgiving."

"You know my sister, Katy?"

"Do now. Sharp woman. She picked clear shots of him, him talking, him watching you doing a back flip, him standing around—the kind of things a guy'd be doing in an airport. But you," he said, shooting a glance at the legs I'd flipped over my head way back then, "were a hot little number."

Who *was* this guy? John had made distrust a way of life and Wallinsky seemed an unlikely exception to such a worldview. I couldn't imagine my brother fronting money to him.

"No record of your brother anywhere within two hundred miles. Not seen at schools, shelters, monasteries, cults, protests, not working trawlers or herding beef—"

"How long have you been on this?" I asked, amazed. It was such a long shot.

"Fifteen years. On and off. Mostly off."

Fifteen years! Something else I didn't know about John. "Steady work for a PI."

"You could say that."

"Could say which?"

"I investigate, I don't do licenses."

"Mr. By-the-Book's been paying you? He might as well wear jeans on his days off."

"Licenses are crap. I'm good: I take a case; I get results. But this Mike thing's different, you know?"

"Yeah." People had always connected with Mike—that was his magic. "Mike's like Gary, but different, smoother. You know Gary, too, right? He's the un-John. Unlike Gary, Mike never plotted things out, at least not in any obvious way. I don't think even to himself. And yet—well, obviously—there were things going on . . ."

"I was counting on people remembering him, hoping for teenaged girls sitting by phones, old guys pleased to see a nice kid. I tried every angle. I hitchhiked up and down I-5, hung around the truck stops, ate burgers in every hamlet here to the Oregon line. This could be a lifetime job. It is for John. But I know when over is over."

I believed him, pretty much, but still . . . fleeting as hope had been, his failure was agony—one less large area where Mike might be, one step closer to none.

I don't like to let myself think that way. So I flip my thoughts to some-thing—anything—else. "Les, you know John. What about the woman he was meeting at Coit Tower? Was she part of this?"

"No one's part of this. There is no *this*."

"So she was just one of his flings?" I threw this out just to see his reaction.

He laughed. "Listen, John may have flung, but to hear him talk, he's so busy toeing the line he can't see anything that's not painted on macadam."

"But you . . ." I hunted for the right term and ended up with the lame, "you liked him."

"Hell no, I don't like John! I respect his commitment and understand his obsession. But *like* him, no way. If I were his kid brother, I'd have been exiting by the second-story window, too."

"That was me."

"Really? He said Mike."

"He's mixed up. *I'm* the one he caught walking across the top of the roof. He cut down the tree in the front yard just so *I* wouldn't leap to it. Mike was, well, more subtle when it came to butting heads with the Enforcer."

"Yeah, well, Mike's got my sympathy."

Now I saw why John had hired him. He hadn't picked the detective he'd like, or feel comfortable with, or even trust. He'd pick the one who wasn't just the most like Mike, but most like the qualities Mike had that he couldn't stand. And didn't understand. Boy, had I underestimated my oldest brother . . . again.

I sat, staring out the windshield at the darkening fields. It hadn't rained in three months. The grasses were tan, dry. The rolling summer hills of the

Golden State. Fire tinder. Here and there a boulder thrust out as if coughed up in one of the earthquakes. In depressions, clutches of scrub brush and live oaks huddled throwing their last shadows in the dusk. It was a surprisingly empty land for the nation's most populous state, the kind of place where you could walk a long way before finding help.

Wallinsky spent time talking about cases he'd solved, techniques he used. I had the feeling he'd sensed my need for distance and was filling the space between us.

"So what about Madelyn Cesko?" I asked, after a while. "And what's with Claire? Is there a cookbook gene?"

"Madelyn Cesko was killed."

"Killed?" I'd remembered something unpleasant connected to her but not that she'd been a rural murder statistic.

"On her farm. Farm in the sense that she kept a kitchen garden for her work. The place is isolated, miles outside town, which isn't more than a couple of stores and a gas station anyway. A brutal killing."

"Brutal how?"

"Stabbed in the chest with her own chef's knife."

"Omigod!" Suddenly the air-conditioning was freezing. The worst that should have befallen her was a collapsed soufflé. "I'm beyond shocked. I mean, my mom had her cookbook! It's, like, people whose books you make apple betty from don't get killed . . ."

"The case was huge up here. I was just out of high school and got involved."

"You were here then?"

"It was my intro to investigating. The biggest thing in Star Pine before or since. People still talk about it like it happened last week, like they were there even if they moved to town last year."

116

"Who killed her? Why?" The truck rattled; outside muted colors whirled by as if unrelated to rocks and grass and bushes. Madelyn Cesko killed with her own knife! Karen Johnson dead on the freeway! I had a cold, foreboding feeling. "Who—?"

"Who killed her? Sonora Eades. A college girl."

I exhaled.

"She was taking a survey"

"Huh?"

"You heard me right—a survey."

"They were strangers?"

"So far as anyone knows."

"Then why . . . how . . . ?"

But he didn't answer. The truck had slowed, the road surface grown rougher. Metal rattled, the seat belt cut into my ribs. Low houses lurked under cover of trees behind fences fifty yards from the road. Wallinsky stared straight ahead and I couldn't read him well enough to guess why he'd suddenly clammed up. The houses were closer together now, nearer the road. A sign proclaimed: "Welcome to Star Pine." The road curved right and became a town street.

"Wallinsky, is this case personal?"

"Seem like that?" he asked, looking not at me but scanning out the window. "It's just part of my history now, same as Mike is."

"What about the killer? That girl, Sonora? Did the state have the death penalty then? Or did she get second degree?" With appeals, either way she could still be alive. "What could possibly have caused her to—"

He jerked the truck to the right and yanked the emergency brake, smack in front of a railroad train.

17

IT WASN'T A whole train, but a single car. The Caboose Café & Bar, announced the sign in shiny green with gold trim and red lettering outlined in gold. Inside, the place was brightly lit and packed with what must have been everybody in Trinity County.

"So, what's your plan here?" I asked, but he was halfway out of the truck.

Wallinsky was an easy guy to be with—undoubtedly his stock in trade. But there was something about him I didn't trust.

Inside, we grabbed two stools at the bar between a couple in their twenties and a dark-haired woman Wallinsky's age who eyed him with interest. It was a tight fit. Wallinsky ordered us beers, burgers and fries.

"Edie, the owner," he whispered to me, as a large red-haired woman three stools to my right, readjusted herself. She sat facing the room, resting one elbow on the bar, and leaning back so a roll of torso rested on the rail. The eight or ten tables were full, with voices battling friends and neighbors and a constant drum roll of dishes arriving, silver being bused back onto trays.

The beers came. We drank, Wallinksy heartily, me on a choke chain till I ate. I didn't know what I was going to say here, but I was damned if I'd blow any chance of saying it. I nudged my companion. He huddled over his glass. Beyond, Edie looked to be eyeing him.

I didn't like the feel of things. But in for a lamb, in for sheep. I took a swallow and said in Wallinsky's direction, "So then, this is the place where"—I let my voice rise—"Madelyn Cesko died?"

Edie stared.

Wallinsky glared.

I hunched down, grabbed my glass with both hands as if it were an offering to her. "Sorry."

Edie straightened up, looked over, and made the kind of sound suited to an offended matron at high tea.

Wallinsky concentrated on his beer.

"Oh ferchrissakes, Edie, go ahead and tell her. You spin it out for every stranger who buys a meal. She's already got a drink," the guy next to me said. When I swiveled to look at him, he winked.

Edie shot darts at him, shifted her butt and leaned around Wallinsky to ask, "You a reporter?"

I couldn't be certain I'd guess the right answer, so I went with safety. "No. Just visiting my friend." I patted Wallinsky's thigh. He had an impressive ability to sink into the background. Edie's attention was on me now. Everyone had gone quiet, watching Edie, as if waiting for the lion to be let into the coliseum.

"You heard of Madelyn Cesko?"

"She wrote cookbooks?"

Edie leaned forward.

"Madelyn," she said firmly, "was not just any cookbook writer. She didn't just churn out recipes. She was an institution." She paused, then said, "She wrote ten cookbooks, five of them bestsellers across the state. She used to create a new dish for The Caboose here every single year. It was a tradition. There'd be a story in the local paper and mention in *The Record Searchlight* in Redding and once, in the *Chronicle*. It was so popular that the first time we made each one there'd be a line outside. One year, we even had to take reservations."

"Wow." I nodded appreciatively. "She was great for business, huh?"

"Well, yes, of course. But what I'm telling you is what a lovely person she was for the whole town. Busy as she was, she took in Claire—that's her niece—when her parents died. A two-year-old! Her with no experience with children! But that didn't faze her. Next year she had a new cookbook and a new dish for The Caboose, too."

"She lived here in town?"

"No, no. She had a little farm about thirty miles from here. She did all the work around the place herself. Her niece, Claire, helped along with some migrants. Even with a garden as small as hers, there's a lot needs doing and she must have worked like crazy, what with trying the recipes and writing them up and all. Don't know how she did it."

"By not wasting time in here, for one thing," someone called out.

Edie took a swallow of beer, staring at her glass till the room was quiet again. I wondered how long she'd been honing her delivery on this story. She waited half a minute until a guy at the nearest table seemed about to speak. "That summer," she said, "twenty-five years ago, this college girl comes to town. Says she's doing a survey for a sociology project on the differences between farm life and city life or some garbage like that."

"Don't need any survey to tell you that. On the farm you work, in the city you sit. Pretty obvious," the same voice explained.

"That's what sociology is—the study of the obvious." The woman next to Wallinsky grinned at us and let her gaze linger on him.

Everyone laughed, except Edie.

"So she—this is Sonora Eades I'm talking about—she drives out to the farm and I guess she asks her questions. But the answer she gets is Madelyn Cesko's too busy to be bothered with stuff like that. If she'd checked before she went wandering out there any of us could have told her. 'Don't go out there expecting her to be the same as she is in town'—not that Sonora Eades would have known how she was in town—but my point is we all knew not to bother her at home."

She leaned toward me, lowering her voice. "But she—*she*—didn't ask anything about Madelyn Cesko. She's banging on doors all over the area. So, out she goes. Not once, but twice at least. We don't know what all went on there because after she killed Madelyn she lit out, leaving poor Claire, her niece, there with the body—and that girl was only fifteen. She was a wreck. Had to go into treatment in San Francisco for months. Never the same afterwards. She was a normal kid—one of my cousins went to school with her, not in her class but in the next grade, and said she was. A normal kid, that is. Quiet, but normal. Isn't that right, Patty?" She asked the woman next to Wallinsky.

"I wasn't in her class either, but it's a small school. No one talked about her before, so she must have been okay."

Three or four of the people at tables agreed. But Patty wasn't looking at them. She was eyeing Wallinsky as if he was a specimen of some kind. Whatever her motive, it couldn't be good.

"What did Claire look like?" I asked, curious.

"Like a waif, a blonde waif, like she'd had the life sucked out of her."

I gasped.

Edie nodded appreciatively.

I could have smacked her. It was a moment before I could say, "But what do *you* think happened, Edie?"

"We're never going to know for sure, not now. Claire wasn't in any condition to talk about it for a good long time. Of course, those migrants vanished like mist on a hot morning. Like I said, Sonora Eades did her killing and got out quick. Left Claire with her aunt's body, dead or near dead.

Poor girl didn't know how to drive. Don't know how long she tried to save Madelyn, if that's what she did. Or maybe she was in shock so bad she just sat there. Whatever, it was the next day before a delivery guy saw her walking along the blacktop. He brought her into town. By the time the sheriff got out to the house, Madelyn'd been dead over twenty-four hours. It was summer. The sheriff said he'd never seen a crime scene bad as that."

"Because her body'd, uh, gone bad?"

"Blood all over the place."

"Everywhere?"

"All over the stoop, the door, the outside of the house. Like it'd been splattered with paint."

"But why? Why'd she kill her? Burglary?"

"Didn't take anything, but that doesn't mean she didn't intend to. Claire came in from the garden and scared her off."

I gasped. "Awful!" I muttered. "How totally awful for her!" I glanced at Wallinsky, but he'd turned toward his plate. For all his history with Madelyn Cesko's murder, it was suddenly as if a few fries were more compelling.

"That's the truth. You can see why poor Claire needed to be sent off for treatment. She's lucky to be as sane as she is now. After the tragedy they were afraid to even send her to San Francisco. She kept talking about the Golden Gate Bridge—you know, jumping?"

As a native of the city, I knew only too well.

"But they do amazing things at those clinics," Edie went on, "and she saw someone in Redding every week for a year or so, and then there was the medication—I don't know if she's even on that anymore."

"Claire's still here?"

"Of course. She's as back to normal as she's ever going to get, able to run Madelyn's farm all by herself. You've got to hand it to her."

"You've seen her? Recently?"

"Of course, I have. Last week right out front here."

Last week was an eternity ago. Three days ago Karen Johnson hadn't been hurled off the fifth-floor slab onto the freeway.

"Claire Cesko's still here," I said aloud, just to make the words real. "She's lived out there alone all this time?" How could she live there alone with the memory? Year after year?

"Word is she thought about going away, maybe to college or to the city, but it was more than she could handle. It's hard running a place like that, but it's what she knows. We see her in town every week or so, picking up groceries and the like. She's not like her aunt when she came to town; Claire doesn't talk more than she has to. Madelyn had a word for everyone."

Edie looked at me pointedly. "If you ran into her, you'd probably think she was rude, but we're used to her. We don't even notice it now. It's just the way she is. Could be lots worse."

"What does she say about Sonora Eades now?" Wallinsky's voice seemed to come out of nowhere.

"Claire never mentioned her, never said the kind of things you'd think. It was way too much for her just to keep on keeping on. I don't think she ever got to the point of turning her fury on Sonora. She just swallowed it and let it eat away at her all these years." Edie gave a mighty shrug. "That's how I see it, anyway—not that I'm any shrink."

"What happened to Sonora afterwards? Why," I said, "was it so clear that she killed Madelyn? It doesn't sound as if Claire, or anyone, actually saw her do it."

"No one there but her and Claire, and the migrants. They came and went. They had no reason to harm Madelyn. It wasn't one of them."

"But how do—"

"Or Claire, if that's where you're headed."

It was. "How—"

"Because"—Edie paused, checked her audience—"the Eades girl's fingerprint was on the knife. On the handle, pressed into Madelyn's blood."

The room went silent. Though I suspected that, as an audience, they were on the verge of applause.

"But—"

"No buts. Not at all. We must've had every cop and every sheriff and all the techs from the coroner's office in here. And the press! That was back when papers had their own reporters, didn't just pick up stuff off the wire."

"... all over town, popping up next to us," an overweight guy was saying. "Every kid and every granny was suddenly an expert! Remember?"

"It was awful," Edie said. "Vultures."

"Kept The Caboose open till midnight," a woman at the nearest table offered. Her companions nodded.

"You remember that. You were here then." This from the dark-haired woman. Wallinsky's neighbor.

Edie was looking at him.

He hesitated.

This was bad.

"You were in school then, weren't you? For a month or so."

Very bad.

I patted Wallinksy's shoulder. Said kindly, "It's been hard enough on you all these years, but I think coming here tonight was a mistake. What do you say, how about some rest before we go?"

18

A VERY bad mistake.

"You went to school here?" I demanded as soon as I slid behind the wheel.

"Get out. Let me drive."

"Oh, right, and have everyone looking out The Caboose window gossip about your miraculous recovery." Restraining the urge to slam into reverse, I backed out slowly, glided down the tiny main drag, not pressing the pedal till we were on the unlighted two-lane. When we hit the first curve, I yanked the wheel hard, smacking him into the door. "You forgot to tell me you lived here for an entire month? What's the matter with you?"

"I did say I'd been here."

"Been here's not the same as lived here! Been here's a raindrop; lived here's a lake. Does John know about that?"

"Listen, I—"

"No, huh?"

"Well, why would he? He hired me to find your brother, not to dig into the Cesko case."

"Nothing like a coincidence." I pulled around a slow car—one doing only the limit—and cut back in close enough to make him gasp. With luck I'd never come face to face with the other driver. As ticked off as I was at

Wallinsky, I couldn't stop thinking of Claire Cesko moving back into the bloody house. Were there still blood stains that had never come out? How could she be discharged from a psychiatric facility and be sent home to the scene of the crime? No wonder she talked suicide.

"Let me drive," he said again.

"Talk."

"Hey, it's my truck."

"Driving is nine-tenths of the . . . whatever."

"You know, you—never mind."

I eased off the gas pedal a bit. "Take your time."

"Okay, okay." He shifted around in the seat. "It was my first job. I was in college, or more accurately had dropped out of college, though I hadn't quite realized it. I thought it'd be a kick to be a PI, do some fast talking, 'loid a few locks,' the whole schtick. Then suddenly, in the school cafeteria where I was spending the time I wasn't spending on going to class, there was an old guy looking for an assistant. Like he'd materialized just for me. If I'd been up to any fast thinking then, I'd have gotten my antennae up when he didn't ask about my classes or why I could take a month off with no problem, or about experience. He just watched me shoot the breeze."

"Because you were what he needed?"

"Yeah. Needed someone who could listen, too. That eliminated most of the others he was eyeing." He laughed. "Anyway, my new boss had a connection, a woman who'd say I was her nephew. She enrolled me in high school.

"Didn't you need transcripts from your 'last school?'"

He shifted to face me. "You think you have to be a genius to fake a transcript from Weehawken High, across the country in Jersey? Nice birth certificate, too."

"So you were what, eighteen? Twenty?"

"Twenty. But I looked sixteen, which of course was why he chose me, not that I would have admitted that then."

"So you enrolled . . . ?"

"Yeah, the idea was to get to know Claire to draw her out. But, of course, that didn't happen because she didn't come back to school. The PI kept me there a month, hoping she'd show, but by the end of the month she was on her way to gagaland in San Fran."

"But you clearly made other friends."

"I did what I could, joined clubs, tried out for teams. I was Mr. Congeniality. I'll tell you, that month in high school really made me appreciate college. Not enough to try to finish the semester, but I understood that the lack of bells and being able to make your own schedule were real benefits."

"Maybe they could quote you in the college catalog."

He snorted.

"What were you after?" I knew, but I wanted to hear him say it.

I could hear him drawing in breath, feel him watching me, trying to stay two steps ahead. "That's the frustrating thing. I don't know. Sounds dumb. *Was* dumb. But I was a kid looking for a fun job and happy to have one dangled in front of me. If I'd known anything about detective work I'd have said, 'Hey, what should I be asking? What am I after?' But I didn't. He told me to go and keep my ears open, not to ask anything particular, but to pay attention when anything useful came up. So I'd call him every night and make a report. It wasn't till toward the end of the month that I began to think the whole thing was a sham—that he was telling whoever hired him that he was up here investigating while all along he was sitting in a Eureka bar. When I got back to town, eventually, after he'd dragged the gig out as long as he could, I told him what I thought."

"And he said?"

"He just looked at me. Didn't even give me the courtesy of any reply, much less an explanation." Wallinsky made a noise that could have been a derisive laugh. "I didn't know who was paying him; I had nothing. So I had him write me up the kind of reference you'd give the head of the class at Quantico. Don't know if it ever fooled anybody, but I've worked steady ever since."

I swung into the motel, cut the engine and turned to him. "Well, it's not fooling me."

The apron of light from the cabins was just bright enough to show an upward flicker of his eyes. He shrugged. "Busted!"

The guy wasn't even embarrassed. "What was the deal?" I demanded. "What did this unnamed employer—oh hell, he didn't exist, did he? It was just you. But you were here. You got yourself into school, and stayed a month. Why?"

"Okay, okay. You're right. The thing is, I wanted to get to Claire. I figured she had to know something she hadn't told the sheriff. Not that she was involved, but just that you don't tell the cops everything, even if you intend to. You forget things, you don't connect Points A and D, and when you finally do, you figure it's too unimportant to go through it all again. Or you don't want to be a pest—or else you just want to forget. Whatever. I figured there had to be something."

"So was there?"

"Dunno. What I said about her being gone, that was true. I never saw her. But I'd left school, taken the trouble to set myself up here, so I stayed, hoping I'd be able to find something out from one of her friends. What I found was she didn't have friends."

"That took you a month?"

"Took me a day. Then I tried to get a job in town where I could over-hear stuff. Only thing I got offered was being a part-time stocker at the grocery. I had every intention of serious eavesdropping, but it's hard when you're shelving canned fruit on aisle one and the conversation's at the far end of aisle two." He reached for the door handle.

I reached faster for his arm. "What were you after? Was there some kind of reward?"

"Nah. It was cut and dried from the beginning. Sonora Eades tried to wipe her prints off the knife but there was still one good one left. The sheriff would have closed the case in record time if she hadn't disappeared—"

"Dammit, what happened to her!"

"Hold on! We're on the same page here. That's what drove me crazy! What happened to Sonora? Answer: she disappeared. End of story."

"Oh, come on—"

"That's the truth."

"You know I find that a very suspicious phrase."

"Yeah, well. But sometimes 'the truth' is true. Like now. I went out there, to the house, three times trying to get a lead. First time there was crime scene tape and I was nervous. Second time the tape was down but there was a patrol car in the driveway. The last time the tape was gone and the driveway empty. But I was still nervous, and with good reason. Sheriff stopped me getting into my car half a mile down the road, suspicious I was looting or up to something an outsider kid shouldn't be. That's when I weighed the pros and cons and went back to Eureka. I talked to kids who knew her at Humboldt State—"

"What'd they say about her?"

"Nice, serious, committed. They said what friends always say about a murder suspect: Not the type to ever kill anyone."

"That's it?"

"I called her father. He was in the Navy when she was a kid and, frankly, he was useless. Hadn't talked to her in months. That's it. Truth."

That might be the truth, but it sure wasn't the whole truth. Still, I wasn't going to waste energy on anymore of his variations on a theme. Tomorrow, I'd have another go at him. "What's Claire like now?"

He shrugged.

"When was the last time you saw her?"

"Hey, lighten up. That was twenty years ago. She was sixteen. I didn't see her then. Haven't seen her since. What do you think's going on?"

"I don't know. Probably nothing. Probably Claire Cesko is a thirty-six-year-old woman whose only interest is which season to feature in her next book. Probably."

It was too late to drive out to her house now, way too late. But I was going to feel a lot better when I laid eyes on her.

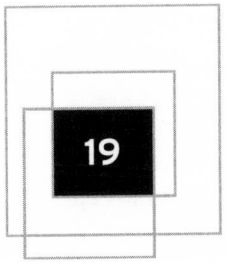

FRIDAY

WE DIDN'T GET much sleep, but I can usually make do on a few hours' worth for several days before I crash. What I needed more than sleep was a long run or a couple hours in the gym—something to clear the mush out of my brain. Strapped in the passenger seat, I felt like a zoo tiger whose muscles were atrophying. I rolled down the window—it was already hotter than it'd be mid-afternoon at home.

Morning eases into San Francisco, usually with a thinning of the night's fog. In summer it doesn't clear till ten, sometimes not at all. But here dawn burst forth. Sunlight glistened off tree, grass, macadam—everything. As Wallinsky sped along the blacktop toward Madelyn Cesko's house (or more accurately now her niece Claire's), I accessed my messages. I wasn't due back on the set for the second stunt till Monday, at least that was the schedule when I left there two days ago. But no word otherwise from Jed Elliot, so that was good.

I checked in with Leo. He already knew I wouldn't be at zazen today. "Anything else I should know?"

"Do you mean have the police been here? Answer's no. None of your family's called."

"Thanks. I should be back tomorrow."

It was 7:00 A.M. when we turned off the hard-top onto a single lane of crackled macadam. "Her driveway?"

"Right."

A frisson of excitement filled my chest. Karen's copy of Claire's cookbook had been signed, not inscribed, but signed. Still, the book could be signed stock and mean zip. Yet why had Karen Johnson bought or brought with her this single book?

Tall grasses, or what might less graciously be called weeds, filled the fields on either side. Ahead, the road disappeared over the edge of a slight rise. But the land was essentially flat. Wallinsky's lips were tense, his teeth pressed together creating little pouches at the corner of his mouth and made his nose knobbier in a disarming way. *The game of life is a kick,* everything about him said. *Hey, I've got a free spot of my team. Here's the ball. See what fun it is!*

We crested the rise and still I saw no house. A few scraggly trees had pushed up amidst the grasses. Wallinsky was checking both sides of the road, as if cataloging the changes in foliage. As if it mattered. Did it matter? As if something had been buried under one of those trees.

"What are you watching for?"

"Habit. Precautionary ass-covering."

"How long *is* this driveway, if you can call this thing a driveway?" I asked. "Quite a distance for a college girl taking a survey to go."

"It's rural."

"There're houses in town, houses on the road leading to town. She could have gotten ten face-to-faces in the time she spent bouncing along this trail."

Off to the right the grasses changed. Lighter. Something like a gigantic letter M stamped the earth a paler color. "What's that?"

"Foundation. Madelyn was about to build a little inn. It was going to be a few guestrooms and a dining room. For her fans."

I glanced back at what was close to rubble now and wondered what Sonora Eades would have made of the foundation—it must have been new—when she drove past it on her way in.

"Okay, so if Madelyn blew off Sonora the first time, of course she'd have gone back. Even if she blew her off again, it'd be worth another try, low percentage as that chance might be. Of course—" I caught Wallinsky's smug expression an instant before he smiled and nodded. "Not 'of course'?"

"You snapped up the story every sheriff and reporter followed."

"And you didn't?"

"I'm not saying it's wrong. Could be a hundred percent right, could be fifty."

"Could be Sonora came here hot for the interview and found something more compelling?" *Something that's still here for the taking?*

Before he could answer the road curved and suddenly a house was dead in front of us.

In the way you realize you've had a fuzzy picture in the back of your head all along, I looked at the house with surprise. It wasn't the vine-covered cottage with smoke wafting out a chimney cooking that I'd pictured for the cookbook author. Nor was it the weathered, overgrown pile of boards I was dreaming up for Claire Cesko. It was the kind of prefab house that could have been at a beach or in a development next to a mobile home court, the kind a truck delivers in two halves.

One step led to a door next to a plate-glass window backed by closed curtains. Smaller windows at the sides suggested one big room in the middle comprising kitchen and living room, bedrooms on the sides. The house was tan, almost the same shade as the flora. The paint was fresh, the windows clean, but the wild grasses grew right up against it. I glanced at the side windows. The blinds were drawn on both. "It's like life outside doesn't exist."

"Or she sleeps late," he said.

"Yeah, or that. Or she's not in there."

The edge of the curtain trembled.

"She's there, Darcy. Let me do the talking."

"Like at the bar?"

As soon as I jumped down from the truck the sun slapped my skin. The air was dusty. The path to the door was dry grass, the kind that had had any moisture fried out of it. I followed in Wallinsky's wake. He knocked.

She didn't open the door. I could hear her inside, not walking around but breathing loudly.

He knocked again. "Claire?" And then, "Claire! Come on, open up."

She opened it, and suddenly there she was. Standing with one hand on the frame, she had her other hand on the edge of the door as if afraid of it being shoved open. Cool air wafted through the doorway. She was tall but almost childlike in her slightness. Her skin was smooth and well-cared for. Her thin blonde hair was caught back in a ponytail neither at the top of her head or the nape of her neck, but the middle of the back as if she'd grabbed a rubber band and carelessly pulled the hair into it. The pale legs of a natural blonde protruded from shorts and her T-shirt had Chinese characters across the front.

But it was her expression that struck me. I couldn't keep myself from staring. Her mouth was firm, pressed in annoyance. Her pale brown eyes peered directly at Wallinsky, but something in the pull of her brow gave them a look of terror completely at odds with the lower half of her face. She seemed undecided whether to slam the door in anger—or run.

"Have you seen the news?" Wallinsky asked.

"No." She was staring at him the way I wanted to stare at her, to examine her. But the fear in her eyes was more pronounced.

"A woman in San Francisco jumped off a building, onto the freeway."

She said nothing, just kept staring.

I didn't correct Wallinsky's assumption about Karen's death. "The only personal possession in the place she was staying was your book."

"Damn!"

"I can understand it's a shock, but why would she—"

"Oh, damn. You're reporters, aren't you?"

"No, no."

"Yeah, that's what they said before when they were all over this place like ants, banging on the door, peering in the windows, parking all over the lawn like they owned it." Her tone was sharp, her shoulders hunched in, but her face was all fear.

"We're not reporters."

"That's how it was before, when Aunt Maddie died. They came like that, like an invasion, cars and trucks and cameras. Like a sandstorm squeezing in through the cracks around the windows."

"I work in the movies. I do stunts." That almost always gets people.

But it didn't snag Claire Cesko. She wasn't thinking about the woman who died, and she sure wasn't paying attention to me; her whole focus was on Wallinsky. "You're not a reporter? But I know you? You look familiar."

What else hadn't he told me?

"Maybe." He was playing for time.

"The delivery boy at the grocery. You weren't very good, were you? You brought the wrong order here twice." She eased backward warily, her hand tightening on the door. "It was a long way to come with a mistake."

Wallinsky hesitated.

"You were putting cans on the top shelves, pulling the old ones in back up to the front where people would buy them." She was smiling but her brows were pulled down even farther in suspicion or fear, as if even the parts of her own face couldn't decide how she felt about him.

I stepped in front. "He was a jerk." I glared back at him. "And he's still a jerk." To her, I said, "There are no reporters. Not yet. Only us and the question why your new book was so important to that woman. She didn't even own a saucepan."

"Some people like to read recipes. They're comforting. Cookbooks make good gifts for all sorts of people." She said this last bit as if it were from a script she'd memorized.

"You could be right. But, on the chance there's another reason, maybe she was—Karen Johnson—a friend."

"I don't know a Karen Johnson."

I wanted to describe her, but how? Blonde, but she undoubtedly had had some other shade. Nice looking, but not natural, with easy-to-spot evidence of face work. "She talked about stepping off a hundred-foot pole."

Claire started. She was looking past me at Wallinsky; his face had gone white.

"You know it, the koan?"

"That's crazy," she snapped. "Anyway, I don't have friends. I've never had friends. I live way out here."

"What do you do?"

"Do? I do what my aunt did, I work. People think writing cookbooks is pulling recipes out of a box and copying them. But it's not easy to come up with something now. Food's been around a long time, you know. To create something new, something that'll make people want to try it, it's not easy, and it damned well doesn't happen on the first try or the seventy-fifth try. It's . . ."

"Frustrating," I offered.

"Damn right, it is."

"How do you do everything? The cooking, the shopping, the gardening?" I asked. "You've got to have help."

"Your aunt had help," Wallinsky added.

"She had to. She had publication deadlines. She had to grow more—different—vegetables here."

"And she must've had help in the house."

Claire let out a bitter laugh. "Me."

"Just you? You were a kid," I said, feeling for her. "And the migrant help, what about them?"

She grabbed the doorknob, ready to slam. "You're one of those damn lawyers. Don't you know what a statute of limitations is? Besides, my aunt is dead! Just leave—"

He ignored her, pushing himself forward.

"Stop it, Wallinsky!" I shoved him aside.

"Hey, I—"

"Get away from her!"

He jolted back.

"Damn it, get away!" I shouted at him. "I only wanted help finding a lead on Karen Johnson and here you are terrifying Claire, who's only trying to help me." I turned to her. "I'm sorry. I know it's been hard for you and we're the last thing you need."

Her hand was still on the knob. Out of the corner of my eye, I saw Wallinsky walking slowly back to his truck.

"Please. Something connects Karen Johnson to you."

"No!"

"To your aunt, then. Look, if I've discovered that, you know the police will. They'll be here asking the same questions. Think! Karen Johnson was probably in her early forties, so she'd have been college age when your aunt died."

College age. A college girl.

"My aunt didn't have friends. I have to work all the time just to do the book, but she worked all the time because that's how she was. She didn't care about anything else. She cooked, she thought cooking, she wrote, she publicized. She could have been Julia Child, could have had her own TV show. She was driven."

"She must have driven you, too."

"Not just me, everyone. She didn't have friends. Ask in town, see if you find one person she ever invited here, a single friend."

"How about Edie?"

"Edie thinks she was a friend?" she asked, clearly amazed.

"She—"

"All I've ever wanted is to live like a normal person, to go to the store, the laundry, the movies. But people stare. People—you!—show up at my door. Go away! Leave me alone! I don't know this person you're asking about. And my aunt didn't. I've spent too much of my life already getting over my aunt's murder. Isn't that enough for you?" She slammed the door.

I trudged back to the pickup, suddenly drained. Wallinsky was sitting in the passenger seat, staring straight ahead. Every bit of his shirt was damp. I walked around to the driver's side and climbed in. I knew the answer, but I put a hand on his arm and then said, "Sonora Eades. She's Karen Johnson, isn't she? How long have you known that?"

He swallowed. "Can't be sure. But age'd be right."

I watched him as he wrestled with what was obviously a difficult thought. For the first time, I sensed, he'd be speaking the truth.

"D'you think . . . Was that always her plan, all these years, to jump?" he said, finally.

"She didn't jump. She was pushed, murdered."

He snapped open the glove compartment, rustled through stuffed envelopes, shut the door, then opened it again and sat back as if realizing what he was looking for was something that would act as a denial of her death. "What did this Karen Johnson look like?"

"People change. But about five eight. The little finger on one hand was twisted so the nail faced away from the others."

"Shit."

20

I DON'T KNOW how long I sat in the truck staring out the dusty windshield into the brown grass of summer. Sweat coated my face, ran down my back. I could have asked him to switch on the air conditioner; I didn't. Karen Johnson a murderer? A murderer with a knife? It wasn't possible, not the woman in the blue linen shell, not the person who laughed about Gary's lack of exercise, not—"She saved a kid from being hit!"

"What?"

"Hit by a car. Not long after I met her."

You can't stand to believe anything bad about people you like.

"A carving knife's so Lizzie Borden!"

Wallinsky didn't answer and I was glad.

The keys hung in the ignition but I didn't touch them. Eventually I got out and walked back to Claire's door, knocked.

No answer.

"Claire," I shouted. "This is important."

Still no answer.

Sweat glued my hair to my neck, ran down under my arms. It was so hot I could barely breathe. "Claire! I'm not a reporter, but trust me, there will be reporters here soon and you don't want them taking you by surprise. You need to hear the news from me first."

The door stayed shut. No sound came from inside. But I was betting she was right on the other side of the door. I said in a normal tone, "Sonora Eades is dead."

The door snapped open. "I don't—Okay, come in and sit down."

I stepped inside, appreciative of the suddenly cool air.

She motioned toward a ladderback chair at a round oak table. With her blonde ponytail at the odd, off-center spot in the back of her head, and her skinny pale legs sticking out of her shorts, she looked like a kid sent to the table to do the homework she'd been putting off all vacation. Her face had flushed but was already losing color, and that wariness I'd noticed before in her eyes seemed like a default expression. After all she'd been through I could hardly blame her.

Karen Johnson had been here? In this doorway? Brandishing a knife? How could that be? How could she talk about us having dinner then steal a police car?

The room had an old-fashioned feel, as if Claire had changed nothing since her aunt's death. Or maybe she'd just never had the interest or attention to give to redecorating. I could picture Madelyn Cesko busily at her six-burner stove. The image I had was some version of what I remembered from that cookbook of hers Mom once had. Was the murder, in fact, the reason it'd disappeared? Mom thinking there was something creepy about it—and who could blame her?

Claire interrupted my thoughts. "What's your name?"

"Darcy, Darcy Lott." I said. "I met Sonora Eades just before she died, in San Francisco, two days ago. She plunged off a building onto the freeway." The memory of her boneless face on the morgue trolley blocked out everything. "It wasn't an accident . . . or suicide."

"But why does that give you the right to try to shove your way into my house?"

It was as if we were inhabiting parallel universes. I had to remind myself she might have a very different interest in the death of the woman who'd ruined her life.

"You want some herb tea?" she unexpectedly offered.

"Do you have black?" What I needed was a drink, or else Renzo's espresso. English Breakfast was hardly going to resuscitate me. "Do you grow your own herbs?" I asked, although I thought I knew the answer.

Still, I was surprised when she said sadly, "My aunt did. I should. I've kind of let things get away from me. For a long time I just couldn't face doing anything she did. It was too painful."

I watched her from behind as she fiddled at the stove. It was a sitter's back, buttocks already flattening so that her shorts sagged at the back and jutted out at the sides. She probably wouldn't grow fat but her pale skin would sag and wrinkle from lack of tone. What did she do with her time out here day after day? Spend it like her aunt, cooking, planning to cook, and nothing else?

Once she'd poured the boiling water into mugs and put the kettle back, she seemed to be moving the mugs without purpose. But her shoulders tightened and she kept her back to me.

The stringed labels were hanging off the side of the mugs when she put them in front of us. The pale water would probably stay so. No aroma wafted up, as if the tea had been in the cabinet for years. "Thanks!"

Claire looked surprised—as well she might. Without pretence of drinking, she put her own cup down. "How did you meet Sonora?" she asked abruptly.

"The thing is, I liked her," I said, and waited for the explosion.

It didn't come. Instead, she stared at me, with an odd expression, and then lowered her eyes. "I liked her, too," she admitted. "I never say that to reporters or anyone; it'd just cause trouble. When she came out here the first time and Aunt Maddie didn't have time to be bothered with her, she hung around and talked. I didn't get much chance to talk to anybody back then, so it was real nice for me. She was a few years older than me and I was impressed she had this summer job, going up to strangers' doors in a strange town, asking questions, when I hardly even ever went to town without Aunt Maddie. I never worked in the garden on my own, either. I always let her tell me what to do. I was like a child . . . I—" She turned away from me. She sounded like she was crying, making me hesitate to come any nearer. "It was all my fault. The whole *thing* was my fault. Sonora would have gone away, gone to someone else's house and probably it would have all been okay. But, see, I wanted her to come back. So I told her I could convince Aunt Maddie to answer her questions, that she should come back in a couple days. If I hadn't . . ."

"How could you *not* want a girl your age back? Isolated like you were out here!"

"But if I hadn't—I knew I wasn't going to convince Aunt Maddie of anything. I never once had, not ever. She wasn't going to talk to Sonora the next time either. The only difference—and I knew this, too—is that she'd be angry. But still I did it. I wanted to see Sonora. I thought after Aunt Maddie screamed at her, I could walk her partway out to the road and we'd talk and she'd understand I was sorry and we'd be, just for a little while, like friends. I just . . . just . . ."

She shifted, still more turned away than facing me. "When she came, Aunt Maddie'd had a bad day. She had a recipe that wasn't working and she was on deadline. Plus, she'd had to get an entire side of beef because of some problem with the butcher. And using even the best knives slowed her down. She was never that good at it." She stopped again, closing her eyes. "So she wasn't in a good mood."

"What happened then?" I couldn't believe I was getting the whole story like this; it was as if a switch had been thrown.

"She drove right up to the door like she'd been invited—which she had. By me, like I said. But before she even knocked Aunt Maddie yanked open the door and started screaming. And Sonora exploded. Really. She just went off! I was so stunned I couldn't get out of my chair—this chair, the one you're sitting in. I was sitting right there."

"She went off like that just because your aunt was screaming? Was your aunt shoving her, or hitting her?"

"No, just yelling, the way she did when she was frustrated. I figured she was going to be screaming at me as soon as Sonora left. I figured I had just enough time to run out the back door before she slammed the front one in Sonora's face. Then I could run around the side of the house and tell Sonora how really, really sorry I was, and maybe she'd still hang around with me a little. I didn't think so after what I did . . . but I hoped.

"But by the time I got there, she was standing holding the knife and Aunt Maddie was a heap on the doorstep." Her hands were quivering but her eyes were dry as she looked directly at me. "You're wondering how I can tell you that horrible story and not break down again, aren't you? In the beginning I didn't tell anyone, except the sheriff, because I'd fall apart before I got anywhere near the end. Then it got so I'd told it so many times the meaning started leaking out. It was just words and I sounded like a robot. If I'd have told reporters then they'd've said I'd had a lobotomy or something."

"But Claire, why'd you tell me?"

"Because this is like normal. We're sitting here like normal people, like we're almost friends."

"And?"

"Because I'm so fucking relieved."

I could barely believe those words came out of her timid little mouth. "Relieved that Sonora's dead?" I swallowed as hard as I ever have in my life, struggling to control the burst of fury I felt. *You're* relieved *Karen's dead? You were the one who lured her back here.*

"Yes!"

I thought she was going to burst into tears now, but once again, she didn't. She looked away, and when she finally turned back we were both in better control. "Ever since—all this time—I've never pulled open that door without being terrified. When Aunt Maddie was here, a knock on the door meant somebody wanting something from her. She'd be polite to them but there was hell to pay after. And then everything had to be perfect so she could get back into her groove. It was always in the back of my mind, the fact that every knock was like an explosion. I was never ready . . . I had no plan . . . no insulation. That's what the shrink in San Francisco said. You know what?"

It was a moment before I realized she was waiting for my reply. "What?"

"You're probably not going to believe this, but I was in the bin there before it even occurred to me that normal people don't resent every knock on the door. The girl in the next room there said her family left the doors unlocked. I assumed she was delusional, I mean seriously."

I lifted my cup and drank to give myself time to consider. Isolation like that was almost incomprehensible to me, the youngest of seven children, growing up in a house where the front door was always banging open and Mom kept stew in the fridge to heat up for any kid or kid's friend who wandered in between meals. It was a rare dinner without a guest or without three conversations going on at once. At least before Mike disappeared.

I felt for Claire, but still, something about her story didn't fit.

"You liked Sonora and yet you're relieved that she's dead?"

"Now I don't have to be afraid she'll kill me, too." She shook her head. "Listen, she must have been a psychopath. One minute she was a cheerful college girl and the next she grabbed Aunt Maddie's knife and stabbed her. So you don't need to look at me like that. Of course she dreamed of killing me, just like she killed my aunt." Then softly, she said, "I don't keep big knives here anymore. None."

She lifted her teacup with steady hands. Why wasn't she more visibly upset? Her neck and shoulders were tight, but otherwise it was as if her emotions were on a separate circuit from her body. She was the one who'd mentioned lobotomy. But it was still Sonora—my Karen Johnson—that was the biggest question mark. What had set her off like that? So enraged her that she'd grabbed the knife and plunged it into a woman's chest? A virtual stranger. Had it been like a blood vessel bursting without warning? Or was she truly a psychopath with such a good façade I'd missed any hint of deviance?

Except, out of the blue, stealing a police car!

Suddenly I understood only too well what Claire was not saying—and maybe not even seeing. "I'm probably the only person you've met who knows just what you mean. I liked her, too, I told you. We were going to meet for dinner. And then, out of the blue, she stole a police car. How can I ever trust my judgment again?"

"If only she'd just taken *our* car!"

Despite everything, I almost laughed. "It must be hard to trust people after that. I mean, second-guessing yourself."

"Why do you think I stayed way out here, alone? I invited a woman here who killed my aunt! I never had a clue. But I'm going to tell you something. You can't learn judgment, no matter how many years you spend in the bin. So don't even try. Look, I let you in!"

Was she making a joke? I couldn't tell. Did she even have a sense of humor, or was she just a mass of quirks?

But suddenly I remembered an important detail. "You and Madelyn weren't totally alone. There was a migrant crew here."

"That's right." Once again, she was regarding me warily. "But they were way out in the garden, on the far side of the house." Then she volunteered something surprising: "There've always been rumors that my aunt kept a lot of cash money around, to pay people, especially once the inn got underway."

"And it's never been found?"

"Of course not. It didn't exist! Aunt Maddie wasn't a fool. She may have been suspicious of banks, but she wasn't an idiot. But people like that guy of yours are never going to believe it. He thinks he's going to get rich."

"Has he been out here before, bothering you?"

She nodded.

"You could have called the sheriff."

A slight flush colored her face.

"You didn't because you were lonely?"

"Bad judgment. I told you you can't learn judgment."

"What can I say?" I was so furious at Wallinsky I could barely think straight. I picked up my cup to take to the kitchen and stood up.

"Wait. I'll make you a sandwich. You're hungry, right? You probably didn't have breakfast."

She sounded like a little kid begging for just a few more minutes of human attention. *Don't leave me.*

But I had all I was going to get here. Hanging around was just putting off driving home and calling Korematsu. "Claire, I'm sorry. I have to go back."

She looked like she was going to cry. Like she'd been controlling herself, or trying to, the whole time I'd been here. Now, all of a sudden, it was just too much.

"Claire?"

"But I was going to make sandwiches!"

Why did the creation of food always make such a difference? Why did the food take on the whole pain? "I'm sorry."

"Promise me you'll come back. I understand—I really do—you've got other stuff. You hardly know me. There's no reason, but, well, I don't know what I'm going to do. I'm so lonely here. Days, weeks, no one comes."

"But you could have—"

"No! She'd have found me in a city! I was safe here. This place I know. No one's going to get me here."

Tentatively, I put a hand on her shoulder. She flinched but didn't shake it off. I could have reminded her Sonora Eades wasn't going to threaten her anymore, but I just couldn't. Despite everything, I still couldn't make myself believe Karen Johnson was a psychopathic murderer.

But looking at Claire, seemingly about to go to pieces, it would have been impossible to say she didn't believe it.

"But now," she forced out, "now I don't have to . . . I can go, do . . . Omigod, I don't even know. It's so scary."

"Give yourself time." I smiled reassuringly.

"I don't know anyone, anywhere. The only place I've been is here."

"You've been to town. If it weren't for Wallinsky outside, I'd be asking you to give me a lift."

"Sure, yes, I'd do that . . . for you. Sure. I even have a new car. I'll show you. No one's seen it. I mean there's no one to show it to." She thought about this for a moment, sighed and then, making some association, and still hoping to keep me, said, "Tell me about your stunts. You said you were in the movies?"

"I'm doing a set now in San Francisco." As we walked to the car, a new silver Honda that made me believe Claire really would free herself from her prison here, I told her about the set-up. "The character I'm doubling is a woman on the run from her husband's killers. She's being chased through the city. She—*I*—screeches around the corner onto California Street, side-swipes one cable car and hits another. Then her car explodes. That's what I'm doing Monday night, the fire gag."

"Fire! Will you be on fire? How do you do that?"

"Why don't you come watch? I'll leave your name with security. I'd like that."

"Really? Wow, that's . . . great!" She looked longingly at her shiny new car. "I could take you for a ride."

"Next time. Right now I have to deal with him out front."

"We could stop somewhere, get brunch, it'd be fun!" *Don't leave!*

"I'll see you on the set, okay?"

I gave a wave as I loped off—glad to be moving—around the house and into Wallinsky's steam bath of a truck. "So you lied to me again. Do you do it out of habit, or do you just lie so much you don't remember what the truth was? Or are you just a colossal pain in the ass?"

"The latter," he said, in a tone that proved him right. "So I've been out to the house here? That's what you mean, right?"

"What else did you lie about?"

21

He shoved the passenger door open. "Get in. I'm driving."

"Fine." *That* wasn't going to be my battle. "You and Claire? Just what was that about?"

For the first time he was silenced. He actually flushed a little.

"You came on to her?"

"Yeah. I needed to get close. It was business."

"To you."

"Me and my boss."

"The boss, as I recall, you did *not* have. So you came on to this poor isolated girl for the purpose of getting into her house and pants?"

"Wasn't like that."

"Wasn't like what?"

"Damn it, I needed to know. How was Madelyn Cesko killed? Why did Sunny—Sonora—pick up that knife?"

"*Sunny?* Omigod, you knew Sonora, didn't you? This isn't just a story that grabbed you, you knew her before. You—you had connections here that got you a local job. You were already poking around this town *before* Madelyn was murdered, isn't that right?"

He didn't answer, which I took as a yes.

"That's why it was easy for you to find a job. Because the grocery owner already knew you, isn't that right? Isn't it?"

"Yeah." He hit the gas and shot down the dirt road, his eyes straight ahead. The truck bounced like a toy. He hadn't even thought to turn on the air-conditioning yet. I flipped the knob.

"So you weren't here to find out about the murder. You were already after something before Madelyn was killed."

He shifted forward, nearly into the wheel.

"Okay, Wallinsky. So, what did you come here for?"

We were doing just under 75, about ten miles more than the road could handle. Amateur drivers terrify me; they're like nervous perps with guns. I checked the door handle location, and the roof supports. If he rolled it, I wanted a fighting chance. Then I lied. "You're not frightening me. I do car wrecks for a living. So answer my question, or you'll hear it every ten seconds between here and Star Pine. What were you after at Madelyn Cesko's?"

With a great sigh, he let up the accelerator. "The migrant crews. They were virtual slaves. Nobody cared. I was hot to be an investigative reporter back then. It was a big story in my mind, but not for anyone else. Not sexy enough. But then I thought of the celebrity angle—to get some editor's attention. Madelyn Cesko was a famous, big shot cookbook writer who was hiring them to do her vegetable garden. 'Celebrity Cook Uses Slave Labor.'" He glanced over at me.

I nodded. It was just about plausible. But, as always with Wallinsky, something was missing in the story. There had to—"Omigod, there never was any survey—"

"Wrong!" He looked shocked by his own admission. "Of course there was a survey. Do you think their sheriff didn't check on that? Sunny was in college, taking sociology, doing the survey, just like I told you."

He looked so smug I had to believe him. And yet . . . "Oh, wait, you piggybacked onto the survey, right? You spotted Sonora—*Sunny*—with this great cover story and you dangled your job, one that someone like her would jump at. You needed her to go out there and investigate it for you. You couldn't do it yourself. Why? Too hard? Too dangerous?" I didn't wait for his answer. "So you sent her out and when she didn't get the goods you sent her off again, right?"

He still didn't say anything. This time it looked like he couldn't. His face was flushed and his lips pressed tightly together.

Now I knew how she had gotten away after the killing. How she'd managed to get whatever fake ID she needed and vanish in those twenty-four hours before the sheriff even arrived at the Cesko house. Twenty-four hours! Still, in a high-profile case like this . . . amazing.

But now I also understood why Claire had thrown him out. "You don't believe Sonora was a killer, do you? At least not in the way everyone thinks."

"No."

I looked over just as he turned toward me. Our eyes met, and, for an instant, everything felt right. "I can't believe it either. Tell me about her. Where she was from. Her parents. School. Everything. What was she like then?"

"Looking back, she was a nice kid. I thought of her as too serious. But that was okay for me. What I needed. She was from one of those suburbs that got gobbled up by San Diego. Father in the Navy. Only child. Mother dead. Sunny hated the military life. She didn't say much, didn't need to, not to a guy who'd dropped out of college. Idealistic but not crazy. She could recite the Bill of Rights. From memory. I've worked for a lot of lawyers since then and not one has come close. But to her it was like a prayer."

No wonder I'd thought there was something between her and Gary. "Was she headed to law school?"

"Probably. But she was only a sophomore then. She could just as easily have gone into reporting. She had a gift for chatting people up. At first, though, she seemed flighty, like she'd never stop talking. And I worried I'd made a huge mistake hiring her. I thought she'd never shut up long enough to hear anything."

Boy, had she changed by the time she became Karen Johnson.

"What hooked her to begin with was the idea of working under a reporter. I listed the notice as an apprenticeship."

"She must have thought she was the one making the mistake when she saw you," I told him. He missed the sarcasm, which was okay. "And not just because you were practically a kid yourself."

"Old enough to be acting on my ideals," he corrected me. "She was a kid from some plastic subdivision. She wanted that story almost as much as I did. I didn't have to twist her arm. Maybe she pressed Madelyn Cesko a little too hard about the migrants working here. I knew she was concerned about Claire out there, so isolated. But I don't know what happened. I didn't force her out there. She wanted to go back there again to see Claire, too. I figured Claire would help me. I was wrong."

"Were you in love with her?"

"With Sunny?"

"Yeah, with Sunny?"

"Hell no. She weighed two hundred pounds."

"God, you are a pig." And this time I wasn't being sarcastic.

He looked over at me as if I'd stepped off another planet.

There wasn't time to deal with his failings; a lifetime probably wouldn't suffice. All I could think of, anyway, was the fact that his description of Sonora Eades was so different from the Karen Johnson I'd seen; I had to question once again if they could really be the same person. "So you know how to get to Alaska, right?"

He didn't answer me. But the set of his face gave him away.

A pig, yes, but he'd pulled off a very tough vanishing act. Still, I wanted to smack him. Instead, I said, "Here's what I know about Sunny afterwards. She had a backbreaking job carrying fish up a cliff in Alaska. By the time she got through she said she could see the outlines of her muscles like she was an anatomy model—"

"You're kidding!"

"The day she died in San Francisco, we ran up the hill to Coit Tower. She was beautiful—blonde, slim, expensive clothes, expensive hair and face. Telling me she was here for a divorce. So, Wallinsky, what happened in the middle?"

"Married money!" he said. Did I detect a note of bitterness?

"Doesn't take a detective to figure that. What else?"

"Won the jackpot?"

"No, that's exactly what she wouldn't—couldn't—do. She couldn't win a lottery because, Wallinsky, she was a fugitive. You can't draw attention to yourself like that. So what else? How'd she get to be a beautiful woman in expensive clothes?"

22

FRIDAY

IN THE ZENDO the bell rings into silence.

Behind and to my left, I could hear the door easing closed and footsteps—slow, careful, as if prolonging the walk to a cushion might somehow make a 7:05 A.M. arrival seem less late than it was. Cloth rustled, knees creaked. I waited till the absence of sound expanded and took on its own sounds—of the birds, of breathing, of a bus hauling itself up Columbus Avenue. I struck the bell and listened to the sweet reverberation—as if a peach had become music—spread through the room and mesh with the silence. I hit the bell the second time, and then the third, listening to its sound melting into the room.

Morning zazen varies from day to day. The unformed day can ease into a noting of breath flowing out and refilling, with the note of each new bird a greeting. Thoughts present themselves—but they can wait. Some days, for me, the pull of sleep is strong, drawing me into a dream from which I awake, dream again, wake again to one scene after another equally real, equally illusionary. This morning Karen Johnson/Sonora Eades was just too compelling to push away.

Driving back along I-5, I'd wondered about her life in Alaska. How terrifying it must have been for an earnest twenty-year-old to wake up every morning as a hunted killer? The crime would have been news nation-wide, till the next monstrous thing bumped it from the headlines. Fleeing, she'd had a head start, but not much of one. Then, to have to watch every word you utter, to scan every face for a threatening light of recognition—she must have been wrung out by the end of each day.

Non-attachment is an axiom of Buddhism. Zen students know that attachment is the cause of misery. We see ourselves led by the nose ring of what we want, what we think we need. And yet we still want. Everyone in the zendo would resist giving up all the things they wanted. How much harder for a twenty-year-old girl like Karen Johnson to step off that hundred-foot pole?

However, it had been eighteen years since Madelyn's death. No one hauls fish up a cliff that long.

So she'd married. Stopped working? Born children? Whatever the state of her marriage, she'd managed a comfortable life. But what had driven her to consider divorce and leave the safety she'd found for herself to return to an existence in which she could never get a driver's license, hold a job that required a social security number, apply for a passport, or draw attention to herself. What could be that important?

Leo was bowing to his cushion. I hadn't even heard him come in. Zen practice is about awareness! I focused back on my breath flowing out, being pulled back in. I wondered . . . This time I let the thought go and noticed my exhale. Meditation, Suzuki-roshi said, is coming back to the breath again and again.

At the end of the period, I rang the bell. The door opened and Korematsu stepped in, standing there and watching as the rest of us chanted the Heart Sutra. *Form is no different from emptiness, emptiness no different than form.*

When I walked out of the zendo, Korematsu was waiting. "Why didn't you call me sooner?" he demanded.

I wanted to talk to Gary. He wasn't at Karen's apartment. It was obvious he hadn't been there all day. Chances were he'd left right after I did and I wasn't going to find him again, damn him. "I'm giving you Karen Johnson's real identity. The better response would be 'thank you.'"

"I've got coffee. Thanks enough?"

I nodded, followed him into the courtyard as he handed me a paper cup. Espresso, a double. Maybe a triple. It did make me think better of him. I sipped, realized it was cool enough and took a long swallow, following the heat down my body the way I'd just been doing with my breath. My eyes opened wider, my head cleared and I noticed how good Korematsu looked at this hour of the morning. Korematsu who'd used me to try to see into John's mind. *Get a grip, Darcy!*

"Talk," he said.

"Karen had a cookbook by Madelyn Cesko—"

"Knife? Murderer vanishes?"

It still shocked me to say it. "Karen Johnson is Sonora Eades."

A thatch of hair fell over his forehead and he pushed it back. Then he said, "Why do you think our Karen Johnson is Sonora Eades?"

I tried to work out what my reply should be.

"Darcy? You creating an answer?" *Busted!* Quickly, I said, "Sonora Eades's little finger was twisted so the nail faced out. Ditto Karen Johnson's."

"That's your proof?"

"Well, yeah! Hard to get clearer proof than that. Plus, now that you know she's Sonora Eades, there'll be fingerprints from the investigation in the database somewhere."

He slammed down his cup. The coffee spurted out the lid. "Fingerprints! Darcy, what is it you expect me to judge them against? Her fingertips are shredded like cole slaw. The best expert in the country's never going to get a match."

"Well, what about the DNA?"

"I asked you a question."

I hesitated. Karen's prints had to be on the desk, the chair, the door of Gary's office, but furious as I was at his disappearing again, I couldn't bear to rat him out either. I compromised—a bad compromise, a semi-ratting. It'd lead Korematsu to Gary, but not right away.

"I'll make you a deal."

"Police don't do deals."

I laughed.

"*I* don't do deals."

I raised an eyebrow.

He shook his head. "I've already stuck my neck out for John. You may remember, he and I are *not* close! We have history. But I covered, waiting for him to stop hiding out like a little kid."

"I appreciate that."

"You should. I didn't do it for him."

"Thanks."

"And it didn't get me any points with Broder. Your brother—would it have killed him to make one or two friends in the department, long as he's been there? Did he research every pet peeve of every guy in the chain of command? Or is he just a natural . . ."

Asshole? I stiffened.

". . . thorn in the side of the universe?"

"Yeah, well, we all have our skills. And, one thing about my family, we don't back down. But I'll tell you this: I don't know where he is. When he surfaces, we both know you're going to have to get in line to chew him out. I want you to have this lead, but . . ." I paused as if I was considering. We both knew otherwise.

He blinked. "But what?"

"You can't ask me how I got it."

"Give me a break! We don't make dumb deals like that."

"Oh, right."

"I can cart you down to the station right now!"

"Give me a week."

"End of the day."

"Instead of a week? Why would I agree to that?"

"Because you want me to use this info of yours to find out about Karen Johnson." He turned and waited till I looked up and he was gazing directly at me with those soulful eyes of his. "Because this is Broder's case and you're lucky to be dealing with me, not him. And the only way you'll continue to deal with me is if you trade something worthwhile."

"Monday."

"If I could, I would. I'm not gaming you. This is a high-profile case. Broder's . . . on the prowl. I'd cut you some slack, but . . . I can't."

"I believe you. I'm trusting you. But—"

"What?"

Can I really trust you with my brother's neck?

"Give!"

"Karen had an apartment in North Beach."

□□□

North Beach was peaceful. Men and women dashing for buses or street cars or to their offices in the financial district beyond the zendo had dashed and were gone. Those who stayed at home were having their second cup of coffee. They might be working; they might still be contemplating working, but, whichever, they were doing it inside.

Karen's place was as empty as it had been last night when I'd swung by on my way back into the city. I'd banged on the door and stretched over the railing to peer in the dark window. Now it was Korematsu knocking and calling out. With a glare at me, he kicked the door in. It was a door even *I* could have kicked in.

The place had looked staged two days ago when the only sign of life was Gary sitting in the kitchen with the cookbook. Now it was just empty. The closets were empty, the dresser drawers were bare, there were no pictures on any surfaces. They hadn't been there before and they weren't there now. The only item left was a wadded tissue in the kitchen trash. "If she was here," Korematsu said, "we can get a DNA match. Maybe from that. Or whatever. Not that it'd tell us anything about why she was here or why she got killed. Did she tell you she was leaving?"

I shook my head. It wasn't her prints I was worried about. What were the chances of Gary not leaving his when he'd cleaned out the place? "You only gave me till tonight, so I'm outta here."

"Stick around. I'll extend it to till one A.M." It wasn't a request. "Don't touch anything."

What had I touched before? Even if I'd had no time limit with Korematsu, as soon as he ran the prints from this place he'd be hauling me in. There are few enemies worse than a confidant betrayed. I needed to get gone quick.

He moved down the hall to the front door, effectively blocking it, then pulled out his phone and called the department.

I took the other way, living room to kitchen to back door. The place was a standard railroad layout. Out back there should've been a landing, rear staircase, and freedom. Luck smiled. A key hanging there allowed me to unlock the back door and step out into the morning fog.

"Hey! I told you to stay put!"

"Just making a call! Like you." I flipped open my cell phone, then turned as if for privacy to check the back stairs. None! This wasn't a third-floor landing, it was a deck! The buildings on either side had back stairs. How could this one not? What did tenants do with their garbage?

"Come inside." He stepped out onto the deck beside me.

"So I don't freeze out here? Or do you think I'm so good at high falls I can leap down three stories?"

"Suit yourself," he said, covering, as if he wasn't as surprised as I about the lack of stairs.

"Okay."

I sat on the railing and patted the spot next to me.

"Uh-uh. These things collapse in this city every summer. You're living dangerously enough." He leaned against the upright, looking less like a cop than a guy who'd stepped out of a party for a bit of air.

I smiled up at him. "Okay, Mr. Play It Safe, here's a *what-if*. No names, you understand, just a question. A public servant high up in rank has a lady friend in a house on Guerrero Street across from a Laundromat—"

His face went blank. "I'm not—"

"No names. Just speculation. One of his subordinates hangs out in the Laundromat, but he's not washing clothes. Others drive by the house frequently."

"There could be—"

"No, wait. It's common knowledge among his colleagues that the woman's involved in some sort of smuggling."

"Common knowledge how?" He didn't even blink at the word "smuggling."

"And since Karen caused the crash on Guerrero, it's got to be just a matter of time—"

He shoved open the kitchen door.

"My *question* is: where are you in all this?"

He turned and put a hand on my shoulder. "I stuck my neck out covering for your idiot brother. He ignored it."

"He didn't know!"

"While my neck's stuck out there, you leave town."

"You didn't mention staying put." I was inches from him, staring at the neck in question.

He grabbed my other shoulder. "You think this is a game. Your family thinks this city's their backyard. Karen Johnson thought she was safe up on the slab and now she's a splat on the freeway. This case, it's serious business."

Gary'd said the same thing, but coming from Korematsu, again, it was a whole different level of warning. I stepped back, pulling free of his hands. "You didn't answer my question."

"I can't."

"You—"

The front door banged.

"I can't!"

Feet slapped the wooden floor, voices called back and forth—the lab techs had arrived. Korematsu went in to meet them.

I sat on the porch railing, pulling myself together. He was right about the Lott family. In my mind SFPD was John's department, the city medical establishment my sister Gracie's, and if I had a legal problem Gary could fix that. Now, suddenly, I was not the protected but the suspected. And somewhere, maybe even in that magic circle that I used to inhabit, Karen Johnson's killer was walking around loose.

My mind snapped back to Gary. Why had Karen gone to his office? What had happened between the time she'd escaped from Star Pine and when she'd become someone else? Where had her money come from? Was there anyone anywhere wondering about her right now? How come—

"Give me your fingers, ma'am."

Ma'am!

The tech motioned me to the table where the ink pad waited. The table was already smeared with black and wiped haphazardly.

I'd been kidding myself thinking it'd take them a whole day to match me. I'd barely be out of here before Korematsu dispatched a squad car.

The tech rolled my thumb.

Why hadn't Karen Johnson left something—anything—in Gary's office? Or had she? That Las Vegas newspaper. With time I could have Googled the news there for missing persons and divorces—Nevada divorces? With lots of time. It was a long shot.

"Other hand, please."

I gave him the left.

He was still holding my fourth finger when the front door batted against the wall again. In the living room Korematsu started. He shot a glance at me as the tech pressed my last finger on the sheet, then turned back toward the hall. There was an unreadable smile on his face as he turned.

I could see Chief of Detectives Broder coming toward him.

"My phone!" I muttered to the tech.

He was waving a towel as I leapt for the back door, grabbed the support beam, jumped over the railing and slid to the ground, leaving a black trail of finger marks.

The yard was fenced. An eight-footer. No problem. I bounced for the top, swung over, found a walkway, and ran till I spotted a cab and flung myself in back.

"Where to?"

"The airport."

As we headed there I called Cass Cassidy in Vegas. "I know it's a long shot. She'll have been missing at least a few days."

"Can't you give me anymore than that? Going missing in Vegas is hardly news."

"Thirty-eight, forty. She lived in Alaska. She was getting a divorce here."

"People don't go *from* Nevada *to* California for divorces."

"She did. She had a flat here, pretty empty."

"A residency address?"

"Yeah." Recalling Karen's surprising football reference on the way up to Coit Tower, I said, "Check football. Start with quarterbacks. She was talking about taking your shot downfield, getting sacked, quarterback stuff. Wait! 'Matt!' she said. 'Matt, my ex.'"

It was a long shot, but being out of town would be its own reward, assuming I didn't end up mired in Vegas right before my gag.

23

MᴄCᴀʀʀᴀɴ Iɴᴛᴇʀɴᴀᴛɪᴏɴᴀʟ Aɪʀᴘᴏʀᴛ in Las Vegas is a casino with planes. As I walked through security, a tall, wiry woman with short-cropped gray hair waved at me from the middle of a row of slots. "Fool's move," Cass said as she deposited a quarter, "but as long as your plane was on time I wasn't going broke. It's so good to see you, my little student-made-good. What're you working on now?"

"Next up's a fire gag. No more Nomex suits. They're using the new stuff you spread on your skin."

"How's it?"

"Good if you get doused within thirty seconds. Otherwise, they scoop on the potatoes and gravy."

Three dissimilar screens bounced into place on the slot. "Damn!"

"Maybe they'll put the proceeds toward more air controllers," Cass said, already half an aisle away. I'd always loved that about her, the sense that the rest of life was in slow mo.

"When I used to walk into your classes it was like life speeded up to normal, like everything was exciting and *now*. So, Cass, what's with you, in the *now* now?"

"Teaching gymnastics. It's a great place for it. Every little girl wants to be in Cirque. But listen, I've got a lead on your guy."

"Really? You're the best. I only called you this morning."

"Yeah, well, we're a small town here, or a collection of small towns, and how many football players with missing wives can there be? How'd you even know Matt Widley's wife was gone? It's not news. Not like he's filed a missing person. I don't even know if he thinks she's missing. She just hasn't shown up at the Flying Femmes meetings. Not at a couple other groups, either. Not like her."

Another thing I remembered about Cass. By the time you got out a question, she was already three thoughts beyond it. "Flying Femmes? Girls' gymnastics?"

"Gymnastics is part of it. Girls' athletics. Flying down the field, up to the hoops, off the high board. We get some charitable funding for a lot of after-school programs here. One's at my studio—where we're going. I want you to see my ten-year-olds. I've got one who'll be in the Olympics in a few years . . ." We got to her van. "Matt Widley?" she said as I climbed in. "You promised you'd tell me why you're looking for him."

"I can't tell you everything—"

"Need-to-know basis?"

"Yup, you got it. I'm looking for the husband of a woman—"

"But where's this woman?"

"Hey, need-to-know! Here's what she said: Good to see grass in San Francisco—"

"Not the first thing you'd notice—"

"At least not in North Beach, where we were. So she must have lived somewhere without grass before."

"Bingo!"

"That and there was a Vegas paper she must have left."

She laughed appreciatively. "Okay, okay, I won't keep bugging you, but you gotta cough up the instant you can, right?"

"Sure." I wanted to grill her about Karen, but I didn't dare. The truth was, I'd already dragged her too far in.

Ahead the fairyland of Las Vegas poked out of the horizon. I'd seen it so often on TV, even the real thing looked fake. "Matt Widley," I mused. "Name sounds so familiar."

"Shame, is all I can say. Great arm, great legs, great presence on the field. Played for one of those cold weather teams. I'm not into football much. I saw him pull out a game in overtime in a blizzard. Home game. Fans went crazy."

"And?"

"Then he was gone. Some kind of scandal. Dropped from hero to hopeless in a deadfall."

"Drugs?"

"Football doesn't bust you just for beating up your girlfriend."

"Did he? Beat women?"

"Actually, not that I know of. There were stories, though, about trashing a casino, demolishing his truck and walking—stumbling—away. Who knows the effect of all that crap those guys inject to make them number one?"

"And gymnasts don't?"

"Not in my gym they don't. Goddammit, not my girls! I tell them over and over . . . Yeah, I tell them: You don't know how that stuff'll twist your brain. You think as long as you get a medal, nothing else matters, but after . . . Oh, don't get me started on this, okay?"

"Back to Matt Widley. How'd he end up in Vegas?"

"Got a cage in the freak show." Her smile faded. She cut right and pulled up next to a single-story building. "Flying Femmes" blazed in hot pink over the double doors.

She reached for the door.

I grabbed her arm. "Freak show?"

"High rollers don't just gamble here. There have to be enticements, extras, amusements to give them something to talk about back home. Like celebrity golf games, celebrity cocktail hours, celebrity et cetera. Matt Widley did golf."

"*After* . . . ?" But she was out of the car and heading inside. I sat for a moment longer, feeling a great rush of sadness. Without recognizing it, and despite knowing about her divorce plans, I'd been hoping Karen Johnson had had a happy life in Las Vegas, that it had been better than time spent with a guy drummed out of pro football and left to pimp himself nine holes a day. But what did I know about her, anyway, this woman who'd thrown my brothers to the wolves, and, even worse, who'd murdered someone with a chef's knife. Who the hell was she? Had it been here, in Vegas, she'd made an enemy who wouldn't give up? Or back in California?"

Cass was tapping on the window. "Come on! Widley's inside."

"Huh?"

She pulled open my door. "You wanted him, you got him. It wasn't that difficult."

That was Cass. Always ahead of me. But what was I going to say to a guy whose wife—probably his wife—had been killed—probably—just after I'd met her? I was going to throw this at a guy who could control himself—probably?

I followed her into the gym. The first thing that struck me was the glorious cold. The second was Widley.

I'm continually surprised at how tall quarterbacks are. But Matt Widley looked more like a linebacker. The hand he shot toward me could have crushed mine. A tattoo ran down his arm, over bulging mounds of muscle. His gray T-shirt emphasized the pecs and shoulder muscles beneath it. I glanced at his legs. I wasn't going to outrun him—ever.

"I'm here about your wife."

Behind him a woman was lifting a tiny girl up to the higher uneven bar. They looked like a different species from him. Farther back, five pre-teens were doing seated Vs on the mat, their arms stretched forward past uplifted legs. Music blared. A man was shouting at a teenager on a balance beam.

Matt Widley glared, watching my eyes for a tip-off of my next move, ready to scramble out of danger.

"Karen—"

"Oh!" He let out a huge breath. "My wife's not Karen. You've got the wrong woman."

"I'm from San Francisco, Matt. Where a woman called herself Karen Johnson. Blonde, about my height."

"Reporter?" he snapped.

"No."

"We don't market our private lives."

That had to be her line; no way had he come up with that phrasing. "I'm really not. I met her running up Telegraph Hill. She was wearing pale blue linen slacks and a matching sleeveless top."

He shook his head slowly.

Of course he wouldn't know what his wife was wearing! "She said she'd hauled stuff up a cliff in Alaska." I shouted over the sudden blare of music for a floor routine.

He looked away, staring at a little girl starting the run to her vault as if it was too fascinating to miss.

"Her little finger was twisted; the nail faced out."

"NOOO!"

Everything stopped, the running girl skidded to a stop, a kid dropped from the high bar, the group holding up torso and legs with their abdominal muscles froze in place. The music—something Russian-sounding—goaded uselessly. Cass stood, mouth actually open. What had she been thinking, to ask this guy here?

"Her finger's fine! It works fine!" He made for the door, yanked it open, left it banging as he shot through.

Works fine? I started after him.

"Don't, Darcy!"

Cass was right, but I ran. I caught him next to a dusty van. "Wait!"

A ring of keys crashed to the ground. I scooped them up. "Wait," I repeated. "You've been worried about your wife, haven't you? What I'm telling you, it's not a surprise, is it?"

He yanked the keys out of my hand. My hand stung.

"I don't know any Karen."

"Your wife was called . . . ?"

"Alison Widley," he said, as if to an idiot. "You know her? Show me you're not a reporter." It was part question, part accusation.

Behind him, the gym door opened. A woman with her hand on the shoulder of a tiny girl peered out and pulled the door shut. I turned out my pockets, thrust my purse at him. "No mike, no recorder, not even a pencil!"

He smashed the keys into the door. "Tell me!"

"I met her Tuesday afternoon. I liked her."

"What'd she say? How'd she seem?" The keys jangled. "Goddamn it! She tells me she's going to scout out San Francisco. She says since she's going to be gone, why don't I hang with Graham and the guys. She hates Graham: I haven't seen him since I agreed to move to California. I'm surprised, but I trust her. She's my *wife!* This is the longest we've been apart since we got married. I tried to call her! She didn't answer . . . I tried." His face was red and twisted. He shouted, "Goddamn it, I have no idea what the hell my wife is doing in that fucking city!"

He took a deep breath, as if he'd been schooled to do just that—or explode. He seemed like the least likely husband for calm, thoughtful, beautifully turned out Karen Johnson—Alison Widley, Sonora Eades, or whatever her real name was. And him, why did his name sound so familiar? He hadn't played for a team in the NFL West or I would have known him. It was a legacy from my dad who'd groused as if playing for other teams in the conference was a sign of degeneracy. Matt Widley? Matt Widley? "Oh! *Stat* Widley! You creamed the 49ers in a game when your miserable linebackers just about killed our quarterback. Montana was already out with his elbow, and Young had a sprained finger on his throwing hand and we were counting on our third-string guy to get us through the season and there he is on the ground! After that, you just piled it on! Touchdown after touchdown! My dad hated you!"

He almost laughed.

I felt like an idiot. A teenaged idiot. "Sorry. For an instant—"

"S'okay. It's the only decent moment I've had since I dropped Alison at the airport." He didn't smile, but his face relaxed out of the hard lines of fear, frustration, bafflement, his body from the need to smash something. There was a sweet desperation in that look, the kind of expression that seduces women into bad decisions.

Stat Widley must have been forty, give or take. He'd been a rookie the year he ran up those huge statistics, feeding on teams like the 49ers and from then on was known in our house as "that-goddamned-Stat-Widley." He'd been a rookie quarterback for some team the 49ers didn't play often, maybe Chicago or one of the Ohio teams. He was local to the area and a big favorite back there, wherever there was. He'd played another year or so and then had some kind of injury—knee or ankle I gathered from his uneasy walk now—and was gone for about a year. When he came back, his arm was better than ever, but by then Dad had died and the list of hated football players faded from family consciousness. Like Cass said, there'd been something about drugs, but that's hardly memorable in pro sports.

"Alison *said* she'd be back in a couple days."

No, wait, it hadn't been the standard drug test failure and the normal four game suspension. Stat's drug thing had been a big scandal. What specifically? Damn, I couldn't remember. If Dad were alive he'd tell me every detail. Whatever, it'd been a screaming sensation in the days before such sensations became the norm. "You were the golden boy. But they cut you for drugs. You were a great quarterback and they cut you anyway. How come?"

"Old news," he muttered.

"Maybe to folks in Cleveland or Cincinnati, but not to me."

"You're supposed to be here about my wife and you're asking about this?"

"Yeah! What kind of user are you?" I stepped back next to a tiny Ford. Wind blew across the empty parking lot, scraps of paper skittered over the macadam. From inside the gym, Russian music blared.

Widley inhaled hard. "You want that dirt, Google it."

"Tell me!"

He was trying to hold himself together, trying hard.

"Tell me, Matt."

"My wife?"

"I need to be sure my woman was your wife. Just answer my question, dammit." *I need to know if she betrayed you like she did John.*

"Okay, okay. I got caught doing drugs. I'd had some injuries, and drugs were easy. I'm not saying teams pushed them, but they shot you up with painkillers so you could play hurt; they called you a coward if you stayed out just because you were going to aggravate an injury. Meanwhile, the guys who played hurt all season didn't get as many touchdowns, got sacked because they couldn't push off on sprained ankles to scramble, and you know what happened to them?"

"They got cut?"

"Damn right, they got cut. Tossed like garbage. But let me tell you, a guy gets injured and suddenly he's healing faster, no one's asking why. No one's complaining about that. No one's bitching if you bulked up. The only guys asking how are the ones who want whatever you're taking. So, yeah, I did it. I got caught. I went from being the hometown hero to out on a rail. That clear enough for you?" His hands were jammed into fists. Veins bulged in his arms, his neck. Sweat coated his face.

"Why you? Lots of guys get caught."

"I was a trailblazer."

"Still, you were the quarterback. They could have hushed it up."

"I admitted it."

Now I remembered. He'd named names, names that took the team out of the playoffs—for years. He'd named a coach, so the team lost draft picks, and that in addition to the scandal'd ruined the team for years. Fans crucified him. I remembered someone saying he couldn't even drive through the state afterwards. "How'd you meet Alison?"

He could have told me it was none of my business, but I had the feeling that he understood the longer I talked, the further he could put off hearing something about her he knew he didn't want to hear. "In a casino."

"Here?"

"Yeah. Where d'you think?"

"What were you doing?"

"Drinking free booze. When you've spent your life being the golden boy and suddenly you're universal crap, the only place for you is Vegas. Everyone assumes pro sports is hypocrisy central. The guys betting are hoping you're taking everything you can plunge or swallow. If you were a mass murderer, in Vegas you'd find guys glad to hang with you—if you could stand hanging with them."

"What—"

"Enough!" He bent over me. "My wife! You know where she is, tell me! Graham kept telling me she was a bitch with secrets. I flattened him. But, damn, he must have been right! Where the fuck is she?"

"I can't be sure—"

He pushed me against the van. "Hey!"

"Tell me where she is!"

"In . . . the . . . morgue."

He let go as if I no longer existed.

"Look . . . I'm not certain. I could be wrong. I want to be wrong. That's why I'm asking you about her. Where's she from? You've been married how long?"

"Six . . . years." He was standing, feet apart, hands at his sides. The blood was gone from his face. He looked like a cardboard cutout. I didn't know whether to squeeze his hand or run for my life.

"I can find out from her family."

"Good luck!"

"Just give me her maiden name or where she's from or—"

He grabbed my shoulders, turned me around and shoved. I went flying back. And then he was in the van, screeching out of the parking lot.

24

"Cass, lend me your car!" I couldn't let him get away.

Not another woman in the world would have flipped me the keys as fast. "Get it back here in an hour!"

"Sure." I raced for her van. It wasn't meant for a high speed chase, but I wouldn't be tailing a Maserati, either. I just hoped Widley hadn't turned off onto a side street. I flipped the ignition, hit the horn and cut in front of a panel truck.

The road was four lanes. Light traffic. Nearly dusk. Night comes fast in the desert. Another half hour and all cars would be one. I drifted left, trying to spot the other van through the traffic. No luck.

My shoulders screamed. I was going to have marks where he'd grabbed me—twice. Once would have left bruises! No wonder Karen wanted out. I stepped on the gas; I'd be damned if I'd let him get away now.

I swung around a truck. Cass's van drove like an ox. Half a block ahead, the traffic light turned yellow. I cut in front of a low, white compact and hit the gas. That maneuver bought twenty yards of space. Three cars ahead in the fast lane was what looked like Stat's van. I slipped in inches from the tail of a silver Toyota and flicked the high beams.

The Toyota sped up.

I flicked again, weaved left, jerked right, flicked.

No one wants a crazy drunk on their tail. The Toyota pulled right. That left a new Mercedes in its place. I cut in front of the Toyota—its driver was giving me lots of room.

Damn! The driver was on the phone. Calling 911? I cut off the Mercedes—luxury cars are easy—settled behind the van, and hoped. Hoped it was Matt, hoped we turned off this road before I got pulled over. Damn him, tailing in the right lane was twice the work.

A truck waddled ahead. Open topped, full of rubble. Old. I pulled up inches from its rear. Splatter hit the windshield. Dirt. Or worse. The van was a car length ahead. I squinted through the muck and the growing dusk.

Jeez! It wasn't Widley! Just a family van! A dog stuck his head out.

I slumped, easing off the gas. Now what? My shoulders ached. Damn him!

I pulled up to the truck's tail, held down the horn, stuck my hand out and pointed. The van with the dog went faster. I honked again. It slowed and I cut in front, waved thanks.

A Mini Cooper, like Korematsu's—who was probably at this very minute squeezing Leo for everything I'd said in the last week—was doing 70. In front of him was—aha!—another van.

Ahead, the light turned amber. The van hung a left. The Cooper slowed. I laid on the horn. He hesitated and shot through.

The light was red. I ran it.

We were in a residential area—one-story houses, eighth of an acre lots. Landscaping. In the growing dark, it could have been an upscale development in San Diego or Jersey. Two-car garages, driveways displaying two or three vehicles. No sidewalks, no people out, and no moving vehicles.

He hung a left. A streetlight showed him—it *was* Widley!—on his cell phone. Was he frantically calling Karen—*Alison?* Or some pal Karen had made someone desperate enough to kill her? Someone still out here.

He turned again, into a driveway, beeped up the garage door and shot in. He barely got the living room lights on before I hit the doorbell. The door stayed shut. I fist-hammered.

"If you care about your wife," I yelled, "you need to talk to me! I'm the one who saw her this week."

The door opened. His face was tight, his gaze unfocused. I couldn't read him; he probably couldn't read himself.

"Show me her picture. Let me make sure it's her before I say anything. Maybe I'm wrong." But I wasn't wrong; he knew that, too. He took his hand off the door, leaving fifteen or so inches between him and it. I slipped through, so close I could feel the heat of his body, smell his anger and fear.

The room was big, with white walls, leather chairs, and Spanish motif. It looked like a cool evening, but with the air-conditioning it was freezing. Temperature set for a big, sweaty guy. "Do you always have it this cold?"

"So leave."

"I'm just asking."

"Yeah, I always have it this cold. I turn it down everytime I come in. Alison keeps it hot. I turn it down, she turns it up. It's a thing we do."

He was stalling, putting off bad news about his wife—or about himself?

"Do you have a picture of her?" I repeated.

He walked out of the room, leaving the front door open and I was relieved. I moved closer.

"Here." The picture he thrust out was a quick shot by a person without skill. The woman in it was half in shadow. The focus had been on her blonde hair shining in the sunlight. Her face was so underexposed as to be barely recognizable. "Is this the best one you have? It's so dark."

"She didn't like being photographed."

I peered closer, eying her for wider shoulders, a more solid stance, anything that would rule her out, as if my discovering Karen Johnson had not been this man's wife would make her less dead. "It's the same woman."

"No! You said it's too dark to tell!"

"It's hard, but I can see enough of her face. Her body's the same, the way she leaned onto that left hip. It's how she looked when I came up to her, when she'd been standing, waiting."

"You can't be sure!" It was a cry.

"The police—"

"You come here telling me—you push into my house, *Alison's* house. You—who the hell are you?"

"Alison died, Matt. She didn't have identification. I don't want to leave her body lying in the morgue."

"No!" His scream echoed off the white walls, the tile floor. It bounced around the room Alison Widley would never come back to.

"Okay, look, let me talk to her parents."

He shook his head.

"Her sisters or brothers? Children?"

"We don't have kids."

He might as well have been holding his hands over his ears or singing loud to keep out my words.

"Where's she from?"

"I don't know."

"Family?"

"I . . . don't . . . know." The big white nearly empty room seemed to echo his frustration, his desperation.

"She must've said something—"

"She didn't!"

"Didn't you ask her?"

"Ask what?"

"Where did she grow up? Where'd she go to school? Did she have brothers? A sister?"

His feet were apart, his knees bent and he swayed slightly side to side as if angling for a way out of danger.

"She came here on vacation. Where'd she come *from?*"

I might as well have been expecting him to query her about the color of her alimentary tract. I took a step toward him, catching his gaze and holding it. "Matt! You must know . . ."

He shook his head.

I was inclined to believe him. She wanted to keep her secrets; he wasn't inquisitive. A marriage made in heaven.

"She's dead?"

"I'm sorry. Really."

"How can she be dead?" he moaned.

"Here, sit." I motioned to the sofa. "Tell me about her. How did you meet?"

He walked like he must have after he'd been slammed into the forty yard line, then dropped full-weight onto the sofa.

I sat beside him. Everything about him screamed *comfort me!* But the bruises on my shoulders still ached. "You met her when things were rough for you," I prompted.

He slumped forward, rocking side to side over his knees.

"Tell me, Matt," I said softly.

"That night, in the casino, it almost didn't happen. There were lots of people who kept hanging around after I was cut, people who wanted to hear secrets, see how much I could bleed. But she wasn't one of them. I saw something in her eyes. We were in the casino. I went up to her. She was polite but scared; she made some excuse and went over to play the slots. I had a drink and made another move. She shifted away again, but she didn't leave. I didn't dare try again, you know? I wasn't ready to be blown off again. I got another drink and stood against a post for a long time, just watching her, not threatening or anything, just looking at how gorgeous she was. Then she came over. We went out for breakfast and we were never apart again. Until now."

Was I wrong? Maybe Karen had had a good life here. A good life till she played her husband for a fool like she had John . . .

"She was so beautiful. I saw other guys eyeing her, this gorgeous blonde in a sexy silver dress. She was like one of those crystal statues my mother kept in a cabinet in the living room so we kids wouldn't break them. Of course, we did."

So her transformation had been before then. But that didn't explain how she'd gotten there. Straight from Alaska, from that job hauling fish up the cliff, or whatever had come after that.

"We ate omelets. It was two in the morning. I expected her to order black coffee and a pastry, not a full plate of eggs and hash. But she did. She ate it all, but we were there hours, her in her silver dress sitting in this greasy spoon."

"What'd you talk about?"

"Me. I was full of me then, but she cared. She was like that with everyone, always interested in them, never carrying on about herself."

So as not to reveal anything?

"She wanted me to face up to who I'd been, what I'd done, the choices I made, that I should be honest with people, with myself. She kept saying to me back then, 'Stat Widley doesn't exist anymore; you're not him now. Be who you are *now*, Matt.' She told me, 'It's like you've spent your life climbing a pole and now you find out the pole's rotten. You've got to step off it. Stepping off's hard, but it's your only chance.'"

The hundred-foot pole! "Where'd she get that analogy? It's a Zen koan. Was she a Buddhist?"

He shrugged. I might as well have asked if she were a Martian. "She meant I had to let go of football and being a star, and even let go of being pissed about the whole drug thing. It was almost impossible. I didn't think I could; I didn't really want to. I wanted to be pissed."

Was that how she'd done it herself? "Because?"

"Because I didn't want to admit I was a jerk. It's easier to have been fooled by someone else than to have done it to yourself. But she kept at it. She kept saying I had to be a new person, not like in religion, but like I'd never played football. She had a rule that we had to do something new every day—go to a foreign movie, wake up before sunrise, rent a tiny car, the kind I'd never choose, lead with the left foot, go to that place that makes waves like you're at the ocean, go to Juarez and walk across the border to Mexico. We never went to the grocery without buying something we'd never eaten." He smiled. "We had some awful meals."

Ah, pop psychology! "You kept doing that, new things every day?"

"Not after I got into the kids' pickup games. You know in Vegas people move into town, and in a month they're gone. Schools barely know who their students are. A lot are illegal. Something like a third of a school class comes or leave in a year," he said, straightening up as if transported back to being interviewed by some radio or TV reporter. "I saw some kids hanging around and figured: Why not some flag football?

But Alison pushed me to do soccer—another new thing. It's not like soccer is brain surgery, but still I had to learn the rules. You can't coach or referee unless you know them cold. If you've gotta stop and think, you're dead. So I set up simple soccer games, just so the kids would have something. And, you know, I had something. I was doing something. Just like Alison figured." He almost smiled.

Pop psych that worked.

"Yeah. But see"—his mouth shook and suddenly he had the desperate look of one grabbing for a safe memory to forestall the truth—"the soccer games were low key, but then, somehow, I realized I could do more. I'd pimped myself, done golf weekends as the attraction. Turns out"— he shrugged—"I was more of a pull than if I'd played out my career and retired. Money guys were curious. Didn't I know all along that the injections were illegal? Where'd the team doctors get the drugs? I mean, like I'd saved the insider secrets all those years just to whisper it to them on the seventh hole. My point is I knew the money types. Most of them coulda cared, you know, but a couple helped out with supplies. And then things got more organized and I made news as 'reformed,' and that meant more chances to raise more money. For kids' sports."

"So you were good at fundraising?"

"What?" he snapped. "What do you mean?"

"Just asking."

"Never mind. It's just that Alison kept asking that, like she didn't believe it, like she kept thinking Graham Munson and the others were using me. Of course, they were. I knew that. I had my lights turned out a few times, but I'm not the idiot people think I am. I told her, but she still didn't believe me. She figured I was blocking out something, like I'd done with the drugs."

"What would these guys get out of using you?"

"Not much. That's what I told her, too. Tax write-off and a bit of sleazy glory."

"But still she was suspicious?"

"Yeah, makes no sense, does it?"

"I don't know."

"Anyway, that's why she kept pressing me to move out of Vegas. She was worried about me being controlled. Graham lined up a feature writer to do a piece on us and the charity, and that did it for Alison."

"A piece on you and Alison and the charity?"

"Mostly me."

"Mostly? But partly about her and she objected to that?"

The front door opened. "This her, Matt?" he said.

What was going on?

The man yanked me up.

I chopped his arm. "Don't even think about touching me again!"

He was nowhere near the size of Widley, but bigger than me. Behind him a woman, a discount version of Karen Johnson, was yelling, "Get out of here! It's private property! You're trespassing!" Matt Widley said nothing, continued to just sit there.

"So, call the police!" I said to the newcomers.

The man jolted back. Then he was in my face. "Out now!"

"Don't either of you care what happened to Alison?"

"Alison"—the woman moved next to him—"is my friend. She doesn't want to be bothered by vultures like you."

I moved back. "You're her friend? Prove it! What'd she like to do?"

"Like?"

"What'd you do together?"

"Shopped. We lunched. We picked up my kids. I don't know, the usual stuff."

Karen Johnson had laughed at the idea of going shopping with me. "Where's she from?"

"I don't know."

"Shut up, Melia!" And to me: "You're out of here!" Her husband reared back, like a wave about to break.

"Munson!" Matt muttered, in a voice that said he should be concerned but wasn't.

"No marks, Graham, honey! Be careful! You're going to leave marks on her."

"You're right, Munson. I'm outta here." I shook free again and strode through the hot night to Cass's van, got in and gunned the engine. My shoulders ached and so did my head. Our voices had been loud but no neighbors had stepped out to help or to watch. I wanted to get clear of here; I needed to get the van back to Cass. But I couldn't, not yet.

The streets were darker now, but just as empty. I drove slowly, as if pacing, thinking about Karen. I kept trying to sketch, retrospectively, a good life for Karen, but this sure wasn't it. Even if Matt cared as much as he said, even if he wasn't a walking concussion now. These people, her friends . . . My hands were clenched. I made myself stop and take a long breath. Were they lying about knowing nothing? Or were they just that self-absorbed? Or, well, both? I'd been with her less than an hour and I knew more. They made it easy for her to hide her past.

Where was I? I peered out the window for a street sign, not that that was going to be much help. I closed my eyes and reran the drive from the moment I'd followed Matt into this tract, the way I do after a new stunt—the first plant, so the next time I do the gag I'll have a mental track to rerun. Now I could feel, rather than see, myself running the red light and hanging a left, then a right, then . . . what? Another left

. . . I was going to have to find that signal and drive, doing the rerun all the while.

It took two attempts, but that didn't matter. When I got back to the house, the Munsons' car was pulling away. The lights inside were off. I didn't know if Matt had gone out to a bar with them, or gone to bed. I reached for the van's door handle.

Cass! I'd promised to be back by now. I pulled out my phone and punched in her number. "Cass, I'm sor—"

"Are you okay? I've been scared—where are you?"

"Sorry. I'm fine. Time got away. I'll tell you when I see you."

"Which'll be what, fifteen minutes?"

"Longer." Broder'd be plenty pissed I'd skipped. He'd be watching the airports, anxious to grab me as a snare for John. I couldn't go back home empty. Not when all the answers had to be here, here where she'd lived. Who Karen Johnson really was, why she gave up this life, who killed her— it was all right here. Had to be. "Another hour, okay."

"It's your neck."

"Huh?"

"I'll try to get through to the police again, Darcy, but no promises. I shouldn't have let you go after Matt Widley, not the way he was. When you didn't come back, I waited as long as I could, then I called the cops. I couldn't tell them you went off chasing him. So I reported the van stolen, maybe a hostage in the back."

"A hostage? Are you crazy?"

"I had to tell them *something* to get them looking. A stolen vehicle might as well be litter in the street."

"Gotta go then."

"I'll raise bail."

189

"Real funny." I clicked off and headed toward the dark house where Matt Widley might or might not still be.

Breaking and entering is one thing, burglary's another. And breaking into a house when the homeowner's there can get you shot.

I'd compromise. I'd just go around back and see if there were lights on in the house. I'd do it quick before the cops might get lucky and spot the van.

25

I JOGGED ACROSS the street at the corner, down the pavement as if I was out for a pre-bed run, cut sharply up next to the driveway, on the dirt, and cut around back. Las Vegas is desert. There's more greenery here than there should be, but not enough for good cover.

A six-foot high wooden fence blocked the backyard. The gate was next to the garage. Gates can squeak; gates can have alarms. Fences can be topped with rows of spikes. But not this one. I hoisted myself over and lowered, oh so softly, to the ground.

The "yard" was almost all pool and pool house—the latter glass-doored and night-lit, showing a good deal less of the panoply of machinery I'd have expected of an ex-jock. Just the basics: Stairmaster, bike, free weights, and butt machine, the devices responsible for Karen—Alison—being in such great shape. The dim light gave the gym a funereal air; it sparkled on the wavering surface, not so much illuminating the pool as creating a shimmering shield over what might be hidden beneath. Water sloshed hopefully over the edges and oozed back in.

On the other side of the pool, the house itself was black. Wind rustled in the distance, in the trees, grasses of far yards, perhaps. Gusts that might have been born in the Sierra crackled dried leaves, twigs, pebbles against stucco block, and cement. Matt Widley could be inside now, snoring softly. If I'd had a phone number, I could have called. Now there was no way to tell.

Wrong. I grabbed a plastic chair and threw it in the pool. Water tsunami'd in all directions. Lights flashed on. I dropped to the ground and jammed myself against the gate, like a draft stopper. Metal clinked, plastic crinkled as I skidded over my fanny pack. Seconds ticked. Water slapped the pool edges. My breathing—slow—sounded like a steam shovel.

The light went off, timed out. Widley could still be inside, waiting to launch his two-hundred-plus pound of muscle at me, but I didn't figure it that way. My money was on him being out. Gone, if not for long.

How to get in? A guy doesn't install motion lights and leave his doors unprotected. I'd inherited a fine set of lock picks from Duffy's former owner, but sadly, they don't let you carry burglar tools on airplanes anymore. Anyway, I wouldn't get near these doors or windows without setting off bells, and sirens going off all over the house. Or worse, at the police station.

My eyes readjusted to the dark and I looked upward. Doors had to be wired, and windows, but maybe not the attic window, twenty feet up, when there're no trees near the house to climb.

I hoisted myself back onto the fence, sprang to the slanted roof, landing flat out. I'd have scrapes on my palms and bruises on my ribs from this one. Asbestos shingles are hard on skin but great for belly-crawling. I slithered up, tense for the feel of a wire, ready to turn, slide, and run if a light came on. But Widley must have done the protection on the cheap, or not at all. No wires here. I shimmied to the top and let myself down head first over the dormer. The window was tiny; if I went in on the diagonal I might make it. Might! I didn't even have a pocket knife thanks to Homeland Security! Credit card?

I checked the window. No credit necessary. The wood was old, the latch rusted, the knob tiny. I twisted. My hand slipped. All I had was rust! I twisted again. The latched moved but the windows stayed shut. I braced my free hand against the house, twisted, pulled hard and just about sent myself back-flipping into the pool. But the little window opened.

The air crackled.

Helicopter! Searchlight! In seconds it'd be shining off my red hair and khaki pants on this dark roof. I grabbed the edge of the dormer, pushed myself all the way to the waist over the roof edge.

The helicopter cracked louder, nearer.

I inhaled, tucked my head and shoulder and shot my arms over my head and in through the window. The air almost choked me. My hips caught. My legs were sticking out the window like a comedy shot. I gave a huge push against the wall, sent myself flying through and landed hard.

Dust billowed up. The helicopter buzzed loud. It sounded like it was sitting on my shoulders. Had they seen me? Seen enough to call in a ground unit?

The attic was closer to a crawl space. Dust was inches thick. I breathed through my mouth. It was dead dark.

The copter light shone through the window. I all-foured away from it and almost cracked my head on a folding ladder, a ladder attached to the hatch door.

I poked the hatch open an inch. Darkness below.

I have this superstition about things evening out. Too much good makes me wary. But bad's like luck in the bank. I cashed the check the helicopter had deposited, opened the hatch, dropped to the floor and turned on the lights like any innocent resident.

Silence. At least inside. No feet running at me; no safety clicking off. The helicopter sounded like it was moving away. A huge sigh escaped me.

I hadn't even realized I'd been holding my breath. If I had any balance left in my luck account, when he got home Widley'd figure he left the lights on himself.

The door from the street was to my left, the living room in front of me, two bedrooms behind.

I scanned the room where I'd sat forty-five minutes ago.

What is it that says who you are? Where you're from? Who you were ten years ago before you came here? What is it you can't bear to leave behind even though you know it may betray you?

When I'd left San Francisco to get away from the memories of Mike and the family that seemed so removed from missing him, what had I taken? Photos. I'd needed a book to comfort me in a lonely bed, to stand guard in case I woke up miserable in the night, to promise me moments away from my misery. My books had been adventures: Alexandra David-Néel's travels through Tibet a hundred years ago; and, later, Zen books. They told me who I was.

But Karen's only book had been the cookbook.

I checked my watch. 9:37! Damn! I hit the bedroom, pulled open drawers, checked the underside, felt behind. I ran my hand between the bed frame and mattress, behind the headboard, slid under the bed. Nothing.

Outside, an engine shifted downward. Patrol car?

I froze. The window opened to the street. No exit from here. I could . . . The car picked up speed.

Karen's closet was a different world. Shiny cocktail dresses like the one Widley'd described. Sexy shoes and lots of them. A drawer full of cashmere sweaters that could have kept her warm even in this freezing house. A soft terry robe, fluffy slippers, sweats and shorts and some shirts and slacks that had the look of L.L. Bean or Eddie Bauer. Mail ordered. The clothes said: sports, luncheons, black-tie dinners. But, mostly, they said: gym.

There was jewelry, too. Diamond drop earrings, a single-row brace-let that seemed to dance in its box, and a sweetheart pendant, the kind that's too schmaltzy to wear but you do because your guy gave it to you for Valentine's Day. And in a leather folder, like a passport case, was a pic-ture—Matt and Karen. They were sitting, smiling at each other. The shot was staged, but not done professionally. It was a snapshot taken in the living room, maybe by a friend, or maybe one of them set the timer then raced across the room and plopped into position. Even sitting, Matt was a head taller than her. His dark eyes, which had seemed to be searching for escape when I was with him, seemed relaxed. He had a little smile, but mostly he looked awestruck, just like he'd told me he'd been. Awestruck and in love.

It was Karen with the wary look. Just a slight one that I hadn't glimpsed in San Francisco. Because she was looking up, her blonde hair hung back, revealing the sparkling diamond earrings. Her smile was slightly amused but pleased, the way she might have looked accepting a gift of wilted flow-ers from a child.

She *had* had some decent times here. A good enough life. At least one memorialized moment. Widley had a temper, I knew from experience. But day to day with him? He looked like he'd loved her and that was something.

I stared harder, trying to discern who she was. The girl who'd swung the knife? The woman who'd pushed the teenager clear of the speeding car? The one who'd betrayed John?

Things change! The first time I saw Leo, he lectured on that. All things change. Things *are* change. In the time—

Time!

The door to the other bedroom was shut. I pulled it open to a wall of photos. Girls playing soccer, boys running, kicking, heading the ball. I spotted Karen bending over a child clutching her knee. But it was Widley who was the star, running on the sideline, calling out, coaching. There were two more shots of the couple, him with his arm around her, her face once again in the shadows.

And that was what he'd really done for her. He'd given her an identity—Matt Widley's wife. In the eyes of the world she was something solid, unchanging. No one was going to think about her even having a past. She was part of an institution here, minor one though he was. For a woman on the run, there could hardly be a greater gift.

I was desperate to study all the pictures, experience what they were revealing.

But I made myself move to the master bath. There I gave the medicine cabinet a quick check, then headed for the kitchen door. A stack of newspapers almost blocked it. *San Francisco Chronicle, The New York Times, L.A. Times, Seattle Post-Intelligencer, The Washington Post,* the *Redding Record Searchlight,* and one from Seward, Alaska. Quite an assortment. I plucked out the Alaskan one. It was small, with big ads. I scanned each page, but nothing stood out. Just another summer week in a one-industry town. Seward, a fishing hub. It had been at least six years since Sonora'd left Alaska, closer to twenty since she'd arrived there. Did she miss the mountains and the water, here in the desert? Or was Alison a different person? That was the question. It was a question that so totally grabbed me, I didn't hear the car pull up.

26

THE BACK DOOR was feet away, but it was already too late.

Munson was with Widley. They were shouting. They were drunk.

If I could get through the hall, I might slip into the guest room and wait till they passed out.

Or—I glanced at the coffee cup in the sink. I'd doubled an actress in a B-movie who'd picked up a cup like that and walked into the fray as if she'd been sitting calmly in the kitchen, waiting, drinking coffee. It had worked for her.

Or I might—

I strode into the living room. "Matt, your wife is dead!"

"What're you—"

"Shut up, Munson!" I said. "Matt, did you hear me? Your wife—she's dead!"

He stared, hazy-eyed. Munson started to speak but Matt silenced him with a glance. Slowly, he picked up a lamp, snapped the cord out of the socket, stepped back like a quarterback going into a one step drop and threw the whole thing across the room. It smashed dead center on the mantel. He grabbed a big urn and sailed it into the same spot. Then a clock. He was moving on body memory, now hoisting a narrow table, throwing it, too, where the other shots had landed.

Munson made no attempt to stop him. Wise move. Next to Widley, Munson looked like the water boy. He looked, also, like he'd seen this kind of thing before. I edged toward the kitchen, just as Matt yanked a picture off the wall. He hoisted a chair and threw it, spun around and spotted me.

He lunged. His hands were around my neck. He lifted me up. I gasped. He was going to pop my head like a wine cork. I slammed my head into his chin. He dropped me, stumbled back, blood flowing from his nose.

I hit the floor hard on my back, rolled, and came up shaky. "Sit down!" I forced out. "Now!"

He stared, sank slowly as if there was a chair behind him, and collapsed onto the floor. He was snoring before Graham Munson stepped out of the bedroom.

"Look what you did to him!"

"His wife is dead! Dead!"

"She can't be."

"Where were you last Tuesday?"

"Where I am most of the time, which is none of your fucking business. What? Did she die on Tuesday? She's really dead?"

"Yes, she's dead. But he's not. Can't you get him to the couch or something?"

"You're the one who head-butted him."

"What do you normally do? Leave him on the floor?"

The guy was the classic jerk; he'd have been the kind of smart-ass in high school who gets a laugh and leaves a girl humiliated. Now he was pushing middle age, dressed like half that, his smug face visiting the lines that would eventually take it over, lines that could have signaled concern but likely didn't—not for Matt, for Karen, or for his own wife. I walked by him, out the door to their car. Melia Munson was leaning against the window. She looked weary of the whole scene—like Karen Johnson might have, had she taken a very different path.

"Come on in. The fireworks are over. But it's going to be a while."

She glanced up, did a better double-take than I've seen in some final cuts, and said, "You?"

"Right. Still here. But it's fine. Now the problem's getting Matt off the floor. Graham insists that's not a one man job."

She looked like she had a dozen different questions, but the most pressing was, "So, it's okay with Graham, me coming in?"

I nodded.

"It's not the first time Matt's been down for the count. The other night I was ready—"

"When was that?"

We were a step from the door. I held my breath.

"The night he got back from San Francisco and there was no message from Alison."

"What happened?"

"He was on our floor, in our living room. Couldn't leave him there; couldn't send him home like that. I knew Graham'd be back by the time he woke up in the morning."

Graham had stayed in San Francisco—when? "Could it have been Tuesday?"

She pulled open the door and I could see it was not Matt, now lumped on the couch like a big wad of blankets, but Munson she was searching for. He was making his way shakily from the kitchen, a glass of orange juice in his hand. "You waited long enough, didn't you? I'm done now."

I took the juice. There were things I needed to know, but not from him. Him I needed gone. "Thanks. I'll deal now."

"Are you a doctor or something?"

"I'm a stuntwoman. I'm doing—"

"A movie?" Melia exclaimed, like we weren't standing in a roomful of rubble and there wasn't a passed-out body on the floor. "Here?"

"San Francisco."

"Now?" Munson looked up, interested.

Were these two living in some parallel, adolescent universe? "His wife is dead! I called the police."

"Why did you—" Before she could finish, Munson grabbed her and shoved her toward the door. She just got the screen open in time.

I hadn't actually called the cops, but I'd have to now before the Munsons headed to Nogales and points south. But which police? John was unreachable. I'd thought I could trust Korematsu before his telltale smile as Broder strode into the North Beach apartment, *after he'd called the station.* So, not John, not Korematsu. Which meant not SFPD. On the other hand . . .

It had been too soon for Broder to have dropped everything and driven over. But more than enough time if he was already keeping tabs on Korematsu.

Did I dare call Korematsu?

Did I dare not?

Matt's cell phone had fallen on the floor. I checked my own for Korematsu's number and punched it into Matt's.

"Yes?"

"*Yes?*"

If I trusted Korematsu and he screwed me and John and Gary and Matt, maybe Matt . . .

"Who's this?"

"I'm having a hard time deciding if I can trust you."

"You called me in the middle of the night to tell me that?"

"I guess so. Reassure me. About Broder arriving at North Beach. After you called the station."

"Broder! Do you know what an idiot I look like to him? After you disappeared—if it hadn't been for the print tech, Broder'd have thought I made you up."

My chest went cold. "So you did call and tell him I was there."

"Of course."

"Of course?"

"Broder's looking for you. Your fingerprints are all over that apartment. You're up to your neck in this. Your only fallback is to work with us."

"Us, being you and Broder?"

"Us, being SFPD. Broder's no fool; he's never going to believe you'll give up John. But if he thinks you're helping us, he'll leave you on a long leash."

"Very kind."

"As opposed to a choke collar." His words seemed to bang off the cold tiles in this cold room. "He can pull you in any time. If he wants he'll have LVPD at your door in five minutes."

He knows I'm in Vegas! It was so much worse than I thought.

Beside me, Matt Widley was snoring, his body twitching as life invaded sleep. Had he killed Karen? She'd thought she'd seen him in San Francisco. He was there. Munson was there. I could turn him in. Broder'd love to nail him. He'd let John off the hook.

But if he was just the innocent husband Karen had cared about—

Karen, who'd betrayed John. I didn't owe her—

"And you, Korematsu, where do your loyalties lie?"

"I stuck my neck out for you, and for your brother. No one's going to be thanking me for that."

You smiled at Broder when he walked into the North Beach flat.

I couldn't accuse him of smiling, ferchrissakes. "Are you still sticking out that neck for me?"

"You mean, after you made me look like a fool with Broder."

"Which you wouldn't have done if you hadn't called him."

"Look, I know the department."

"I know what trust is."

"So?"

"I just don't know about you."

"You were at Cass Cassidy's school. LVPD is *not* on her doorstep."

Maybe. The room was suddenly icy; Matt's snores thunderous; my hammering heart about to break my rib cage. I needed to trust Korematsu, but he was a by-the-rules guy and I was skirt-the-rules all the way. Did "fair" even mean the same thing to him? "Okay"—although I was not okay with this—"I'm here with Karen Johnson's husband. I told him she was dead—"

"You told him? You compromised an investigation?"

"Hey, I found you the husband. After I gave you *her* identity. And gave you a house with her fingerprints. Don't posture around with me. You got a lot in return for that short neck of yours."

He didn't argue.

"I didn't make free with any details, just said 'died.'"

"Don't, okay?"

"He's a wreck. Tied one on after I told him. He's sleeping it off now. How soon can you get here?"

"First flight. I'll send a local unit out now."

I gave him the address and hung up.

Then I shook Widley awake. "Matt, why were you in San Francisco this week?"

"Couldn't stand it—her gone. Went looking for Alison," he said, more asleep than awake.

"On the spur of the moment?"

"Umm."

"Did you find her?"

He shook his head. Every part of him—mind, body, burst of dreadful memory—dragged him back toward the comfort of sleep. I jerked him just far enough back so he could focus on my questions, where answering them was the path of least resistance.

"Why was Munson there?"

"To help me."

"And?"

"Business."

"What kind of business?"

"Kids . . . the kids."

"In San Francisco?"

"He called . . . woman . . . soccer tour." His eyelids drooped.

"Matt, wake up! This is important! It's for Alison!"

"Alison! I was dreaming she died." He looked over at me, his face knotted up and then he was sobbing, bracing his big head in his hands. "Love her . . . She can't be dead. Not gone." For a moment I thought he was going to howl again as he had earlier, but the sound he made was closer to a child's wail. He looked like an enormous little boy, and I could imagine Karen being drawn to take care of him. I could imagine her trying against all logic to make the hundred-foot drop safe.

I felt so bad for him. I wanted to—but LVPD would be here any minute. "Matt, listen! Tell me this: What did you do in San Francisco?"

"Bought a phone."

"Didn't you have one?"

"Left it here. Had to get one of those pay-ahead ones. Called Alison. Kept calling her till the time ran out. No answer. Never! Drove me crazy that she was there; I was so close, but couldn't get to her."

"Did you call from the airport?"

"Airport, rental car, standing outside—" He slumped forward again.

"Outside what?" I was almost yelling.

"House."

"Why were you there?"

"Graham was inside dealing with the Asian bitch."

Omigod! "The house, Matt, what did the house look like?"

"Old. One of those houses like in the pictures of San Francisco . . ."

"A Victorian?"

"Yeah. Gingerbread. You know."

"Was Graham talking to the Asian woman about girls' soccer?"

"Um. Tour to Thailand."

"Did you see Alison?"

"No. I told you, no! I never saw her at all! I thought if I was there . . . but that'd be like spotting someone in the crowd at the far end of the field. It was stupid. I sat there in the car thinking how stupid it was—me sitting in San Francisco with my dead phone—how she could be calling home right then and I wasn't there to pick up the phone. While I'm standing there, worried out of my mind, a car crashes into another one like feet away, brakes squealing, metal banging, horns and all. Car spins, almost hits me. I think: this whole trip is nuts. So I walked up to that big main street, threw my useless piece of junk cell phone in the trash, got a cab, and flew home."

The crash outside Guerrero. "Did you see the driver?"

"The two guys who got hit, yeah. They were steaming. That's part of why I left."

"The other driver, the one who hit them?"

"Nah. By the time I turned around, it was heading off."

"And Graham?"

"Left him a note."

"You flew to San Francisco and only left your rental car, when you got out to find a cab, is that it?"

He nodded.

"Then you came home and checked you messages?"

"I called her back. Hit redial til the battery ran out."

"And then?"

"I drank."

I picked up his cell phone, the one he'd left behind and eyed his list of saved messages and scrolled back to Tuesday. It took me a moment to find the one from Alison:

Matt, pick up! Matt? Matt? Damn it, honey, this is important. Get out of San Francisco now! Now! Just do it! Now!

I shut the phone off, put it on the coffee table, and was out the door, into the van, and far enough away the police car I could see in my rearview mirror as it pulled up in front.

I trusted Korematsu, but not enough to fly back to San Francisco.

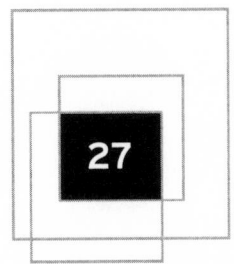

27

SATURDAY

CASS DROPPED ME at the airport at 5:00 A.M., but, oddly, my mind was in San Francisco. At the zendo.

I didn't normally have *dokusan*—interview with the teacher—on Saturdays. That was the time for his other students. Certainly I never had it this early, since he was barely up. He'd be brewing coffee, sitting there on the second floor landing taking his first sip. I wanted to call him, but what were the chances of my phone *not* being tapped?

With a nod to Matt Widley, I bought a Virgin cell and dialed the zendo.

"Leo, sorry to disturb you."

"But it's important?" I pictured his gray eyes crinkled, his grin wide.

It was important; it also wasn't the first time. "Yeah. But don't ask me anything you can't repeat."

"My nasty habit of answering truthfully?" He'd be sitting on the landing, his feet on the steps, his back propped a bit awkwardly against the corner. It would have been more awkward had I been there. The little second-floor hallway begged for cozy discussions, but we hadn't quite found our spots there yet.

"Leo, who are you?"

"Coffee cup in hand, itch on the back of my neck."

"Who were you before?"

"Sleeping."

"What's the connection?"

"Memory."

"Nothing else?"

"Karma."

"In the sense that . . . ?"

"Things happening cause other things to happen. I knock over my cup; it causes the coffee to splash down the stairs. You jump off a third-story porch in North Beach; it causes Korematsu to come by here three times."

"I'm sorry."

Leo laughed. "That makes five times this week; even my students don't come that much. It's going to cause him to start pondering Buddhism. Not all bad."

Hmm.

"But your question: What makes a woman change from what you thought she was?" He paused, giving me time to protest. I could have tackled the 'you thought she was,' but now I wanted to know what he saw as my basic question.

"You're thinking of life like a pearl necklace—pearls strung on a thread. Wrong. Life is"—he rapped the receiver—"this moment"—rap—"this moment"—rap—"this moment. Nothing more. Only pearls. No thread. Moment, moment, moment, nothing between."

"And yet—"

He'd hung up!

Only pearls, no thread. I knew it, intellectually, but still I couldn't stop believing I was the thread. That Karen was a thread. And what was driving me crazy was how one end of the thread became the other.

I understood why she'd gone to San Francisco and had a good idea why she'd stolen the police car. But I was no closer to knowing who killed her. I just hoped that what she'd done in Alaska, those pearls between the Star Pine pearls and the Las Vegas pearls would hold the answer.

SFPD'd find out about my flight, but—with luck on my side—not till I was heading out of Anchorage toward the Kenai Peninsula. The plane was scheduled to make a single stop in Seattle. I could have started worrying, but once it lifted off I was asleep.

The plane bumped down in Anchorage just after 12:30. With no luggage and eager to run, even if it was only to the rental counter, I scored a compact, and thus within a half hour was on the lookout for a fish joint so I could make up for the breakfast and lunch I'd slept through.

Any other time I'd have stopped at every scenic overlook on the drive along Turnagain Arm and down the Seward Highway through Moose Pass to Seward itself. The mountains, the inlet, the vastness of the place; it's hard not to slow down to stare.

I made it there in a bit over three hours. It was just about 5:00 P.M., but between my binge and bust sleeping habits and the endless July sunlight, it looked like noon. Sun sparkled off the waters of Resurrection Bay and the fishing boats eased back to the docks. Pickups crowded nearby and clutches of men, women, and dogs waited, ready to select their dinner. The briny smell sent a flicker of homesickness through me. How long ago was it that I drove Duffy to the beach in Gary's car, his paws on the dash?

But, no time for that. I headed up to the edge of town. Wind whipped my hair and crackled my windbreaker as I walked to the rocky edge of the cliff, stood for a moment looking out across Resurrection Bay at the sharp snow-strewn mountains, hollowed out as if the gods had run their dessert spoons up the sides. It was the perfect place for a woman on the run to reincarnate as just another immigrant who'd left an unsatisfactory life in the lower forty-eight for a fresh start in a town looking toward tomorrow.

Still, she'd been twenty years old, hiding out, and beginning to understand that she'd never again be able to see her family, her friends, anyone she cared about. She'd have trudged up the hillside, the smell of dead fish filling her nostrils, slime coating her skin, realizing that she could never become the lawyer she'd probably intended to be, never get a passport, never hold a job long enough for an employer to discover the social security number she had was fake. She'd have shifted the load knowing there'd be no better jobs for her, no decent salaries. After work, if she stopped in a bar, she dared not drink enough to chance a wrong word. Later, she'd go to bed, reminding herself as she drifted off to sleep that she could never, ever let down her guard, never relax, never be honest with anyone.

The drop was way over a hundred feet and straight down. How often had she considered that, standing here after she'd dumped her load? Had the cliff beckoned? Had she wondered if stepping over was the sensible end to a life on the lam?

Having worked long days myself, just as Sonora had, I knew where to go for gossip.

It took me just ten minutes in the Yukon Bar to find it. Didn't even cost me a beer. Burt and Rikki Jessup already had dark ales. The couple had that look of years together—wearing the same kind of plaid shirts, and the same brown fleece vests over the back of their chairs, his gray hair sparse, hers long. They'd settled at a corner table away from the microphone. It was too early for music, but the place was already packed. Plates rattled, glasses clinked, voices bounced off the wooden walls.

I pulled out Matt Widley's picture of his wife. "The bartender said you were folks who might know my friend. Does she look at all familiar? She was heavier when she lived here." She may not have been dressed the same here. She may not have *looked* the same except for her eyes and some inef-fable something, her stance, the angle of her head, the way she held her hands behind her back.

Rikki eyed the shorts and halter and laughed. "Nope."

"That the best picture you got? I've seen less blurry shots taken out the truck window." Burt nodded in agreement with himself.

"She hauled fish up the cliff to a packing plant. I'm thinking it has to be the old Emerald operation just outside town."

"Closed for years."

"Fishing's declined that much?"

"Not hardly, honey," Rikki said.

"Then?"

"Owner died."

Damn. I took a pull of the beer. It was worth the drive from Anchorage, but not a flight from Vegas. "No heirs? Didn't anyone want to buy it?"

Rikki leaned forward as if she couldn't believe anyone in the world didn't know. "Bad luck operation. Harris Henkley, the guy who owned it, he was up to his eyeballs. Owed everyone he could still see. Been up to his hairline if he coulda found anyone who didn't already have an uncle or cousin he'd stiffed already, and if he'd had any hair. Nothing left to sell."

Damn. "Couldn't his creditors have sued?"

"Not worth it. Too many claims in line already."

"Couple fraud claims from buyers. Two sex harassment claims."

"Sex claims? Is that common in that type of place?"

"Hands on your ass? Back then no one raised a fuss," Rikki said. She was older, stockier now but she had the look of a woman who'd known those hands. "You weren't surprised, you didn't complain, and if you couldn't take care of the problem yourself, you stayed out of the way. And you didn't talk about it to strangers."

What you didn't repeat was exactly what I wanted to hear. But Rikki and Jed clammed up and it took me three long casting couch tales, one with a particularly sweet revenge, to convince them I was simpatico. By the time I guided the conversation back to the Emerald operation incidents, a crowd had gathered.

"Folk who worked there weren't about to go to the law," Burt said.

"Because?"

"Because, hon, Harris hired by the week, paid by the week. No withholding, no records, no questions asked."

"But two women did file papers with the court." Behind me someone rested their hands on the top of my chair. I could feel breath hitting my hair.

"Caused a lot of talk. 'Course the cases went nowhere."

"Because?"

"'Cause Harris died."

"Inconvenient."

Rikki shrugged. "Those girls weren't going to get anything, settlement-wise. They just filed because they were fed up with him being such a pig."

I nodded. Above, dollar bills tacked to the ceiling fluttered in the breeze from the door. "And then he died. How'd he die?"

Rikki snorted. Behind me, there were a few more laughs.

"Hey, a man died. Show a little respect."

"Oh, right, Burt." She turned to me.

"See, hon, the way he had the path set, he was at the top and the girls had to go right past him. They're carting big loads of fish and they're watching their step because it's a long way down that cliff and Harris didn't waste profits on maintenance. Those girls, they're worn out, so they're too beat to be skipping out of the way if he sticks out his paw and grabs ass. That

212

grab, it was his m.o. He had other tricks, but that was the one drove girls crazy. Still, good money in a tight job market, what're you gonna do?"

"Yeah. But then he died."

Rikki grinned. "Story was he tied one on Friday night, grabbed for ass that wasn't there and shot all the way down to the water. Didn't find him till Monday morning."

"What'd the police conclude?"

Burt shrugged. "They didn't. No witnesses. No one was sorry to see him go."

"Yeah, afterwards, the stories that came out. Wasn't just ass-pinching. Like Burt said, no one was sorry."

"Didn't people lose their jobs?"

"Well, yeah, but the season was over. Lot of 'em just moved on."

"When was that?" I asked, holding my breath.

"What was it, Rik, fifteen years ago?"

"Sixteen. Because, we'd just gotten Scout. Remember he chewed up the paper when you were trying to read the story? Scraps everywhere—you were in a fit."

He grinned. "Yeah, but what could I do. Can't blame a pup."

Sixteen years. Three years after Sonora Eades made her escape from Star Pine. I took a long swallow of beer and said, "If one of the women pushed him off, would anyone have been surprised?"

"They would have cheered."

"Who wouldn't have?" a male voice behind me asked. But he was asking a question, not just chiming in agreement.

Burt and Rikki looked up, wary.

I knew that voice. I tensed but didn't turn.

Rikki said, "No one bitched then. No one's squawked since. Weren't even heirs fighting over the cannery."

"Yeah," Burt said. "It was like throwing trash over the side of the boat: It floats a minute then it sinks. In another minute there's no sign it was ever there."

"Do you recognize the girl in this picture?"

I still didn't turn around. Of course it was Karen Johnson, Karen Johnson when she was Sonora Eades sitting for her high school year-book picture. Sonora Eades with hair that looked like brown kale, pulled back in bunches and caught at the nape of her neck. Other girls must have agonized about what to wear, but Sonora's plaid shirt looked like she'd grabbed it out of the laundry bag. Behind her defiance there was an earnestness, a yearning. She must have been such easy pickings for Wallinsky. I could see her overwhelmed with outrage at possible abuse of migrant workers, of Madelyn's treatment of Claire. And yet there was something in her expression, something I couldn't place, that made me—like Wallinsky—wonder.

The newcomer held the picture out for Burt and Rikki. "Do you remember her?"

Rikki jerked back, grabbed her beer and stared into the glass a few moments before she took a swallow.

"Never seen her," Burt said.

"Really? High school pictures of strangers make you people this nervous?"

"Don't know her," Rikki muttered.

He put a hand on my shoulder. "If you—"

I slapped it off and turned around slowly to face my brother John. "Who the hell are you? We said we don't know her. How clear do we have to make that?"

John hesitated. Then he grabbed the photo and stomped off.

I thought I saw a glimmer of admiration in his eyes.

28

"WHEW!" I TOOK a sip of my beer and tried to gauge Rikki and Burt. What did they know? Did it incriminate Karen Johnson, or them? Or had John's heavy-handedness just gotten their backs up? I waited for them to comment, to wrap me into the tribe of the offended. They sipped, too. Rikki stared intently into her glass. Burt turned to watch the stage where a guy was positioning a mike. I glanced around to see if John was trying his number at some other table, but he was out of sight. He wouldn't be far, though. There was so much I wanted to know from him, not the least of it being how he ended up here. Having him lurking nearby should have been a comfort, but chances were good it would end up being a problem.

But I'd underestimated John. A guy in a house T-shirt plunked down a bottle of Irish and three shot glasses. "Compliments of some dude who said he pissed you all off."

"From the looks of you, Keith, he must've given you city money."

"Yeah. A real L.A. tip. If he wants to insult you again, drag him in here."

I laughed, trying not to overreact. I was having a hard enough time not reaching for the bottle and pouring. But it had to be one of them who made the move and tacitly accepted the gift, one of them who became my host and answered my questions. Rikki and Burt seemed fine; they'd been decent to me. People like them were the reason I'd washed out as a PI's assistant in New York, interviewing a suspect's parents, trying to get them to reveal something that would incriminate the entire family and destroy their lives more than their lowlife son already had.

"Where is he, Keith?" Burt asked, meaning John.

"Gone."

"You sure?"

"Saw him walk out, why?"

Burt shrugged, then reached for the bottle and poured.

"What was he after?" I asked.

"Same thing as you are."

Damn! Was it that obvious? "Harris Henkley, you mean?" I took a smaller swallow than I wanted. I have a good head for liquor but I didn't dare push it.

Burt nodded. But Rikki drank the whiskey and laughed. "He's Seward's Judge Crater. Every couple years we get a reporter like that, or a guy doing a feature. Once it was for *The New Yorker.*"

"Woulda been if he'd found out anything. We tell 'em: nothing to find. They think we're lying, so they spend a week in town irritating people—"

"But buying drinks. Bartenders love to get a whiff of them. I got a damned good lunch once at that fancy place by the marina, the one that went belly-up—"

Burt laughed. "Too bad for it there weren't more reporters, huh?"

"But who was the girl in this guy's picture?" I asked.

Burt put down his glass and eyed me anew. "Just what is it that brings you to Seward?"

"Scouting a location. I'm a stunt coordinator now." That line always worked.

"Movie location? You mean a movie about Harris Henkley?"

Any advantage in that? "Not per se, no. The movie's fiction, but it deals with a similar kind of story, so, you know—that packing plant? Could it be a location? I mean, is it still there? Doesn't it look like *real?* Can you show me?"

"Now?"

"Yeah."

"Rik? You want to?"

"Let me finish my drink."

The drink turned into two, but when I climbed into their old black pickup, I wasn't sure whether they'd bought my story or the drinks made the whole thing seem like a perfect foray for a slow night. It'd be a good story for them tomorrow, whichever.

By the time we reached the path up to the Emerald Packing Plant out-side town, night was finally coming on in this northern outpost and the light had changed. Civil twilight, the bridge between clear afternoon and the first shadow of dusk, the last time you could see clearly without arti-ficial light. I wished I'd known how little seeing-time I had left. The cliff was more rock than earth, more dirt than grass and almost vertical. The path, or what I could make out through the haze that coated it, was sharp switchbacks. It looked endless. "Omigod!"

"Believe it. Damn thing nearly killed us. We started right here." Rikki pointed to a dirt-browned cement slab.

We! "You call this a path? I'll just follow you."

Burt leaned against the truck. "You girls go right ahead. I'll catch you if you slip."

"Burt's got no head for heights?" I asked Rikki.

"That, and the bottle in the trunk."

I hoped he settled in with it, kept an eye on the path and wouldn't spot John, who'd surely tailed us.

217

Rikki headed up a switchback trail of dirt, mud, and the remnants of wooden stairs. The cliff was like a wall, the trail narrow. "What kept you from falling right off here?"

"Desperation. It was a little better back then. Henkley didn't want to end up paying hospital bills. Rope rail then, but the damned thing burned your hands so bad you only grabbed it if you were going to fall, and then you just hoped it wasn't frayed."

Wind snapped my shirt, gusts smacked my face. "This is crazy. How long did you do this?"

"Me? Just that season."

"That last season?" The season right before it closed?

She mumbled something. I couldn't tell what.

I was right behind her. It wasn't dusk, but shadows blurred the steps. She was moving more slowly. I tried to remember how much she'd had to drink, but she'd already been in the bar when I arrived. If she lost her footing, we'd both go shooting down to the bay. "I'm in good shape, but I'm panting. How could you do this with a load of fish?"

"Like . . . I said . . . desperation."

"You were *all* desperate?"

She made a move I took for nodding.

"The girl in the picture, what about her?"

Rikki didn't answer.

Had I pressed too fast?

The path curved back, even steeper now.

"There used to be . . . stairs here. Hard enough with them."

"I can't believe you did this every day. How many times a day?"

"Sixteen. Eight hours. Two loads . . . an hour."

"The girl in the picture did this, too? She sure didn't look in that good shape."

"Not when she got here."

Bingo! "But by the end of the season. Yeah, I can imagine. The gym of the damned, huh?"

"We're almost . . . at the top. Here's . . . the place he . . ."

"The place Old Harris was waiting to grab ass?" The path veered inward. Its steep dirt surface passed a level cement slab. "Fucking bastard! If I'd worked here I would have dreamed every night about taking one good swipe and knocking the shithead clear off his little perch."

She plopped on the weeds at the top, panting. "You and everyone."

"Like it must have been Topic A in the powder room."

"You mean the outhouse . . . over there?" She rolled to her left and pointed to a pile of rotted boards.

"It'd be so easy to shove him off. Irresistible."

She rolled back, pushed herself up, and suddenly she had me by the shoulders. I was on my knees. I couldn't get my balance. She shoved me hard. I grabbed for her leg and flung myself on the ground, digging my fingers into the dirt, imagining the two of us shooting over the cliff and down into the water.

She moved to face me, her mouth contorted in anger. "There's no location site, is there? Goddamn you!"

I was inches from the edge. One angry shove and all the grass on the ground wouldn't save me. I pushed up.

"Don't you move."

"Rikki," I said with more bravado than I felt, "are you making my point for me? It'd be so easy, wouldn't it?"

Her body went stiff and then, suddenly, she was shaking.

I backed away from the edge fast. "I'm sorry. Really. Okay, I lied. You're right. But I didn't come all this way for curiosity. I knew that girl in the photo, went running with her. Now she's dead."

"Karen died?"

Karen! So this was when Sonora Eades became Karen Johnson. "Karen Johnson"—I waited till she gave a slight nod—"yes. She fell off a building."

"She killed herself?"

I shrugged and sat down on the grass, motioning her to sit beside me. "Tell me about her. Did Henkley go after her particularly?"

"No," she said slowly. "Dead? Karen?" She shook her head. "Damn, it shouldn't . . . things . . . should've been better for her."

"They should have. Definitely." I took a breath. "But you were saying about Henkley?"

"He barely bothered with her. There was tastier meat around."

"Then why—"

"I don't know. She didn't start hanging out with the rest of us till the season was half over. She was close-mouthed, but, you know, everyone had secrets. You didn't work here otherwise. But Karen, it wasn't like she was running from a crazy boyfriend, or like she'd cut out before doing thirty days for shoplifting. None of the common things. It was like she'd climbed the wall from the convent or something deep like that."

"Had she relaxed more by mid-season? I mean, when she started hanging out?"

"Yeah. Well, in the beginning. It was like, you know, you gauge yourself, figure out how much you can drink and still keep your business to yourself. It's a stage. Then you figure out Seward's a good place where people'll watch out for you. A boyfriend's not going to come asking questions and beat you to a pulp. Petty crime in Arkansas's not going to follow you here. It takes a while to find out you're safe, longer to trust it. Nothing's total, but still."

"*In the beginning.* Then what happened?"

"She tightened up again. For a while she stopped hanging out at the bar altogether. Then, it was like she'd decided she couldn't give up the one release we all had, so she came back. But it didn't relax her. It made her tense in a different way."

"How?"

"Like she was choking on something all the time."

"Anger?"

"Yeah, I guess."

"And then?"

"Nothing."

"Rikki, Karen's dead. Don't leave her with the stigma of killing a man for no reason. What happened?" She hadn't said Karen killed him, not in words. If I couldn't get her to admit that, I had nothing.

She crossed her legs, staring down toward the choppy water. Wind-whipped hair covered her face, but I could see the indecision in the movement of her jaw.

"I know Karen," I insisted. "She had a reason."

Still she hesitated.

"I liked her, Rikki. She fell onto the freeway. *The freeway!* I saw her body afterwards. The bones in her face were gone. There was just skin. She—"

"Stop! I don't want to—" She inhaled. "The day before he died, he went after me. But I was tougher than he thought—I took a swing at him. The fish basket swung me around. I was lucky I didn't go shooting right down. I ended up needing twelve stitches in my face." She pulled back her hair, so I could see the scar over her eye. "The next day I was so zonked with the painkillers I could barely put one foot in front of the other—"

"He didn't fire you?"

"Nah. He knew I knew he'd be waiting for his chance to get even. He loved that. He knew I couldn't tell anyone because . . . well, because."

I didn't ask why she'd come back. I knew that answer. "How do I know you didn't kill him?"

"I would've. I really think I would've. But by the end of the day I wasn't here." She pulled out a dental bridge with four front teeth. "After he got even, he told me to take the rest of the day off. Mr. Magnanimous."

"How do you know it was Karen?"

"She told me. When she helped me down the path with my mouth bleeding. She told me he'd never do it again. I said yeah, he would, because what else was I going to do? She just repeated that. The way she said it, so matter of fact, it was the calmest I'd ever seen her."

29

GETTING RIKKI to talk to John took some maneuvering. He might have managed it by heavy-handing her but I couldn't let that happen. It was the least I could do for her.

I checked in with the stunt coordinator to make sure my gag was still on schedule and there were no last minute changes in equipment or layout. Suddenly, what had been distant was looming. Tomorrow! I'd done fire gags before, but then I'd had time to eyeball everything, check the fuel mix—diesel and unleaded gasoline—and double-check the Nomex suit to make sure there were no tiny holes. But this time we'd be using a gel that was new to me. The gag had been story-boarded a month ago and I'd picked it apart looking for flaws. There was nothing more to do, except the mental run-throughs I knew I'd do over and over on the plane. I trusted Jed Elliot, but still it'd be my skin in the burn.

I got some cold drinks, a couple burgers to go, and ate mine while I waited. I watched the fishing boats waddle in carrying loads a lot bigger than their San Francisco counterparts. And I thought of Karen Johnson, wondered what had gone through her mind as she'd sat here, looking at her beautiful bay of exile.

When John finally pulled open the car door, he greeted me: "What the hell are *you* doing here? You could get yourself killed! It's not the movies where you've got a catcher net." He shook his head. "Slide over. I'll drive," he instructed.

I laughed. "If you get out now, you'll be hoofing it back to Anchorage. Here, I got you a burger. Eat and be grateful." I pulled into traffic. "What'd Rikki say?"

"Don't ask."

"Hey, I'm the one—"

"It's nothing you don't know. But if there's an inquiry, you want to be able to say you're clear." He pulled something from his shirt pocket.

"You taped her? She agreed to be taped?"

He shrugged and started to unwrap the burger.

"You mean: didn't know."

He chewed.

"Dammit John, I just about had to beg her to talk to you. If she'd seen that recorder—"

"She didn't. Do you think this is the first time I—It's harder for a man; a woman puts her purse on the table and *voila!* Man's got to . . ."

"Find a man-bag?"

"Watch the road, will you?"

"That tape's not going to be admissible."

He didn't even bother to answer.

I turned all the way toward him. "So, what're you going to do on this drive, John, drink water and stare out the sunroof into the dark?"

"Try to have our flights moved up, if you don't get us killed first." John, for all his annoying heavy-handedness, was a welcome addition so long as that hand was pressing someone else. Even so, he couldn't get us a flight till midday, and he spent the next half hour calling motels.

I followed the road out of town onto the highway. I couldn't bring myself to talk about Karen, not yet. I didn't know where to begin. Trees clustered around me, pressing in. They hadn't done that on the drive down, before I knew Karen Johnson had—"John, I just can't believe it. Henkley was beyond disgusting. But for her to kill . . . again. I mean, I wanted to believe somehow she didn't kill Madelyn Cesko, that there'd been homicidal migrant workers like Wallinsky thought. But now—"

"You don't know what to think."

"Yeah."

"You're trying to find some good reason, some excuse—"

"Such as?" *I'm not a complete moron!*

"The thing with you, Darcy, is you can't bear to see bad in people you like. I've pointed this out before. You see what you want to see. If someone's your friend you don't want to believe bad's really bad. If it's Mike—"

"Give it a rest, John. It's not like you didn't spend a fortune on Wallinsky alone. Hunting for Mike where Mike is not and never has been supported Wallinsky for a decade."

He made a show of eating, like chewing was some new and challenging task.

But I was being forced to believe bad about Karen Johnson now. Like her or not, two people were dead. Wallinsky had questions, but he didn't know about Harris Henkley. "I wonder, after Madelyn Cesko, was it easier to just push a guy off a cliff? No mess, no bother?"

"Not according to Rikki Jessup. Good burger. That period here before Karen killed him, when she pulled back into herself, Rikki figures she was trying to deal."

"Trying to decide if she could just move on? Not kill him? Just forget about his constant abuse? You think?"

"Rikki thinks. Murder one."

"D'you agree?"

"Yeah." He sounded not as shocked as I was, but as sorry.

"It was a big chance to take."

"Why? Alone with a guy who's had a long free ride and wouldn't see it coming. One shove. Easy pickings."

"Still, after Madelyn Cesko she was lucky to get away."

John start to speak, but didn't. Second-guessing himself wasn't like him.

"So she wasn't lucky?"

He cleared his throat. Unconvincingly.

"Oh, wait, she got away—but not by luck, right?" I knew it, myself, but I didn't know John had suspected Wallinsky. Then the lightbulb went on. "It wasn't chance that Gary gave me Wallinsky's name, was it? You're behind that! You wanted me to check out Wallinsky! How long were you going to wait to ask about him?"

No answer.

"Ah, you want to know, but don't want it to be known that you know, right? What are you going to do if I start telling you how Wallinsky got her here? Put your hands over your ears and hum loud?"

"Watch the road! You're almost over the line!"

"Never mind," I said, suddenly tired of poking at him. Instead I just drove. For the first time since I'd faced my fear of the woods, I let myself play with it. Since the moment I'd gotten control, not a year earlier, I'd steeled myself each time I'd driven through Golden Gate Park or across the bridge to Muir Woods. Now I noted the dark looming shapes, willing the panic to rise in my gut. It was better than dealing with the reality that the woman I'd felt I'd known as Karen Johnson I'd never actually known at all. "She played me."

"She played us all, kid." His voice was barely audible. It was clear that the loss that stunned him wasn't her, but the loss of his trust in his own judgment.

I reached over to touch his arm. How long had it been since he'd call me kid? Since before Mike disappeared.

The headlights showed movement. I hit the brakes. "Moose! John, look! A moose!"

"Where? Oh, that tail?"

"Hey, you gotta be quick." I speeded up. "The thing is, John, we're not total dupes. Yeah, I've given friends the benefit of the doubt, ones you thought were full of it, and sometimes you were right. You gave your ex-wife more than you should've, point of fact. I didn't say it, but I'd never have trusted her. Look at the big picture—between the two of us we're not taken in often, so—"

"Why Karen?"

"Because . . . Because, damn it, she came with Gary's seal of approval! Why shouldn't we believe the woman he foisted on us?"

He started to say something, but I was on a roll.

"That's what you were doing, isn't it? Of course! You had this same question: why'd Gary guarantee her? He vouched for her; you bet your career on her. Now you're in deep shit with the department."

He laughed. "I'm always up to the neck there." I had to laugh, too.

"So, what'd you find out?"

"Nothing till I got here."

"John!"

"That isn't what you think. Believe me, I'd be a lot more comfortable telling you I'd uncovered, ferreted out, and deduced all the answers about Karen Johnson. But I didn't have the Sonora Eades connection until you made it."

"How'd you find out about Seward?" I didn't think I'd mentioned her comment about hauling the fish up the cliff. Even if I had, there's more than one cliff in Alaska.

"Newspaper."

"The one in her house in Las Vegas? Just what was the chain of information there?"

"Slow down! You're twelve miles over the limit."

"Don't worry, you're in good hands." I thought for a minute. "I just can't believe you're in contact with Korematsu."

"Yeah, right, like we'd be having tea."

"Doesn't matter. He couldn't have gotten to Vegas in time. No, oh! Omigod, you've got a source in LVPD! That's right, isn't it? But why? And how'd he just happen to catch the call on Matt Widley? Oh, wait! Didn't 'just happen' did he? He—"

"Stop! I'll tell you. But it's just between us."

"We're in the middle of the woods in Alaska."

"I'm taking that for a promise."

I rolled my eyes and waited for his explanation.

"You know San Francisco's a center for human trafficking. Slavery in our own city—it's disgusting. I came into a piece of information—don't ask how. The way cops do. It's not important. The money piece is that I know there's a switching house in the Mission—"

"The Victorian on Guerrero. Broder's babe's place."

I could have sworn he did a double take, but I was watching the road, mostly. "Yeah. So I needed an airtight—"

"Omigod, you're setting up a sting *there*? You're planning to take down Broder? No wonder you went to ground! Omigod!" The audacity . . . the danger! "Jeez, John!" I was stunned, and yet on another level I wasn't at all. It was just the kind of single-minded, righteous move I knew he was capable of. Like making us mow the lawn and sweep the sidewalks before we could ride our bikes on Saturday. How long have you been planning this?"

"You don't want to know. No details. Safer."

"So, it's just you and the guy in Vegas?"

"Vegas, Miami, a few others."

"So, your guy in Vegas hears the call for Matt Widley's because he's been keeping an eye on him. Why? Is he trafficking? I thought it was Munson."

"I know, you don't want to think ill of—"

"Proof? Give me proof."

"It's connected to his sports charity. The soccer. Some of the girls have flimsy family ties, or parents on drugs, or else parents who got deported. Street kids. They say they're sending these girls away to school, but no one's going to follow up. And then they turn up at the Victorian on Guerrero."

Human smuggling.

"I've been waiting for a girl we ID'd in Vegas to show up there. I was expecting her the night Karen crashed my car and blew the whole sting. Now everything's wait-and-see till the next time."

"But you had to have a source . . . Oh, I get it! Karen! It was Karen, right? It had to be Karen! Right? Right!" I was almost jumping with relief. "That's why she felt comfortable stealing your car. I mean, not good to snatch the car of a cop friend, but a whole lot easier than taking one cold from a cop on the street who'd show no mercy when he caught up with you. You were waiting for her, you just weren't expecting me, and that's— oh yeah—that's why you were such an asshole to me about Mike. You were trying to make me mad enough to leave. Doing a helluva job, too. If I hadn't promised Gary about Karen, I'd have stalked off. But I couldn't. And then Karen nipped the car. Why'd she do that?"

"Got me."

"Oh come on! After all this, you don't know why she stole your car?"

"No."

Was he playing me? "What do you *think?*"

"That I'm no smarter than you. She fooled me. She was key to the set-up and then, bingo, she takes the car, crashes it and alerts everyone in the house. I have no idea why."

"Wait. She checked her messages while we were talking. Matt had tried to reach her. She'd seen him in town. She knew he was with Munson. She'd gone to the huge hassle of getting a divorce to protect him. She hadn't gone to all the trouble, just to have him stumble into the sting because he's with Munson."

"Good guess."

"Not a guess. She left a message on his regular cell phone, begging him to get out of town. Obviously he hadn't answered the call and she hadn't known if he'd gotten the message. So what other option did she have but drive over there?"

"In my car and destroy the sting? There are things called taxis. Would it have killed her to spend fifteen minutes hunting a cab?"

"Apparently."

John grunted and leaned back, leaving me to peer into the growing darkness and follow the headlights on this road I might have thought better of taking in the dark. *Why steal the police car? Why not wait and—*

"The stunt, John! My stunt! The roads were about to be blocked off. She couldn't have gotten through later. Not without weaving through other parts of the city, getting caught in traffic, and who knows what." My hands clenched tight on the wheel. "I told her, John. I told her the streets would be blocked. If I hadn't—" I swallowed.

Now his hand was on my shoulder. "Don't! You can't see the future. Things happen."

"You sound like Leo."

230

There was nothing more to say. I drove down and off the Seward Highway back onto Turnagain Arm, watching the road, thinking about John and Gary; about Karen racing to the Victorian to ward off danger to Matt. The lights of Anchorage were shining in the distance when I remembered that she'd had another person in the car when she turned the corner after causing the crash. Matt? I couldn't believe—Munson? Lure Munson up onto that fifth floor slab and shove him off? No one could have been better prepared than she. None of those pesky questions about how to get near enough, when to do the shove, how to avoid getting tangled up with the falling victim. Piece of cake.

Unless she was overconfident. Let her guard down. Or Munson somehow knew about her past.

30

SUNDAY

JOHN AND I barely made the flight for phone calls. He to Charlie Abrams, his guy in Vegas, me checking messages.

"My gag's been moved up an hour. I'm going to have to go right from the airport."

John's mouth twitched. "You going to tell Mom?"

"I'm working up to it. Doing the easy call first." I punched in Claire Cesko's number and lucked out. It was the answering machine. I left instructions on how to get her set pass. "I'll have to stick around till the director's sure it's a take. It's a fire gag, so after I'm clear, I'm going to be a while cleaning up. Could be a couple hours. No need for you to hang around."

"Now Mom?" John prompted.

I hit speed dial. "Hi, Mom. Listen, my stunt's been moved up. Things are really rushed there. They're not going to send the car for Duffy."

When I clicked off, he asked, "So?"

"She said she'd go to the beach with him to take his mind off missing the stunt."

He shook his head.

"You know, I wonder about Mom. I can never quite tell when she's serious and when she's having a laugh at me."

"Join the pack."

The first clump of passengers were boarding. "That's us. Come on!" John hoisted the carry-on I didn't need help carrying. I'd honed my skill at sleeping in odd moments and places while waiting on sets, but this brother was a real pro. He was out before the seat belt lecture was over. What had he been doing all night while I was sacked out in the motel? Four hours into the four-and-a-half-hour flight and he'd never opened his eyes, merely shifted position.

"You're not asleep, are you?"

He didn't move.

"You've done everything but pull the covers over your head. What're you avoiding?"

He was hardly about to answer that.

"It's not as if you've ever hesitated to tell any of us to mind our own business, so you can't be playing possum for that. Maybe you're planning something you don't want me to get wind of, even a hint." I was watching his eyelids, but they didn't move at all.

"Are you—"

"Dammit, leave me alone! This whole thing has blown up. My sting, my career—who knows how it'll hit Gary. Karen's dead, and yeah, for all the questions I had, I did care about her and she's in fucking pieces on the roadway. San Francisco's still a hub for trafficking and those girls we were trying to save are going to end up in Dubai. Yeah, I'm depressed about it." He turned away, clamping his eyes shut, and there was not a thing I could do for him. I couldn't even tell him that, yet again, I'd misjudged him. Maybe I always had. John, The Enforcer. Mr. Just So. He had been so easy to blame. Maybe he'd never wanted to be The Enforcer at all. But I couldn't even tell him I'd guessed that.

He didn't budge till the plane touched down.

"The sting, John, what now?" I said before he could leap up. "Those girls, where are they?"

"Don't know."

"Munson flew back to Vegas. He couldn't have taken them back."

"We'd know."

"So they're still in the city, then."

"Most likely."

"What're you—"

He heaved himself up and yanked down his carry-on. "Gotta go."

"Hey!"

He shoved by three passengers. The door opened and he was gone.

He was headed to Portland and from there to Oakland, Sacramento, Santa Rosa, or San Jose, someplace he could deplane without Broder's men waiting.

I couldn't let him go like this. I raced into the terminal, to the counter. "Where's the Portland gate? The one the guy with the short black hair wanted?"

"I don't—"

"He's even pushier than I am."

"To the left, halfway."

I ran down the aisle, skirting rolling luggage. "John!" I caught up with him.

"Darcy, I've got a flight in fifteen—"

"Those girls, we know some of them are illegal. Once they disappear, no one's going to be looking for them. Karen died to protect them; she died because of this sting. We can't just let it go bust. There's got to be some way to save it."

He stopped. A woman barely missed him with a stroller.

"And you? How much did you put into the set-up? You can't let it go—"

"I'm not."

"What's the plan?"

"You're not involved—"

"Please! If I was deeper in this I'd be entombed. The plan?"

"Munson was supposed to bring the girls to the Guerrero house Tuesday, but something stopped him. Maybe Widley's carrying on. Something. So no girls. But I have a message from Abrams. Munson's flying back to SFO today. He's got both girls with him. They're on their way to the airport, to SFO."

"When's the transfer?"

"We'll have to follow; but before it was set for nine."

"Where?"

"They won't use the Victorian this time. They'll go for somewhere public and crowded, like Coit Tower. Munson'll be standing with the girls; then a woman will join them. They'll stand there like a couple and two daughters, then he'll walk off."

"Coit Tower?"

"Just an example. Single exit, too easy to block."

"Fisherman's Wharf?"

"Single exit. I'm not saying—dammit, I don't know where. Like I said, Darcy, we just have to follow."

"How're you going to—"

"I'm not, not if you make me miss my flight! Abrams'll meet me, bring the reports and we'll be in SFO by sunset."

"But how—"

"Gotta go! Trust me, it'll work."

He was barely down the gangway when I realized where it would be. "John! The set, John!" But, of course, it was too late. I had my phone out before I remembered his hadn't answered days ago. I didn't know what number he was using now.

He was gone and there was no way I could reach him.

The set was perfect for Munson—dark, crowded, lights and camera focused on the take. He'd even perked up when I mentioned the movie.

I also couldn't handle this alone. I had to have help from the SFPD.

I ran to the end of the terminal for the hell of it. It felt good, just nowhere near good enough.

I reconsidered. Did I absolutely need help?

I drank a latte—also nowhere near good enough.

Absolutely. But I was no closer to trusting Korematsu than before I called him from Las Vegas.

Still, a pig in a poke is better than no meat at all.

I dialed Korematsu.

31

I'D MADE IT back on the plane to SFO with three minutes to spare, then sat staring blankly out the window, searching for flaws in the plan. There were plenty. But too late now.

Two and a half hours later, descending into SFO was like flying into a glove. A dark gray glove.

Almost twilight! The plane was late! I'd never make it to the set on time. I pulled my pack from the overhead.

"Please stay in your seats till the plane has come to a stop at the gate."

Maybe the filming was behind schedule. Thin hope. My stunt had already been moved forward an hour.

The plane jolted to a stop. I sprang into the aisle. "Excuse me! Sorry! Sorry!" When the door slid open I burst out and ran up the passageway.

"That's her!"

"Come here, Darcy."

For a sweet moment, I thought it was a limo driver. But it was the opposite, and the worst of all possibilities—Chief of Detectives Broder. I flashed on him walking into the North Beach apartment and me leaping over the porch railing; flashed on his girlfriend, the trafficking ring, the sting that was thwarted by Karen's death; him looking at prison time if I—

"Where's John?"

"Don't know." I could barely breathe. How many cops did he have with him? Half the station? I had to project confidence, not look like a cornered deer.

"He's on this flight."

I shrugged toward the gangway. "Feel free."

"Are you saying he's not here?"

"Right. Check with the airline."

"We will. Stay here."

"Can't. I have to be on the set in twenty minutes."

"The movie'll wait."

Five uniformed officers were behind him. A road block. Travelers were skirting them, creating a crush at the sides. My heart was going double-time. It was all I could do not to run. I planted myself in front of Broder and said, "Detective, the city film commission got me this job. If I don't show, the city looks bad. And the next film goes on location in Montreal."

"I don't care if the next ten films are shot on Mars. Wait . . . here." Broder shot a glance at the uniformed officer to his right and strode to the counter.

I eyed the uniform in vain hope he might be one of John's cronies, few as those were in the department. But he was a stranger. I smiled. He didn't. Definitely not on John's side. Still . . . "Where's Korematsu?"

The cop took a wider stance, folded his arms across his burly torso, and eyed Broder as if he was the suspect. As Broder walked back, the officer unfolded his arms.

"Double-check the plane. Lott could be using an alias."

"Yes, sir."

"He's not," I said.

"I'm not asking you."

"The airline'll tell you. He got on under his own name in Anchorage, got off in Seattle. It's in their records."

"Stay here."

Broder strode to the counter again. His flunky hesitated, then strode onto the gangway. I didn't look at the other cops, just turned and walked through the line of watching civilians. Then I ran full-out, threading through passengers as if I was dodging bullets, just hoping none of the cops had reacted before I got a lead, hoping they'd give chase, not call ahead. Just hoping.

Small chance Broder wouldn't nab me at the curb—or before—but it was my only chance! The gate was—of course!—at the end of the concourse. Clutching my pack in one arm, I skirted a family pulling luggage, raced between passengers emerging from the gate and friends hurrying toward them, around a motorized cart, onto the moving sidewalk and past anyone dawdling on it.

The moving sidewalk ended a hundred feet ahead. In front was a large security guard. I waited till I was ten feet away, leapt the railing and spurted around and onto the next belt, skirted three women and leapt the railing. In minutes there'd be a dozen guards here. Speed was everything. I raced through the lobby, almost smacked into the glass doors before they opened, and skidded to a stop at the curb.

Now what?

A cab pulled up.

I jumped it.

"To the set?"

It was Webb Moratt.

"A gift from John?"

"Big gift. You know how hard it is to stay ready to pick anyone up, circling around, how damned near impossible, with the traffic guys fussing?

You can't tip everyone. Hell, there're some won't even take it, like they don't know what the job's for, you know? I had to . . ."

Moratt shifted lanes and kept on complaining.

The biggest gag of my career was coming up and I was going to be late. I'd gone over it again and again, tweaked the choreography days ago, but planning can't take the place of a run-through. I needed to focus.

Moratt ranted on.

Suddenly, I just needed to talk to Leo. I pulled out my phone and hit 1 on the speed dial. "Leo—Roshi—I need to ask you a question."

"Where are you?"

"In a cab from the airport. On my way to the set to get thrown out of a burning car."

"Ah." I could picture the smile that wiggled at the middle of his wide lips but didn't make it to the sides.

"You always say, 'Don't complain.'"

"I did."

"Why?"

"Why not?"

I sighed.

"Don't complain. Sighs count."

"But, Leo, it's so frustrating."

"Don't complain."

"But—"

"Don't—"

"Okay! Okay. But if I can't complain, there's no way I can talk about it."

"Exactly."

"Leo!"

I could hear his exhalation. He was considering, thinking about giving me a hint.

I didn't dare speak. "Talking about it isn't *it*."

"Oh. Right."

"When was *it?*"

"Oh. You mean *it* is in the past. Not now. Focusing on *it* means . . ."

The phone was dead. He'd hung up. I turned my own off so I could think.

"Dammit! If you're gonna crawl, get a crib!" Moratt swung around a yellow van, cutting back into the lane with inches to spare.

"That was the 280 exit!"

"Asshole made me miss it!"

I laughed.

"What? What?"

"Just thinking of Leo." *If you hadn't been so busy complaining* . . . Whoops. "Get off at Vermont Street. With luck, you'll still miss the worst of the back-up."

"Like there won't be trucks and double-parked . . ."

If *don't complain* meant stop entertaining yourself with complaint, get out of your thoughts and do something, then Karen was a master. But it doesn't mean act on the spur of the moment. It's not: don't prepare. It's choreograph your gag ahead, run the tape in your mind, make it part of you, and when the start comes, don't think back to that—*do* the gag. It's not steal a police car because your mind is in the past with Matt or his possible future. It's now, now, now, don't dwell on the past, don't complain, be alert, and ready to do. It's see a girl talking on her phone in the street and shove her out of danger. It's see the chance, maybe because you've choreographed for weeks, and push Henkley, the abuser, off the cliff. It's not meet Madelyn, look for a knife, though. That still stopped me. But was it, see Munson, the abuser, open the car door and beckon him in?

Was it: hire Gary? Why *had* she contacted him? She wasn't in danger of being discovered. She had to be turning herself in, here, for her California crime. Why now? Because it was the only way she could stop the trafficking? And protect Matt while she worked with John? She alerts John to the trafficking. But if the sting uncovers her, a murderer, the traffickers would get lost in the flurry. Who'd believe her? On the other hand, if she turns herself in first, then she's got cred. She'll stand trial after trial, but the first won't start for months.

But why the divorce? How much would that really keep Matt out of the spotlight? Why have everything hang on getting the divorce?

"You married, Webb?"

"Divorced. Cost me a freakin' fortune, too."

Nothing near what trial after trial would have cost Karen's husband. It would have left him bankrupt. "Thanks."

"Huh? Hey, don't slow! Get through the damn light. You can—shit!"

Something still didn't feel right.

"Webb, you got John's cell number?"

"Not working."

"Not his old one, the one he's got with him now."

He hesitated.

"Tell him the sting's at the movie set. I set it up with Korematsu."

Moratt pulled around the corner. Ahead Market Street was blocked just as it had been Tuesday. Fog blurred the streets, veiled the set. On the sidewalk was Munson. I pressed against the window trying to spot the girls. "Stop over there!"

"Here? How'm I going to get out of here? Back up here, in this mess? You could've—"

"Here! Dammit!"

I slammed the door behind me. Munson was gone.

32

WHERE WAS MUNSON? I didn't dare look around for him, or for the girls. Broder wasn't here, not yet. He'd have raced out of the airport as soon as he heard I was gone. But I had the advantage: he wouldn't have been running, or have a cab waiting. I gave him ten more minutes. There were police all around, but none of them seemed to be looking for me. Yet. When he did get here, he'd have half the force ready to pounce. It would make the perfect diversion to allow Munson to pass on the girls.

I headed through the checkpoint onto the set. The lights were brighter here. Beyond it everything was dark. I glanced at the camera guys. Two of them should be police techs, one watching for Munson, the other for his contact. They'd be ready to record the whole transaction. Assuming Korematsu had arranged this part of the sting, assuming I could really trust him. I squinted as if that would clear the fog. Korematsu was nowhere in sight.

But Jed Elliot was right at my shoulder. "Where *were* you? You're late. Never mind. We're holding the entire gag for you. Never mind. Wardrobe's over there."

"Sorry." I ran to the trailer.

Today the cable car I'd driven into before was farther down, nearer Market. In the final cut, sixty seconds would have passed before tonight's scene. The sports car would have bounced back, the cable car caught on fire and now it would be rolling out of control toward Market Street, threatening to jump its tracks and crash into a bright orange trolley. Cable car aficionados would scream about accuracy, but fiction is fiction. As I jumped into the trailer, I glanced back, trying to gauge the distance between the cable car and the trolley, but the fog was too thick and all that stood out were the fire engine lights and the ambulances.

The wardrobe mistress grabbed a tube. "We're not doing the Nomex suit, hon. Just the skull cap under the wig."

"So I'll burn but my hair'll survive? You're using the new stuff?"

"Yeah, the Canadian gel. You can have the fire burning off your skin with this one. Start smearing, Casey."

Her assistant, a stocky woman motioned to me to lift a foot. "We don't want to miss anything."

"One patch of bare skin and you're fried."

I hated to distract them. "This stuff's not freezing like the gels I've used before." *In burns that took split seconds, no longer.*

"Nah. Doesn't need to be refrigerated. You'll be real glad."

"It works how long? Twenty seconds?"

"Give or take."

"Uh huh."

She handed me the denim shorts and red hibiscus-flowered halter I'd worn Tuesday. "Careful. Don't rub the gel off."

As if!

"Remember to keep your eyes closed in the fire. You don't have gel in your eyes."

Eyes closed in a gag I'd only run through in my mind? "Thanks."

The icy wind hit me as I hurried out of the trailer. Jed and the crew were swaddled in heavy jackets. The fog was gusting now, creating momentary clears. "Bitch to film," one of the cameramen grumbled.

"Bitch for a fire gag!"

Outside the cordon, civilians looked like the winter follies. In one of the clears I spotted a couple watch caps and one tasseled hat. But I wasn't cold. My worry was sweating, sweating the gel off.

"The set-up's changed." Jed pointed to the convertible. "We'll do the insert in studio. It'll look like this jobby"—he smacked the orange fender—"got tossed over here when you hit the cable car. Like I said, we'll take care of that in-house. The accelerant's on the strip beside the car, but the car's going to go, so this is a one take."

I eyed him for some sign he was in on the sting, but he was all business. Korematsu must have told him . . .

Forget Korematsu. Think about the gag! You're going to be on fire!

It's good to have a second or third chance, but this was one time I was all for a single take. I glanced nervously at the gel. I'd read the script, choreographed the gag. The seat cushion had been replaced by the spring board I'd be crouched on, the one that would send me into the flip. I'd do a 360 in the air and land on a pad five feet from the engine. On film it would look like the car exploded, the force throwing me out. "Windshield's been switched with breakaway glass?"

"Of course."

"Give me ten minutes to do a check."

"We're running late. I've already gone over the car, the accelerant, the landing pad."

"If you were me, would you take someone's word? Even yours? Ten minutes. Five to check, five to get my mind in place. Ten minutes, real people time."

"We're—"

"Hey, it's one take."

"Okay, yeah. Sure."

247

The grips were rolling lights to the far side of the car. Behind the director's chair I could make out some of the first unit, one of the actors who'd been at the dinner with the second unit the other night. I had the impression the crowd beyond the cordon was two or three thick, but I couldn't be sure. Was Broder there? The fog would be good cover for him. But here, for me, it was like having my eyes taped shut.

One of my ten minutes was already gone. *Concentrate on the gag. Focus!* I bent over the landing pad, eyed the tie-downs, the weighting, felt the heft of the air pressure. The pad was softer than a high-fall pad. I'd be doing a flip like a gymnast over the pummel horse, but I wouldn't be landing on my feet, I'd be coming down head first, tucking and landing on my back so I could use the time in the air to appear out of control. I'd land full out, but I'd be on fire. The pad had to hold long enough for me to get off before it caught fire, too. "Seems good," I assured myself. It wasn't like doing the set-up myself, though. No one is as careful as the person with the chance of dying.

I stepped into the convertible. The spring board was a fourteen-inch square, the steering wheel replaced by a breakaway facsimile. I squatted down on the board, tried to run through the gag in my mind, but I couldn't. I kept peering into the distance, hoping for the fog to clear an instant, to show me Broder.

I'd never *not* been able to do a mental run. I couldn't take a stunt like this with no prep.

Wind whipped my hair. The fog cleared. I saw—omigod—not Broder but, was that Matt Widley? Widley had no business here at all! Had I misjudged—was Korematsu with him?

"You ready?"

"No! Jed I have to do a live run-through. Can you spot me?"

He hesitated. "Sure. If you've gotta, you gotta. Of course. When you're ready."

"On three. Lemme know when you're a go."

I stood up off the spring board for a moment, then crouched back down, felt for the spring board release, ran through the gag in my mind. "Okay Jed."

"One . . . two . . . three!"

I hit the release lever. The spring board sent me flying up. I pulled my shoulders hard forward, hips forward, saw the ground, splayed my legs and landed on my back on the bag. Too close to the front edge, but on the bag.

My eyes were open! I'd forgotten to keep them closed. If this were real, I'd be blind.

"Great! Can you get a little more leg action?"

"Sure, Jed. No problem."

"This is it! We can only burn the car once. No second takes."

Don't need to hear that twice. "Gotcha."

I rechecked the bag, stood beside the car, and ran the gag through, focusing on the extra torque I'd need for the leg action. The wind gusted, ruffling the edges of the bag. I could hear murmuring from the onlookers, but I didn't dare let myself look. I shut my eyes, saw myself sailing up in slo mo, arching over, kicking in the air—wider than before—landing in the middle of the bag, rolling off into the arms of the tech with the fire extinguisher.

"Places!"

I stepped onto the spring board. The wind gusted. In the clearing Claire Cesko stood waving. *Waving!*

"Darcy. You go on three after we ignite the car."

"Gotcha."

"In ten . . . nine . . ."

I crouched, hand on the lever.

". . . two . . . one. Fire!"

The accelerant on the hood shot up flames. I pressed the lever. Nothing! The lever jammed! I stomped. Still nothing! Flames roared off the hood. No time! Screw the lever! I pushed off hard as I could, pulled my shoulders forward. Legs up, head down! I was too low. My face was in the flames! I was going to land on my head! I slammed down on the hood. Flames shot up around me! *Keep your eyes closed.* I flailed my legs and arms. The hood was too hot! The metal was burning me. I reached back, flung myself forward onto the ground.

The gel—twenty seconds. I stumbled forward, toward what I hoped was the camera.

"Cut! Hose her off! Quick! You okay, Darcy?"

Water hit me from all sides, slithering down my body with the gel. Cheers broke the tension.

"Fine. Lever stuck. I should have double-checked. Had to improvise."

"You got it?" that to the camera in front.

The cameraman looked as shaken as I felt. He nodded.

"Won't know till I check the monitor, but I've got a good feeling. Good save. Yeah, great save." He threw an arm around my shoulder. "Trust me, it's going to be great! Good work, girl! Go get yourself cleaned off. You look revolting."

I grabbed a handful of wet gel that had been dripping off my elbow and rubbed it on his cheek.

Around me the crew, the onlookers were shivering in their down jackets, but I was roasting inside the cocoon of gel. The sting had to go now. Onlookers were already drifting away; in minutes the streets would be empty and the necessary cover gone. I was desperate to look toward Market Street, to where I'd spotted Munson before. But I didn't dare. The timetable wasn't mine. I walked toward the wardrobe wagon, pulled open the door.

Lights burst on behind me. I turned. Across the set, at Market, I could see the tableau. Two small figures, a slight, dark-haired woman pulling open a car door. "Police! Freeze!" Munson ran; a cop tackled him and threw him to the ground. I could make out John now, running in. The woman shoved the girls into the car. John was almost there. She slid into the driver's seat. He was heading straight at the front of the car. *She won't stop! John! She'll hit you and keep going!*

The engine roared, the car jolted. John leapt around it, yanked open the door and pulled her out. The crowd didn't know what was happening, but they gasped and then they cheered. I leaned back against the wardrobe wagon and smiled. The onlookers cheered John. And it was all on film. A clip Mom would show every Thanksgiving and Christmas, till we all put our hands over our eyes and the star actually blushed.

I turned back toward the wagon. Something moved in the distance, in the half dark. I stopped, peered across the street. It was Broder, striding away from the scene, moving fast, but not running. At the curb, thirty yards in front of him was a dark car. An unmarked?

I started to call out, but John would never hear me.

Broder was picking up speed. He'd be out of town before anyone realized he was gone.

Frantically, I looked around for Korematsu.

Broder was twenty yards from the car. Dark-suited man in the night fog.

He was now almost running.

I grabbed a handful of gel, smeared it on my arm, set my towel on fire and ran toward him. "Help! Fire!"

He stopped.

I was slipping from the gel. I leaned forward. "Help!"

I could hear calls of *Fire!*

Broder turned, ran for the car.

My feet were sliding. I was too far forward, going to fall. The flaming towel flapped near my face.

Broder was almost at his car.

My feet flew out from under me. Dropping the towel I fell, skidded and slammed into him.

33

THE ONLOOKERS WERE mostly gone by the time I finally got a chance to get into the wardrobe wagon, clean up and dress in clothes suitable to the season. When I emerged, fog had reduced the world to a square block. The crew was packing up fast.

"Dinner's in ten. Drinks on me, to celebrate." Jed slipped an arm around my shoulder. Every class I took, every gag I auditioned for, every broken bone and torn ligament, every scut job I'd had all these years was for this. I wanted to bask in the camaraderie, lap up the praise and be part of the crew, but there was still Karen Johnson. Despite everything I'd learned about her past, there was still something I needed to do for her in the present.

I walked across the nearly empty street. The police who, minutes ago, had filled the area with flashing lights and loud arguments till John produced a couple of feds, were gone. John was gone, too. The crew was already at Harrington's and all the tourists had vanished. All but one.

"Claire, I'm so glad you stayed." She was leaning against her car, her loose hair blowing in the gusts of fog. She was wearing black slacks and a thick gray hoodie. She looked as nervous as I was. "At least you knew enough to dress warm."

"When I was being treated here, it was summer. I spent a lot of time shivering then. I thought it was the drugs. But I wasn't cold tonight. Not with all that was going on here. You were amazing."

"Thanks."

"No really. Tell me!"

"Sure, but listen, Sonora and I were going to go for dinner after my stunt the night she died. You and I are the people who cared about her, so let's go have a drink for her, a fancy drink, something special."

"A drink to her?" Claire nodded, considering, as if this new plan required adjusting the creaky mechanism of her mind. It reminded me how sheltered she'd been growing up under her aunt's thumb, being institutionalized, and then living back in that isolated house. "Yes. Yes, that would be really nice. My car's here. We can put the heater on high."

She pushed open the passenger door for me. "Are you okay? I thought you were on fire when you ran into that guy. And then the police, what was all that? You must be wiped out?"

"Yeah, actually." I leaned back against the seat. "The guy I was running toward, Broder—it was the only way I could stop him. Draw attention. The one who got to us first was my brother. He's a detective."

"Your brother's a detective?"

I didn't know if she understood I meant police as opposed to private like Wallinsky, but I just nodded.

"So that's good, huh?"

"Yes and no. Broder's in custody, but getting him meant John had to take his eye off Graham Munson, Sonora's husband's friend and a pretty bad guy. Of course, Munson vanished. Now he and Matt, her husband, could be anywhere, and pissed at me."

I thought she might show some surprise or ask who Sonora married, but she was focused on me. "Like they might be coming after you?"

"If they're smart, they're already out of town."

She glanced over at me—as if she was waiting for an opening to ask some key question—then pulled away from the curb and cut across three lanes into the right lane.

"You drive well in a city."

"It took a while, but now I do. Where to?"

"Take a right on Embarcadero." A car started up behind us. "It's impressive what you've done, Claire. You've really got your life together. Your own cookbook. Lots of people would give their right arm for that."

She nodded. "I'll never stop feeling guilty about Sonora, though. I should never have let her come back to the house."

The Bay Bridge was almost overhead but the fog obscured its lights. It was a moment before muted disks of headlights shone in the side mirror.

"But her survey, it was just a shield. You know that, don't you? She was investigating the migrants. The ones that worked for your aunt."

"I don't know." She crossed over to the right. "Maybe. I guess. They weren't much different from me." She was leaning forward, peering through the windshield, as if trying not to out-drive the headlights. "What did Wallinsky say?"

"About?"

"About Sonora."

So that was her question. In another day, when word of Seward hit the news she wouldn't have had to ask me anything.

"Sonora worked for Wallinsky. Your aunt must have known him, right?"

She glanced in the rearview mirror. "She wouldn't let him near the house. She thought he was a reporter . . . Sonora worked for him. Huh. He must have liked her."

That was a leap. "Yeah, he did. He liked you, too. That's why he kept up with what you were doing."

"What'd he think?"

"About your aunt's death?"

"Yeah."

"He couldn't believe Sonora killed her. He thought one of the migrant workers did it." I paused. "What do you think?"

She hesitated, as if yearning for that theory to work but finding it wanting. "No. She killed my aunt."

"But you didn't actually see it, right?"

"I went out the back, was running around the side of the house. I—I may have stopped. I shouldn't have, but I was afraid." Again, she checked the rearview. "Someone's following us. Do you see the lights?"

I looked back. "You're right! Could be someone following your tail lights because the fog's so thick."

"No. They've been with us. I saw them as soon as I picked you up."

"From the set? Really?"

"Yeah. It's a man driving, another in the passenger seat."

"Can you make out a face?"

"No. Why?"

I craned my neck, trying to see.

"Too foggy. Why are they interested in you? You really think it's them, Sonora's husband and his friend?"

"They had a trafficking scam going and I helped bust it up."

"People trafficking?"

"Yeah."

She hit the accelerator. Behind, the headlights stayed steady. "Omigod. This is serious, isn't it?"

"Claire," I said shifting to face her. "They were both here, in San Francisco, the night Sonora was killed. They flew in from Las Vegas. Her husband left that night."

"Are you saying . . . they killed her?"

"I'm thinking . . . I've been putting together a plan . . . I wasn't sure it would work, but now there are the headlights behind us. They'll keep following us. My idea, it's extreme, and dangerous. But it could tell us who killed her."

She swung into the right lane in front of a bus. The wipers were on but the windshield was fogging inside. I cracked my window, but it didn't help.

"You can say no, Claire. Not a problem. There's no reason why you should endanger the good life you've built for yourself. I don't even know what made Sonora throw away the safe life she'd built. Okay, wait, this is crazy! Forget I even mentioned it!"

"No. Wait. What?"

"Headlights. Other lane now."

"I see them. What's the plan?"

"Lead them to the scene of the crime. Drop me off. Wait'll they get out, then you follow and be the witness. It's a big open slab five stories high. You must've seen it on the news by now. It's dangerous up there, but Matt Widley's a big guy, he's not going to worry about me. Munson either. If it's him in that car, he'll figure he can handle me. He'll be desperate to find out what I know, glad for a dark open space. I'll take the elevator. He'll use the stairs to surprise me. You need to come up the stairs, too. But keep quiet, stay in the shadows. If things go wrong, you have to promise me you won't try to help me. Do you have a phone?"

"No. I didn't think—"

"Here's mine. But this is too risky . . . too crazy . . ."

"It's okay. Sonora gave me my life. It's the least I can do for her."

"You sure? Things could go seriously bad. They could throw me over the edge, too. Then you'd be alone with them . . ."

"No! I want to. This way I can maybe get my life back."

"Okay. Turn here." I pulled out my phone—all or nothing!—and put it in the cup holder. "There's the building. Pull up into the lot. Drive off fast. Park around the corner. Don't forget the phone." I got out and didn't look back.

The building was dark. On the ground, the site lights barely blurred the thick gray of the night. Crime scene tape across the driveway had fallen. Yellow plastic strips flapped listlessly in the wind. I ran up the incline, into the elevator and pushed 5. The plan wasn't perfect, not by a long shot. Why did I feel so sure the killer would actually turn up on the dark open construction slab?

The elevator inched slowly upward, rattling loud enough to be heard across town at the zendo. Had it been this sluggish before? A guy could do the five stories faster on tiptoes. I hadn't factored this in at all. *Be quick, Claire!*

The door opened. Ahead was gray-black nothingness. For an instant I thought I was in the Bardo, the Tibetan passage between death and life. A sharp wind strafed my face. Distant creamy circles of light were nothing more than dots in the darkness. I thought there'd been a light by the elevator, but if so it was burned out or broken.

I walked straight ahead. My eyes were adjusting, turning the black to fuzzy shades of gray.

Anyone could be climbing the stairs; I couldn't hear footsteps. Anyone could be behind a pillar, staking out their claim on me.

I walked on. The edge was twenty feet away, visible not by a fence or even tape, but by the darker gray of emptiness. *What was I doing here?*

I stopped, strained to hear distant rattle of the elevator below. Was there a rattle of metal below? It sounded more like a car grunting up the incline. I leaned in, as if being two inches closer would make a difference.

A car. It sounded like a car.

A car like the one that sent a woman flying to the pavement below.

I walked on. An updraft poured over the edge. I saw Sonora's face in my mind's eye.

An engine raced. Being gunned on the turns. Definitely a car.

Only one reason to drive a car up the ramp of an empty construction sight in the dark.

I stared around, peering at the huge support poles, hoping to spot a figure half in shadow behind. I was desperate to call out: Are you here? Yet it would take more than a single would-be rescuer if . . . headlights veered around the elevator cage, shining on the ceiling, turning the cement slab below black.

Focus, damn it! Focus.

My feet were inches from the edge. I leaned over into nothingness, peered down, looking for something to grab for if things went bad. But there was nothing. Nothing but a straight shot five floors down.

Headlights hit the floor, shone on the unmarked gray cement, on the thick pillars, on me. They seemed warm on my skin, but I had to be imagining that.

The car picked up speed.

I didn't move.

It shot between pillars, coming right at me. I was inches from the edge, from the five-story drop. The roar of the motor reverberated off the cement ceiling and floor. The headlights were in my eyes. I didn't move.

It was thirty feet away, coming fast. Twenty feet.

My heart was thudding.

Ten feet.

The brakes screeched. Too late!

I leapt away. The front tires slid slowly over the edge, with me watching in horror.

Wrenching open the driver's door, I yanked Claire out, threw her to the ground and fell on top of her. Then, as with the Titanic, the car sunk into the dark. I braced against the crash, but there was just a dull clunk, like it no longer mattered.

Claire was whimpering. I flipped her and jerked her arms behind. "Sonora trusted you. You took her by surprise here. You didn't surprise me."

"Screw you!"

"She gave you your life! She trusted you. You were the only one she would have come here with. Because she trusted you. *Because* you owed her!"

"Owed? *Owed!* She was going to send me to jail. I have a life now, finally, and she was going to ruin it all."

I couldn't believe it! "Sonora took the blame when you killed your aunt."

"*She* killed her."

"That's crap!" I yanked her arms back. "You're the one who hated her. You're the one who'd lived under her thumb, was her slave for years! How often did you dream of killing her? It's why you begged Sonora to keep coming back, isn't it?"

She didn't answer.

I pulled her arms tighter. "Isn't it?" My head was starting to throb.

"Her fingerprint . . . it was on the knife."

"She tried to pull it out, right?"

"Only *Sonora's* print." She sounded smug.

I could have throttled her. "Then, after she left, she bought you time, to wipe the rest of the prints, to come up with your story."

She gulped for air, giving a sort of laugh. "No one'll ever believe you! Just like no one would've believed her! Get off me!"

I dropped her on the cement. With every bit of control I had left, I stepped away and let her roll over.

Claire sat up and rubbed her forehead. "Now I'm going to look all bruised, because of you."

Was she crazy? "Listen to me! Sonora's *dead!* She let people believe she killed Madelyn—for you. She spent her life hiding out, to protect you. She cared about you. She was your"—the word caught in my throat—"friend! Your friend," I repeated, my voice almost inaudible. "She didn't have to, but she called you, warned you she was turning herself in, right? *Because* she thought she was your friend."

"Friend! Big fucking deal! Big fucking magnanimous deal! She never suffered like me. I lived with—under!—that bitch my whole life! She had it coming."

"But Sonora—"

"I was a slave. A goddamned slave!" She glared up at me. "Damn right I used to lie awake at night thinking of getting rid of her, how I'd do it, how I'd *love* doing it. When—finally, *finally*—the moment came and I drove that knife into her chest, it felt . . . so good!" She was smiling.

"Sonora—"

"She'd had it easy. Not like me! I killed that old bitch—and still I wasn't free! I got carted off to the locked ward 'for my own good.' After that, all those god awful hours with smarmy therapists, me having to watch every word so I didn't screw myself. Reporters badgering me. Always waiting. No one was my friend. I managed to kill her and get away with it, and nothing changed. Not till my book came out and things got better. For the first time in my entire life things were good! And then out of nowhere, there's Sonora, still trying to save someone. Saving some girls, it's so all-important, she thinks it's just fine to take away my whole life. Like my life was nothing."

She sat there, glowering at me. In the dim light I could see that odd contradiction of her face: her mouth firm, almost smug, her brown eyes wild.

"She calls me to give me a 'heads up' . . . that she's planning to ruin my life. Of course that's not what she said. She was all high and mighty, noble, just like before. But what it really means is that suddenly, she's got some other girls she's all concerned about and so now I'm worth shit. The deal is I'm supposed to meet her there and chat, get reacquainted, buddy-buddy, whatever—before she throws away *my* life."

"You got there early?"

She chuckled. "With my life on the line? Yeah, I got there *plenty* early. I was there for an hour, watching, waiting, planning, ready to jump in her car when she came. It was way too easy! She never suspected a thing!" She pushed herself up. "I'm done here. There's no point in stopping me. No one's going to believe you."

Korematsu stepped out in front of her.

34

By 10:00 a.m. Friday, the fog had already burned off and the sun was warm. At Renzo's Café, small white cups and saucers were on the table outside, with Duffy underneath it.

"You could've told me!" I glared at Gary.

"Privilege," he muttered over the top of his cappuccino.

"Privilege be damned," John grumbled.

"Right. You knew Karen and I'd run into John. Would it have killed you to let me in on that?"

"Or me! If you'd—"

"And you"—I looked hard at John—"would it have killed you to . . ." but I was feeling more kindly toward The Enforcer. "I mean, just to say, guys, that if you two had trusted me—"

"It wasn't that . . ." they began, the one echoing the other, and stopped. Gary grinned sheepishly. John said, "We didn't want you to be involved."

I laughed.

"Any more involved, then."

"I'm in better shape than either of you. I can go places you can't, find out things no one's going to tell you. Why can't you just admit that I'm an adult? I'm not your *baby* sister—"

"But you are." John looked so abashed that I reached over and patted his arm. You can't teach an old brother new tricks.

Gary was making a show of stirring the foam back into his cappuccino, but there was a wistful look in his eyes. I wondered about him and Karen and what might have been. But I wasn't going there. Instead, I turned to John. "So, Broder's been arrested. You've been the flavor of the week. Mom's dined on your glory for days. I've even heard rumors about the board of sups."

Gary snorted. "Just the guy to be making compromises in city hall."

No way to argue that. "You going to be chief then?"

They both laughed, surprisingly, the same kind of laugh. It was John who said, "Turning in your boss doesn't make you popular."

"Ask Korematsu." Gary grinned.

No way was I going there either, not with both of them ready to pounce. "So you're back on in detective division?"

"For the moment."

"What does that mean?"

John hesitated before saying: "Don't know."

"That's the much respected Zen reply," I pointed out.

He shrugged it off. It was his kid sister's comment, after all.

ACKNOWLEDGMENTS

ONCE AGAIN, I am indebted to stunt coordinator and director Carolyn Day, to writer Linda Grant, and to my superb editor Michele Slung. And, as always, to my agent, Dominick Abel.